DOWN UNDER

DOWN UNDER

GEORGIA FAYE

MOONSCAPE PRESS

DOWN UNDER
Published by Moonscape Press
San Diego, California, U.S.A.

Down Under is a literary work of historical fiction, based on true
events. An adventure romance about a free-spirted woman who
seeks to find herself in the mid-seventies in in Sydney, Australia.

All incidents and dialogue are products of the author's imagination
and are not to be construed as real. Where real-life figures appear,
the situation, incidents, and dialogues concerning those persons are
entirely fictional and are not intended to change the fictional nature
of the work. In all other respects, any resemblances to others living
or dead are strictly coincidental.

Library of Congress Control Number: 2021904352

FAYE, GEORGIA, Author
DOWN UNDER
GEORGIA FAYE

ISBN: 978-1-7366717-0-2 (paperback)
ISBN: 978-1-7366717-2-6 (hardcover)

FICTION / Romance / Action & Adventure
FICTION / Women

QUANTITY PURCHASES: Schools, companies, professional
groups, clubs, and other organizations may qualify for special terms
when ordering quantities of this title. For information,
email info@moonscape.press.

This book is printed in the United States of America.

Book Design by Michelle M. White

Buddha once said:

"What you think, you become
What you feel you attract.
What you imagine, you create."

Ode to a Memory

Written by Sam to Brad

Listen my love to the babble of the creek and the cry of magpies,
I left my small footprint in the clay surrounding a billabong.
I left my heart in images you whispered in my ears and set in my eyes
My soul still belongs to where the heart has gone.

All that we played, explored and said
Replay in dreams that time has robbed.
Like the cold wind from the North that crossed our bed
It blew our moment into the distant fog.

But the questions of fate or the challenges of choice
Leave us questioning our yearning hearts still.
Setting our footsteps on different continents to voice
What our unborn children were meant to fill.

How does one question what fate has in store?
Or how time has never been a friend?
We are not the first to seek answers for more.
The question is never to be answered by mortal men.

1

The Lancaster

The plane's nose loomed high in the air. She had aged but she was proud, almost defiant. Sam tip-toed under her shadow, feeling her courage. She felt her touch as though she could hear all the stories she could whisper. Eeriness circled Sam like a slow-moving fog. *Was she feeling the voices of the dead?*

Slowly, she walked under the fuselage and tripped on a large wooden block holding the *Lancaster*'s wheels in place. *Splat*! Sam was spread-eagle under the greatest bomber the Royal Air Force had ever made. She looked around nervously to see who may have witnessed the event. *No one, thank God.* Suddenly she heard the drone of a single male voice. She focused on its direction, stumbled up, and walked over to the others.

"The *Lancaster Bomber* was a British four-engine heavy bomber. It was used by the Royal Air Force (RAF) out of Manchester, England in WWII," stated the docent.

Suddenly there was a crashing sound, followed by another. Sam jumped and turned to see the metal drinking bottle that had been in Cassie's hand skip three times until it landed next to Holly's foot.

"So sorry," Cassie said softly to the docent. "Please continue."

He looked over at Cassie and nodded. "Over 7,000 aircraft were created at this time; however, an estimated 5,000 were brought down during the war." The docent followed the eyes of the audience, especially the four recently retired female teachers standing in front as they glanced over the length of the aircraft in Hamilton, Ontario.

Jack, the docent, was in his early seventies. He filled everyone's imagination with stories of "the boys." They were mostly lads of eighteen who joined the war to fly these bombers that held many of the larger blockbuster bombs. She was known as the *Lanc* and was the most successful night bomber of the Royal Airforce.

Sam saw Cassie fidget as her shoulders drooped under a large weight, "My father died flying on a *Lanc*. I often try to imagine the gunfire and commands given right before their plane came down. I was only three when they found his body floating in the sea off the coast of Norfolk, England." A serene silence followed her statement like the smoke from a fired gun.

"Oh . . . I'm *so* sorry, Miss. Unfortunately, that was the tragedy of many of our fine lads. Yah, in the beginning we were using a smaller caliber of fire power than the Germans." Sam looked over at Cassie, her eyes appearing sad. *This information was not helping Cassie reconcile her father's fate.*

Now Jack was even more captivated by the ladies in their sixties. He realized this visit had a personal connection for them.

"Well, I'm so happy you are visiting our museum to learn more about the details on how we won the war."

"Well, actually we're here today to get the lay of the land. Two of our group from Sydney, Australia will be flying on that very bomber this coming Saturday," Sam said pointing. The docent turned to Cassie. "You came all the way from Sydney, Australia to fly on the *Lanc*?"

"That's right."

"Are you going as well?" the docent asked turning to Sam.

"Sadly, no," she said, "only two, Cassie and Brad. We are all here enjoying a reunion. $2500 is a little over my budget for a one-hour joy ride."

"Yah, it is pretty expensive," Jack said. "But many captivated followers of this WWII aircraft come here just for that thrill. It's a unique experience ya know. I wish I could afford it."

"Me, too." Sam chimed in sighing. She couldn't think of any better experience that Cassie and Brad could share together. They both did a bit of traveling together after Sam left. She thought how their special friendship must have allowed them many years of sharing the world together. Sam was clearly jealous but hid her feelings behind the excitement she was feeling around the reunion. *It was certainly my own fault that I didn't get to share all those memories*, she thought.

Cassie, Holly, Patty, and Sam wandered about the museum taking photos and trying to imagine Saturday. This was their third day of the reunion and they hadn't talked about Brad once.

Later that evening, they were enjoying their evening tea in the century-old farmhouse that belonged to Patty's family. They all examined the photos of them posing in front of the *Lancaster*. That same eeriness surrounded Sam. As she peered at the photos under the wing of the aircraft she was shocked to find that all their faces were bathed in white light. They stood out defined only by the black jackets they had all purchased in the gift shop.

"It must be a sign," Sam said out loud.

Sam was a firm believer in the Universe. She thought it very strange, though, as they were all out of the direct rays of the sunlight in that photo. They were all at a loss for words viewing their ghost-like faces on each of their cameras.

Giving up on the photos, they moved to the living room and sat around the old fireplace, wearing pajamas, soaking in the bed and breakfast charm. The farmhouse had been a beautiful productive dairy farm back in the day. It was the house Patty and her sister were raised in and it was the house Brad lived in with Patty's mother in 1981.

The ladies spent that evening sipping wine and dancing to the music of Joe Cocker's, "With A Little Help From My Friends". They shared the sweet familiar feeling of camaraderie. It was as though thirty-six years had never passed. They simply picked up where they left off. It was amazing how people remember things. Someone would recall a moment like, "Remember when we all . . ., or Remember the time we . . .," and details were added. It was like someone was drawing a sketch and the others would join in adding the colors to the picture.

"I remember sitting in the living room of Gladstone Street cuddling up with your dog, Sam. What was his name?" asked Patty snuggling into the couch by the fireplace.

"Toby," Sam reminded her.

"I loved that dog," she said.

"I mostly remember getting ready for all the parties we went to every weekend. They were great fun, eh," shouted Holly.

Cassie chimed in with stories of students they had all shared, "Remember Lenny," she said. Then she would go on with an amusing incident that occurred during their teaching days in Australia. But **not once** did anyone mention Brad. It was somehow off limits. Without uttering a word about him, they knew it would take on a life of its own when he arrived.

Both Holly and Patty shared all their carefully-cared for photo albums from the life-changing year of 1981. Any remnants of photos that Sam had now remained buried in plastic boxes deep within a storage facility in San Diego. She threw everything of importance to her in there after her two sons left home to do their thing. She did away with condo life to go live on a smaller footprint, a thirty-six-foot motor yacht in San Diego Bay. The boxes laid in their same disarray all these years, maybe never to be opened again, deteriorating, melting, turning yellow, claiming a faded past.

Honestly, the real lure for Sam was when Patty gave her information about the reunion and told her that Brad was coming. Patty wasn't certain whether Brad's wife was coming or not, but Sam figured what the hell, maybe it was time they all met. There was no way Sam was going to resist seeing him one more time. No way in hell. Their lives were in need of closure. She began to wonder how she might begin to explain why she made the choices she did. How could she explain her choices after all these years when she still didn't really know *why* herself? She resisted thinking about him constantly throughout the day, but the old feelings were still there. They truly had never left her heart, not for a moment.

2

Leaving New Jersey, September 1975

Sam didn't really know if she had been spending her entire life running away from home. It is a question she often thought about. Like the song made famous by Lee Marvin: "I Was Born Under a Wandering Star".

Sam's parents were pretty grounded people. Her mother was a second-generation Jersey girl from an upper class Irish Montclair banking family. Her father was a self-identified dandy, part of a second-generation family from Jersey City, New Jersey.

That was reason enough to get married in Jersey after WWII. Her father served in Patton's Third Army and was ready to start a family as soon as he returned from the war. One day he got on a bus and met Sam's mother. They got married after three months of dating. They bought a cozy Cape Cod house in a small suburban North Jersey town fifteen minutes outside of Manhattan, New York. Sam's father joined the police force and her mother became a bookkeeper. They had three children and Samantha was the oldest.

Sam knew very early on that she wasn't going to live in New Jersey the rest of her life. She remembered when she was about nine and her brother was seven, she was plotting to run away from home. She shared her plan with her brother in their upstairs bedroom. She had thought carefully about how she would get out of the house from the bedroom window and escape over the roof of the garage and jump to the ground below. One night, she had decided she was definitely going. She told her brother she was leaving. She was packing some clothes and he began to cry uncontrollably.

"Why are you crying," she asked.

"I don't want you to go."

"Why? Nobody will care if I go."

"I will," he said sobbing.

She began to think more about him than herself. She was hit by the fact that she might hurt someone by this decision. She didn't know he cared that much and that she would leave a void in his life. She thought to herself, *Okay, Sam, what is your plan after you jump from the roof? Where are you going? Oh, by the way, you have no money, and if they catch you . . . well, you probably will be grounded for life.*

Her brother had given her time to pause and think things through instead of just running on instinct. She crawled back into bed and decided she was just going to be patient and put together another plan. It would take another seventeen years before she finally managed to run away.

Sam's father's way of raising children was authoritative and controlling. She attended a private Catholic school through high school. She never experienced adolescence with any social interaction. She essentially became a wallflower. It wasn't until she was in a bathroom stall in her high school one day that she overheard a group of girls commenting among themselves that Samantha Giblin was attractive. She remembered walking home from school, thinking about this comment. She certainly didn't look like the models in the magazines or even the popular girls in school. Why did those girls think *she* was attractive?

She thought long and hard about what attractive meant. It must have a scale from zero to ten with cute, pretty, beautiful, and gorgeous being near the top. Sam decided she must be in the middle somewhere.

The motivation to better herself was coupled by her father's repeated scrutinizing of her appearance before she walked out of the house saying, "Remember, first impressions count, young lady."

She was shy and awkward around boys, but even with a mouthful of braces her dimples and Natalie Wood eyes would often elicit a look from others. At five foot five, she was athletic, big-boned and carried a few extra pounds. She was definitely a tomboy who hated her first name, Samantha. She once asked her mother where she came up with that horrible name. Her answer was that she read it in a novel. So Samantha decided to go by Sam. She liked boys' names for girls better. The name George, for Nancy Drew's best friend, was her favorite name of all.

Years passed. She was only allowed to attend a local university and had to commute. Her parents didn't have the money to send her to college so she took out loans. She worked after school to have some spending money, always thinking she needed to have money if she was to get away.

Around the same period of time, Sam met a nice guy named Daniel at university. He was the president of his fraternity. They hung out together, got pinned, got engaged, and by the fall of her first year of teaching, they were married; after all, this was the way things were done, weren't they? They didn't really think much about if they were a good fit as a couple. He was fun and they got along—what more was there to know. They bought a house at the Jersey shore. One day Sam brought up the topic of when they might have kids.

"Sam," he said. "I don't think this is a good world for raising anything, least of all children. I really don't want to have *any* kids."

"Are you serious? I have known you over four years now. Why didn't you tell me you were adamant about not having children?"

"Well, it didn't come up until now."

"So, where do you see this marriage going? I mean, what was the purpose of us marrying other than obviously moving away from our families? We could have just committed the mortal sin of all time and live together." Sam was visibly shaken.

"We have a nice life, we have friends, and our family is our Westie puppy."

"Sure," she said shaking her head. "Sure, that will do it."

Sam thought she was back to square one. A life that had no future, no promise, and she was still stuck in New Jersey! She was not happy. She began to let Dan know that the marriage wasn't working. Sam had already moved out when suddenly she saw an ad in the *New York Times* for teachers needed in Australia. Sam walked into the Rockefeller Center office in New York City during the Thanksgiving holiday and signed on the dotted line to be a teacher in New South Wales, Australia.

Daniel was sweet and would always be a hero of sorts to her. He did whatever he could do to let her follow her dreams to escape. They both knew their marriage had been her first big plan to escape life under her father.

Soon after Sam filled out the application, she received a letter. It described that in this program, a married woman wouldn't be allowed to enter the country of Australia. However, the same letter stated that a married man *would* be allowed to bring a wife. The letter from the Australian Immigration Commission was clear—they would not tolerate a situation where a job could be taken from an Australian male. The injustice of the situation infuriated Daniel.

He told Sam he was going to help her solve this problem by getting one of the new quick no-fault divorces that New Jersey had just put into effect. The divorce was going to cost $5,000. He told her that if she came up with half the money he would supply the other half. Her desperation to escape was making him unhappy, too. After three years of marriage, they decided to move on with their separate lives. She decided they were probably too young to get married. *People shouldn't get married before thirty.* By July, they were divorced and by September 9th Sam was boarding a Qantas 747 for Australia.

Sam's mother and sister had lunch with her the day she left and drove her to the airport. This was a surprise and a welcome. They all had experienced a few rough years. Sam's parents divorced in 1970.

One day during her parents' separation, her mother knocked on her father's apartment door. She knew that he was at work. Sam was living there because it was the closest spot for her to commute to college. Her mother knew that her father was dating someone and by now, so did everyone in town.

Sam didn't think about how desperate her mother must have been to approach that door. She only knew that the incident was ugly.

She answered with a friendly, "Hi, mom, are you here to see dad?"

"No, I'm here to see you."

"Do you want to come in," she asked pointing to the beautifully decorated apartment her father had set-up for himself.

"No, what I want to say I'll say right here."

"Okay . . .," she said stepping backwards.

She stood there and screamed and pointed her finger at Sam.

"*You*'re the reason for this divorce!"

Sam reeled from the accusation, "What are you talking about?"

"You always knew he was cheating on me and you never told me. The two of you were in cahoots together," she screamed.

Sam was in shock. "Listen," she said, "The two of you didn't get along for years. You slammed cupboard doors every morning in front of me in frustration saying, your father, this and that . . . and now you want to blame *me* for a bad marriage? I had nothing to do with the failure of your marriage. This isn't fair; you can't come up and blame your daughter for your divorce." Sam just closed the door sobbing.

Those who knew Sam's mother loved her. They always talked about how she was so sweet. Sam thought she obviously brought out her mother's bad side. She realized early she wasn't one of her mother's favorites.

Sam's first learning experience with a woman's jealously was, in fact, with her own mother. In her teenage years, Sam and her father spent Sundays in deep discussions over Civil Rights or the political climate of the 60's, usually taking opposing views. They were always heated arguments, but fun. She looked forward to them. She felt safe arguing with her father but never with her mother, because she didn't appreciate Sam's relationship with her father and she could not hide her feelings toward Sam.

The divorce in 1970 was brutal for Sam and her siblings. They all became pawns to the deceit and the play-by-play action to the terms of divorce. Sam's father was in love and wanted to get married quickly. He came to the hospital one day where Sam's mother was admitted for a leg injury.

He walked up to her brother Lenny, paused and handed him a brown envelope, "Here," he commanded. "Take these papers in to your mother. I need her to sign them today."

"What are they?"

"They are the final divorce papers," her father barked.

"You want to serve her with papers, do it yourself," replied Lenny refusing to take the envelope. "I'm not going to perform your dirty deeds for you."

Sam's father stood even more erect and glared at her six foot two-inch-tall brother. He pointed to his holster with his .38 caliber Saturday Night Special and said, "Listen, son, I *gave* you a life and I'll take it away."

Her father must have been pretty desperate. The line he was quoting was right out of a Yul Brenner movie that she had seen on *The Million Dollar Movie* just that week. All three siblings eventually escaped in their own special way. In the end, Sam felt her option to run away was the least harmful.

When she crossed the United States for the first time, Sam knew she would never return to Jersey again to live. Many thoughts were confronting her as she walked through the companion-way door of the Pan American Airline flight that was to be the porthole to her future. She was armed with twelve years of private school upbringing and Irish Catholic guilt. She felt ready to take on the world.

She'd hoped her decision to leave would help her find exotic places and perhaps find that special soul mate who she imagined she would travel the world with, maybe even sail around the world if she got really lucky. *Wouldn't that be living the dream?*

Sam sat back in her seat and ordered a glass of white wine to toast her future with her inflight meal as she picked up a pair of aircraft headphones and clipped them over her ears. The first song playing was the long version of the song "Freedom" by Richie Havens from Woodstock. It was a sign. *Change is good.* Sam thought of the old saying: if you do not create change, things are doomed to remain the same.

Sydney, NSW

Author's drawing
Not to scale

3

Arriving in Sydney

Sam wandered around San Francisco for two days by herself. She thought it would be fun exploring a new place, but she decided being alone had its drawbacks. *Not connected, empty, lonely*. When she got to the airport, she checked in early and began to make conversation with people her own age.

A very tired short girl slammed down several overweight travel bags in the seat beside her. She wore a pair of jeans, a peasant styled shirt, and a pair of high platform shoes. She took a quick look at Sam and dismissed her, most likely thinking she was a businesswoman. Sam wore a cream-colored tailored dress, a professional page boy haircut with matching beige high-heeled shoes.

"Where are you traveling to?" Sam asked, intruding on the tired girl's mood.

"Sydney, Australia," she answered curtly.

"*Really*, so am I. Are you signed up to teach there?" Sam asked.

"Yup."

"My name is Sam, what's yours?" she said, extending her hand.

"Lyndsey," she responded shaking Sam's hand in return.

"Where are you from?" Sam asked.

"Upstate New York. Where are you from?"

"Jersey, fifteen minutes outside of Manhattan."

"Well, at least we are both from the East Coast," She moved her bags over and took the seat next to Sam's.

She looked Sam up and down, "That probably explains the clothes. One quick question, if you knew this flight was fourteen hours long, why the hell did you wear a dress? I mean, why not wear a pair of jeans?"

"Well," Sam uttered softly, "I don't really own jeans." Lyndsey looked at Sam weirdly.

"It's true, I don't, but I also thought this was how people dressed to go on planes," Sam answered naively. "At least this is how I have always dressed before when I traveled on planes."

"Well, other than my flight out here from New York, this is my first flight. Oh, and by the way," Lyndsey continued, "I *live* in jeans." *Perhaps, Sam thought, she was letting her know they had nothing in common.*

A minute later an attractive-looking guy in his early twenties with sandy blonde hair came over and put his bags down across from the two of them, one of which was clearly a guitar. Lyndsey took over and made the introductions. He nodded and said, "Hi, I'm Robert Snowden from Upstate New York. You can just call me Robbie. He shook their hands. "I'm signed up to teach school in Australia."

Lyndsey answered, "Yeah . . . us too. I don't know about the rest of you, but I *need* a drink. Where is the nearest bar?" Sam volunteered that she remembered passing one in the waiting area. They promptly left their bags on the seats. However, as an after-thought, Robbie went back and grabbed his guitar, "I'd really be upset if someone stole my Martin."

Robbie and Lyndsey got bar seats together and asked for a beer. Sam ordered a gin and tonic. A slim brunette grabbed a seat to her right. Sam was captivated by her long curly brown hair. It was amazing how she tossed it about her head. She was also heading to Australia.

Lyndsey turned to Robbie, "So why did you sign up for Australia?"

"Lots of reasons. To get a quick job, get out of the icy cold upstate New York, meet new people, learn to play music surrounded by a different culture," he spouted sipping on his cold beer.

Lyndsey chugged her beer down fast, slamming her glass on the bar. "It was the only way I was ever going to get a job right out of college in our small town. I would have to wait for years to get in that system," she said ordering another beer. They both turned to Sam. She lowered her head not wanting them to know that she was older than they were. "Well, if I didn't get out of Jersey right now I might never get a chance to leave," she said.

Helen, the girl with the curly brown hair shook her curls and said, "Same, I needed to get some job experience. They have a shortage of teachers in Australia and we have an over-abundance of teachers in the States. It would be years before I got a job." The four of them continued to drink until they were called to board the plane.

The seating on the plane was set by gender and arranged by alphabetical order. Marsha Ross sat next to Sam. She was from Pennsylvania—a natural beauty with long straight blonde hair. She was beautiful, wholesome, and friendly and she talked about her college life. A short time into the flight, a very tall, handsome athletic type recognized Marsha and came over to talk to them. His name was Lance. They had both attended the same college.

Halfway through the trip Sam could hear a girl vomiting in the bathroom which happened to be adjacent to their seats. After her second bout at the restroom, Marsha attempted to say something to her. "Are you okay?" she asked sympathetically.

"No, I'm not. Do I look it?" she growled, "I want to go home." The girls looked at each other and said nothing. The unhappy girl moved her way back up to her seat in the forward section of the plane.

"Maybe she never left home before," Sam said.

"There isn't much any one can do about her problem this many miles over the middle of the Pacific Ocean," commented Marsha.

"I guess it is safe to say not everyone is excited to be heading to Australia," Sam said.

After fourteen hours, the descent began. The stewardess suggested that the passengers look out the porthole in the direction of the Sydney Harbor Bridge and the Opera House. It was surreal to see these images for the first time outside of a magazine. Sam did notice the large expanse of waterways below and that *all* the roofs were made of red tiles. Sam thought, *we definitely aren't in Kansas anymore.*

After they made their way through customs and picked up their luggage, the 300 new teachers who were on the 747 walked to the buses waiting to take them to their youth hostels in Sydney. Sam noticed that the girl who had been throwing up in the bathroom was already at the Qantas desk asking about returning flights home. *Damned if I would be jumping back on an airplane for another fourteen-hour flight.*

To their dismay, there were picket lines of young people protesting the arrival of the Americans, screaming, "Yankees go home! You're taking jobs away from Australian teachers." Lovely, Sam thought. This adventure may have a challenging start. *Well, one step at a time.* Sam had signed up for a minimum of two years and if all goes well, maybe more. No one said life in another country was going to be easy.

From the moment Sam arrived in Sydney, she never had any intention of leaving Australia. She had found the perfect spot to call home. It was a blend of American and British culture. It was a country the size of the United States with less people than New York City. Sam was 10,000 miles from New Jersey and unreachable. She found herself in Sydney not knowing a soul except for the five people who met in the airport. They made a pact to have dinner together each night so they could compare notes after each day's orientation.

The first week was spent in a small bedroom with two twin beds in a youth hostel with another girl. The number of teachers who had been brought over to fill the needed positions easily filled two hostels. Sam walked into the tiny room and ran straight for the bathroom.

"It's *true*," she screamed with excitement to her roommate. "Come over here and look. The water does go down the drain counterclockwise!"

"What," she said. "What are you talking about," she mumbled walking away from the toilet.

"The Coriolis Effect. You know, because of the earth's rotation, the water currents flow clockwise in the northern hemisphere and counterclockwise in the southern hemisphere. Just look."

She didn't share Sam's excitement. She shook her head and walked to her bed where she had a copy of the *Sydney Morning Herald* that she had already purchased from a newsstand. *She knew the drill.* As soon as they went through their daily lectures that covered such topics as: money systems, culture, history and colloquial phrases, Sam's flat mate would take off for points unknown and contact local realtors to find a place to rent. She made it very clear she wanted to live alone. However, Sam realized that if she didn't start looking soon she was going to be in deep shit. By the following Monday all teachers were expected to start their first day in the school where they were assigned.

Sam's last name began with 'R' for Rothbauer—she had kept her married name. All the newly arrived teachers had to fill out forms stating past teaching experiences, such as the grades they were best suited for and where they might like to teach. Sam had already made contact with many of the placed teachers. It wasn't rocket science. They had run out of honoring requests after the letter 'M' and everyone after that was given whatever positions were left. *It wasn't fair.* Sam was placed in the Outback somewhere and it wasn't going to work for a girl from the outskirts of New York City.

She soon made an appointment with the head of the Ministry of Education. *She needed to at least try to get a change.* The man who was in charge of the placements was Mr. Wagner. He listened patiently to Sam's observations and complaints about being given a kindergarten placement in the outback town of Quirindi, 700 miles north of Sydney. "I was an intermediate science teacher and kindergarten class just won't work for me," Sam explained.

Mr. Wagner gave a deep sigh, "I'm very sorry, Miss Rothbauer, but when you signed the dotted line for this contract, you said you would teach *anywhere* in New South Wales as well as whatever grade you were qualified to teach."

"I understand that, sir," Sam argued, "But that would all be fair enough if you had created a lottery system that was fair for everyone." Sam knew she was out on a limb and he could easily just tell her to take the next plane home. *I need to stay calm and not get my Jersey up.*

"Listen, sir, I'm a single woman. I am here alone. I've spent my whole life living fifteen minutes outside of Manhattan, New York. I'm a science teacher for primary schools. I will not survive teaching kindergarten in an Outback town with one pub. *Please,* sir." Sam was pleading, begging, placing her two hands together in a prayer-like motion. "Isn't there *anything* closer to Sydney that will persuade me not to return home in a year's time? You will just have to be looking again for another replacement for me."

He breathed another long sigh. "I have one job to do. It's to place not only *all* of you Yanks but every single teacher who just passed University (Uni) by this Monday. Okay, listen, if you can find me a person who will take your kindergarten placement in Quirindi, I will see what I can do for you."

There was a God, *there was hope.* "Thank you *so* much, sir." Sam took a taxi directly to the great hall where everyone gathered in the mornings. She'd need to have a lot of conversations with her fellow migrants if an exchange were to happen quickly.

She began yelling like a fish monger at the swarm of people whom she had never met and would probably never see again. "Hi, does anyone want a kindergarten placement," she screamed. The process didn't take long. A cute young blonde yelled, "I do. I do!"

"So, where were you placed," Sam anxiously asked.

"I'm placed in a fifth grade class in Bourke." It was even further away in the Outback.

(Sam knew right away that she wasn't going to jump for the straight trade.) "Well, I'm placed in a kindergarten class in Quirindi, let me know right away if you're interested."

Within ten minutes, Jane, the little blonde teacher, found Sam and seemed very excited, "I'll take it!"

"*Really!*" Sam said with equal enthusiasm. She explained that she could get on the rail line from Quirindi and could visit her friends in Sydney most weekends.

"I'm just so excited to teach kindergarten, older students scare the shit out of me," she said.

"Can you come with me right now? We need to report to the Ministry right away before this offer expires." They took a quick taxi together and caught Mr. Wagner just before he was done for the day. Excitedly, Sam explained how she found someone to take her position.

Sam stressed the fact that Jane had only taught kindergarten. "She will be very happy with the job there."

Then Mr. Wagner asked Jane where she had been placed.

"Sir, I was given a fifth-grade class in Bourke."

"Perfect," he said turning to Sam, "Then, Ms. Rothbauer, *you* can report to Bourke on Monday."

"*NO*, sir," Sam squealed. "I'm not reporting to Bourke! You promised that if I found someone who would be willing to take my position, you would find me a placement somewhere near Sydney." Mr. Wagner just grumbled at Sam.

"So, who the bloody hell is going to take her position in Bourke by Monday?"

"I don't know, sir, maybe some big strapping bloke who would love to hang out in a small town with a pub. All I know is I wouldn't survive there, I would leave and that wasn't our deal. Come on, sir, have a heart, please!" *Sam felt as though she was pleading for her life.* She had never begged before, and found it to be a humbling experience.

He looked at the two of them who stood fixed with pleading eyes and he looked at the clock on the wall for the time. It was late Thursday afternoon. School was back in session Monday. He flipped through some sheets.

Finally, he looked up and said, "Here," shoving a name and address in front of Sam. "Leave, the both of you. It's a placement for fifth grade in a small public school in the western suburbs. You both need to report to your schools on Monday."

Sam and Jane both skipped out the door and hugged each other. "What an ordeal. I know we will probably never see each other again, but I wish you all the luck in the world," Sam said as she and Jane hugged goodbye.

"You too," she said. "Good Luck," she screamed, as Sam watched the back of her head rush out the door.

On Friday morning, Sam ran into the great room for the last time. People were heading off by noon to start looking for appropriate accommodations. Everyone was hugging and saying goodbye. She ran into Robbie who was eager to teach in Broken Hill. He had his guitar and seemed quite happy for the new adventure. Sam told him she was able to negotiate a placement in a suburb of Sydney and asked him to stay in touch. "I'm meeting with a rental agent in Bondi. I'm desperately trying to find a flatmate today. Any ideas?"

"Try over there." He pointed to a brunette who was surrounded by a group of people. "I was just talking to her. I think she may be looking for a flatmate."

Sam approached the girl slowly. She was telling a story to everyone about her exciting weekend in an electrifying manner. People were flocking to her effervescence. Sam wondered if *they* might be a good fit as flatmates. She was certainly colorful. They looked like they could be sisters—about the same height, brunette, both East Coast women. *Oh, come on Sam, take a chance, you are looking for some excitement in your life.*

She was telling everyone how she had gotten off the plane and jumped into her first adventure with a guy named Barry, who was a photographer. They had spent the weekend together in Surfer's Paradise getting the feel of the land. She said she had fallen in love with him the moment he jumped in the hotel's pool to save a young boy.

Sam waited until she was alone and introduced herself. "Hi, my name is Sam Rothbauer," extending her hand. (She decided to get right to the point.) "I've been placed in the suburbs of Sydney and I hear you may be interested in finding a flatmate."

"Hi, I'm Lacy," she smiled back. "Yup, you're right, I need to find a flat." She immediately began retelling her Barry story.

"Well," Sam interjected. "I think I found a good flat in Bondi Beach. It has two bedrooms and is just two blocks from the beach. I don't know how transportation will work to get us to our schools but my thought is that we could rent a car for a week. This way we can look at the flat and figure out what furnishings we need and commute by car for the first week until we figure it all out. What do you think?"

"Well, you're in luck, Sam. I'm *way* too lazy to go out and try to figure out all these details by myself," she chuckled. "It looks as though you may have found us a good spot. You have a flatmate."

"Great," Sam sighed. "I hate to rush you but we need to go quickly and rent a car and check out of the hostel. The realtor is expecting us to sign a lease today and put the money down on this place. We need two months in advance payment. Are you okay to help with that?" She nodded as she raced after Sam.

When she saw Sam nervously heading for the car, Lacy smartly volunteered to take the wheel. She was able to maneuver the right-hand drive and stick shift better than Sam ever could. It was definitely going to take some time to adjust to driving on the left side of the road and Sam wasn't a confident driver. *We all have our skills.*

On the way to Bondi, they rode through Paddington taking in all the handsome two-story laced townhouses. *This looks like New Orleans.* They continued the drive through Bondi Junction and slowly descended the rim of a wide cliff that took in the entire view of the horseshoe bay of Bondi Beach. They both gasped at the same time.

"Oh my God, is *this* where we are going to live!" they screamed in unison.

By Sunday they had found some used furniture stores in and around Paddington. They spent the next two days carting two mattresses, a kitchen table, chairs, and some wicker furniture that they were ready to call a living room set. They moved in, constructing their new flat on Gould Street and creating the beginning of their American expat family.

To Sam, it was shocking that teachers were on strike in response to the American arrivals. She began to ask around as to the reason for the severe teacher shortage in Australia. It seemed that becoming a teacher was not a prized occupation in Australia. Students went to *Uni* for higher level business or engineering jobs, basically careers that paid well. Most other students apprenticed and interned for skilled union labor jobs, which paid far better than teaching careers.

When the shortage first reared its ugly head, the government offered the Australians a deal. The government would supplement their income, grant them a teaching license after two years of training and only asked that the participants sign a three-year contract. After a year of teaching, some had money in their pockets and took off for Europe. They were bailing on their contracts.

As a response, the Government of New South Wales first invited exchange teachers from Commonwealth countries such as England, Canada, and New Zealand to fill the gap. When they got desperate, they advertised for more teachers from other places including the United States advertising in many of the colleges.

4

Venturing Outback

Sam would grow to love her little school in the western suburbs. There were only six teachers who shared the second floor of this small primary school and one of them took Sam's breath away. His name was Brad. Sam immediately learned he was married, so she kept her boundaries.

Cassie, Freddie, Kristi, and Sam were single and tended to check in on what parties were going on in the area each Friday evening. They had different tastes in parties. Cassie lived in artsy Balmain. Kristi hung out with a British expat crowd more like flower children from Berkley. Freddie came to many of Cassie's parties for he knew many of the same crowd, but his crowd had many men who liked men.

In the staff room, Sam's fellow grade level teachers, Brad and Cassie, both described the Outback in ways that suggested Sam needed to get out there.

After four weeks, Lacy and Sam began their first venture outside of Sydney with a flight to Canberra to visit Barry. It was an invitation to a Halloween Party placed in an old abandoned Outback pub.

Lacy always seemed to arrive late to planes. It was *Lacy Logic*. She always said, "Why sit bored in a lobby when you can be running for a plane." More than once Sam found herself running as the flight attendants held the doors open for them.

They arrived in Canberra late Friday afternoon. Barry, who borrowed a friend's car, drove them through the countryside to get to his flat in Queanbeyan.

Magpies flocked every tree creating the familiar echo of Australia. The landscape seemed arid and sparse save for an occasional Eucalyptus tree. Their eyes darted everywhere for signs of a kangaroo, but they were told they were still too close to the city.

That Friday night there was a party at Barry's flat. Lacy joined Barry in his room. The flatmate Tim suggested, "You don't need to sleep on the couch, I have plenty of room over here in my room."

"Thanks … that's alright, the couch looks comfortable enough," she said making a quick bed with the blanket and pillow handed to her by Barry.

That Saturday evening, Sam and Lacy prepared for a "Fancy Dress" party. In Australia, this is any party in which people dressed up in costumes (not to be confused with how the Aussies use the word costume, which in Australia means a bathing suit). Sam rode in the back of an open-air jeep that Barry borrowed. This was somehow the best part of the evening. The smell of the countryside, the moon, the air flowing across her face. It was tantalizing. They arrived to the old stone pub which was damp and stale with the smell of old beer. The old wooden tables were lit with hundreds of candles, lively fiddle music played in the background. Sam sipped her brew slowly from a plastic cup and tapped her foot to the rhythm of the music.

Everyone was pretty drunk within the first hour. Sam conversed with a few groups of people during the course of the evening, mostly expat Americans who had also chosen to come out to Australia to teach school.

About midnight, the party was emptying out and Sam wandered from room to room looking for Lacy and Barry. They were nowhere to be found. Then from behind a door appeared Tim.

"Hi," he said. "Do you need a ride?"

"Well, I might. I've looked everywhere for Lacy and Barry."

"Oh, they left hours ago. Here, I have my car outside; come with me I'll give you a ride back." *Do I tell him now that I'm not going to sleep with him? No . . . I'd better not.* He was pretty wasted, definitely swaying. It would be smart not to say anything that could inflame the situation. *Oh, the decisions we are forced to make sometimes.* He walked Sam over to a little red sports car, a two-seater Triumph. Tim said, "I think the quickest way for me to get back to the flat is through the city." Sam gave no input and just obediently got into the convertible.

It was after one in the morning. No one was on the road. Sam began conversing about his car to make small talk. "So, how did you manage to pick up such a sweet car?"

"Pretty easy. One of the other American teachers who was returning back to the States needed cash fast and I bought it from him. Look at the pickup she has." Suddenly, he stepped on the gas and pushed the pedal to the floor. Sam was beginning to get *real* nervous.

"Don't you want to slow down a bit?"

"Why?" he asked, "Nobody's on the road." They began heading into the second set of circular road patterns when he screamed out, "Oh, *no,* we're going to crash!"

As he said those words, Sam was thinking to herself—*if you think we're going to crash, why can't you just stop it!* She braced her hands on anything she could grab, slouched her body down in the seat, and closed her eyes. This was going to be her first car accident and there was absolutely nothing she could do to avoid it.

It is a funny sensation when you're engaged in a traumatic event. Everything moves in slow motion. Sam remembered the jostling but not the flip and the roll. She thought she must have hit her head because she could feel her head throbbing. Her eyes were suddenly opened as they came to a stop. Her seat belt was still on, the windshield was cracked, but not missing, and she wasn't dead. *I'm alive!*

Sam heard Tim's voice from far off, "Sam, are you okay?"

She nodded.

Then he said, "We have to get out of the car. It might blow up." Sam tried to move but shook her head slowly.

"I can't move. I can't get out," she said.

"Try, *try!*" She tried everything to get anything to move but all she could do was move her mouth and eyelids.

Sam could hear a police officer talking to another officer. "She's in shock, we'll need to pry open the door to get her out." Then, one of the officers lifted her up like a rag doll and put her into the ambulance. Sam woke up to a big bright light over her and an officer questioning her about what happened as she lay on a gurney.

"We were going fast and then there was an accident. I didn't see much on how or why it happened. I had my eyes closed most of the time."

"We are charging your friend with reckless driving while under the influence. He gets out tomorrow, unless of course you file charges against him." Sam just stared at the officer blankly.

"Do you understand me?" the officer's tone was harsh, "You *need* to press charges." Sam thought for a second. Tim could possibly be sent back to the States if she pressed charges. Maybe she would be too. *I'm still pretty mad at him though.*

"No," she said slowly and calmly, "I don't want to press charges."

The next morning an emergency room doctor visited Sam. She was still covered with broken glass and her head was pounding. The doctor said she was a lucky girl, "You just have a mild concussion." *Oh God yes, thank you Lord, I'm not paralyzed.*

Sam asked if there was any way she could get something for her huge splitting headache. *I didn't think I was asking for too much.* He said he would send a nurse with some aspirin. The attending physician told Sam, "I will let you go midday but you should take a week off work."

"I have been working for just a little over a month sir and now I need to ask for a week off, is there a way you can write me a note to justify my absence? They are not going to believe me without a doctor's note." she pleaded.

The following day Sam got into Barry's car with Lacy and he drove them back to the airport. They arrived in Sydney late Sunday evening. Sam walked through the airport with her head the size of a basketball sporting a large black eye.

After her first adventure out of Sydney, she looked for events that would bring her closer to the feel of the local Outback. Lacy was also keen to join her as well. They saw flyers for a Ned Kelly Festival just beyond the Blue Mountains. They didn't know much about Australian history, but they heard that Ned had a history very similar to Billy the Kid.

A few weeks later, Brad asked Sam if she would like to bring some of her 'mates' on a Saturday trip with him and his wife, Sheri, to Jenolan Caves in the Blue Mountains. This was Sam's first time to be walking through limestone stalactites and stalagmites. Lyndsey, who joined Sam on the trip with Marsha pulled Sam to the side as they left the last cave. "Brad is sweet on you," she said.

"Naw," Sam looked embarrassed feeling the blood rise up throughout her body. *There was really nothing I would have cared for more.* "He's married."

"Well he may be married, but he couldn't take his eyes off you all day. I think this trip was set up for him to spend some time with *you*."

"Oh go away. That is your imagination running away," Sam commented quickly to shut her up. The last thing she wanted was a married man interested in her. However, she *was* enjoying the flavor of the attention. Sometimes fantasies can be a girl's best friend.

5

Creating an Expat Family

It was November, the beginning of the Australian Summer. Sam was standing at the bus stop in the morning with Lacy outside their Bondi flat to wait for the bus to school. It was beginning to get hot and Sam was getting irritated by the swarms of black flies in her face and eyes.

One morning Sam shouted out. "Does anyone know why there are so many flies?" The entire bus stop of about twenty people just stared at her. This happened to her a lot in the beginning. She just didn't have a clue.

One bloke spoke up. "So you don't know the Australian wave yet, do ya miss."

"Nope, I'm afraid not. What is it?"

He curved his right hand to make a cup and scooped it in front of his eyes left-to-right and did the same with his left hand in the opposite direction. "There you are, Miss. It'll come in handy through the six months of the bloody warm season we have coming our way."

"Are there this many flies everywhere?" Sam asked.

"No, Miss they are denser in the Outback, but they are bloody dense pretty much everywhere here in Australia in the summer months."

So flies came with the perfect country she was now calling her new home. She knew she'd have to get used to them. Now she understood why she kept seeing pictures of the Jolly Swagman with his hat that had corks hanging from the brim. She kept humming the music to "Waltzing Matilda" to truly get into the feel of the country she was growing to love.

On the first day she walked into school, she introduced herself to the Headmistress, Miss. Find, and the secretary, Mrs. Armstrong. Miss. Find introduced Sam to the class. Only twenty-four students. Great, she thought. Her last class in New Jersey was thirty-nine. Before she left, she whispered, "They can be a bit cheeky, especially that big blonde lad at the end of the second row." It took all of twenty minutes for him to begin cat calls, whistling, and making rude statements. Sam called Trevor up to the front and immediately told him her three strike rule. *No way did you want to get to strike three.* Then she made him her first mate for teaching her Australian terminology. They made a 'T' chart with Aussie and Yank words on either side. The class was enjoying the education.

"Trevor, what do I call this here?" she pointed to the black hand-held article at the bottom of the blackboard, "In America, we call this an eraser."

"It's a duster, Miss." Sam was getting a crash course on Australian slang: duster, bin, beauty, brolly . . . just to name a few.

Sam also began working on her own Jersey girl slang. In the metropolitan area of New York, the word *fuck* was like a comma in most sentences. What the fuck, fuck you, and the middle finger was used liberally. Soon she learned that bloody was a good substitute here in Oz, and the swipe of two fingers sweeping up took the place of the middle finger. *Not that she did that very much.*

On her first months in the staff room, the six teachers in grades 3 through 6 usually shared lunch together. The school was overdue for renovation. The staff room was a small narrow room no bigger than a broom closet. One long enameled table took up the middle and they had to shuffle around chairs to make it to the fridge.

The staff were not jaded against her being an American. They were engaging, witty, and often comical. They were having fun toying with Sam. She felt (or hoped) they were going to give her a chance; she never took it personally. Their curiosity about Americans was equal to her curiosity about Australians. Whenever she left the staff room, they would chant together, *"Have a nice day!"* Sam would turn around and throw both arms up in the air and shout, *"Fuggetaboudit* (that's Jersey for get stuffed.)"

Sam still didn't know if she fell in love with Brad at first sight or just thought he was one of the handsomest men she had ever met. She would look up from her lunch often and find him staring at her. She would slowly move her head up to meet his eyes and give a wink and smile back. It was an innocent nonverbal flirt. She did sense their attraction was mutual but both knew there were lines they couldn't cross.

In the narrow staff room was also Cassie, lithe and unflappable; Frank, who was tall and handsome; Linda, a strict tyrant of a teacher; and Kristi, petite, sweet, and pretty. Finally, there was Mr. Melrose, the second in command and an older married gentleman. He was also witty.

Often at work, Brad would love to share stories of all sorts of encounters he had with critters over the years. He was a witty storyteller. Some tales were tongue-in-cheek. Sometimes he would intentionally tease Sam, saying, "Really, Rothbauer, did you think I was serious?"

Brad shared that he grew up on a dairy farm near a country town north of Maitland. Sam didn't know whether to believe half of his stories, but she was hungry to hear more about his life. During one lunch period, he told a story about a snake. He described how he needed to walk a mile up a country dirt road to retrieve the mail each day.

"Once, there was this humongous bloody brown snake. It must have been over six feet long. The most poisonous of them all bolted out of a nearby bush and began chasing me up the road. I guess I had disturbed the bugger's midday nap. He was so bloody fast, he almost had me by the heel twice. I ran close to five kilometers before he quit."

"No, you're pulling my leg," Sam said avoiding his eyes.

"S'truth! Rothbauer, when are you ever going to believe me? He chased me forever. I was in bloody fear for my life." At that point Cassie walked into the staff lounge.

Brad turned to Cassie, and said, "She won't believe the story about the giant brown snake chasing me up the bloody road."

"Ah, yes . . . ," Cassie said in her slow even keel voice, "The brown snake story, yes, that one *could be* true. He tells us that one often enough. But, you're right, if I were you, I wouldn't believe many of his other stories."

"Great help you are, Cassie," commented Brad.

The next morning Sam came in before the start of the day very troubled asking the group, "Does anyone here know what a funnel web spider is?"

Cassie sighed, "Ah . . . yes. They're the most dangerous spiders in all of Australia."

"Are they *really* here in Sydney?" Sam asked nervously.

"Bloody well right, Rothbauer," spoke up Brad. "There was one in my car just last weekend."

"What?" Sam screamed in disbelief, "Really!" She wasn't sure if she should believe this story but Cassie was present, so she felt it was valid. Cassie sat herself down across the table from Brad to hear the story herself.

"Yes, this last Saturday, my wife, Sheri, and I were out doing our food shopping. Sheri saw something crawling out of the air vent of our vehicle onto the dashboard just above the glove box. She began screaming bloody murder, so I pulled the car over. She immediately jumped out. I yelled, "Where are you going, it's just a bloody spider!" However, on closer examination it was not just one of your household types, like a brown recluse, red back or big black. It *was* a bloody funnel web.'"

"Really, are they as bad as they say?" Sam asked.

"Well, I would advise that you better get as far away from those buggers as you can."

"So, how did you deal with it? I mean, you couldn't just abandon your car. What did you do," Sam asked with eyes as big as headlights? She really did want to know what to do in such a situation. There had been radio reports recently that a housewife had been killed by a funnel web. She had been changing the sheets in her home in North Sydney. It was lying between the bottom sheet and the bottom of the bed board.

Brad went on to describe how the funnel web, which is about the size of an American quarter, could jump and dig its fangs through someone's thumb nail and drive the venom into their body killing a full-grown man.

"Well, I finally got the bugger," he went on. "I trapped him. I got a discarded coffee cup and held it over him and slid a piece of paper below him and emptied him outside in a nearby bush. You know that trick don't you, Rothbauer?"

"Seriously, you just spilled it out in a bush!" Sam asked incredulously.

"Yes, what else do you think I was going to do with the bloody thing, make him a pet?"

"Why, *kill it* of course."

"Kill it. Why, would I attempt to put myself in danger by killing it?"

"Well . . . because someone else might get jumped by the spider," she suggested.

"Not bloody likely," he said, "But it wasn't going to be me."

<hr />

Lacy and Sam often arrived home late in the evening. They didn't spend much time talking about their day. They brought food home and Lacy often brought home company for dinner. She had a talent for picking up folks along the way. Lacy sensed Sam might be too serious to be around alone.

It was always a party. In those days, they were all trying to sow their wild oats. Sam had never gone away to college and was the oldest of their group by a year. She had already been married *and* divorced. Wild oats were different for many. Some saw that being away from family and friends in another country afforded them a past they would not run into in the future. Sam's opinion was that the past you always run into is yourself.

Lacy was only a year younger than Sam, but she was a wild child. Sam knew that if she was ever going to learn how to figure out how to branch out from her former strict upbringing, Lacy would teach her how. Sam wanted to test her boundaries. She had a sense of what they were. She knew what she might try and what she would not.

In Australia, your party beverage was limited to wine or beer. People usually didn't drink hard liquor. Beer killed her gut so KB and Tooheys were out; it was wine for Sam and there were only two choices. Riesling was Sam's box of choice; Chablis was *way* too sweet. She brought a box to every party and drank plenty of it.

The flat filled each weekend with three East Coast girlfriends, Marsha, Lyndsey and Jersey City Kat, who were all living in the western suburbs. Marsha and Lyndsey roomed together and came at Sam's invitation. Lacy invited Jersey City Kat who she befriended on the plane. Kat was a buxom blonde with a low sexy kitten-like voice and a strong opinion on most everything, which she was always ravenous to share.

This was the beginning of their American expat family. Often in foreign countries 'birds of a feather flock together,' a cliché, but true. As the girls got to know each other, they tried not to cut each other off at the knees. Sam wasn't big on judging people's actions, but she was always being judged for hers. She came to understand it is a dog-eat-dog girl's world. Though she had a little sister back in the States, they didn't grow up together because they were years apart in age. She had no experience with women other than those of her even-keeled childhood neighborhood friends.

The lure of coffee at the kitchen table on a typical Saturday morning always drew her into a hornet's nest. After an adventurous Friday evening at The Bondi Beach Hotel Pub, Sam would walk into the three women sharing stories about their escapades from the evening before. They were always colorful. Sam enjoyed listening but remained quiet as she had no desire to share anything that would cause her to become a target. Around men Sam wasn't a huntress. She enjoyed being hunted. However, her American expat family refused to leave her be.

"So . . . Sam who was that cute bloke with the long brown hair you were talking with in the corner of the pub all evening?" questioned Lyndsey.

"He said his name was Patrick, he's visiting from Ireland," she answered not letting her eyes meet theirs.

"So, did he take you back to his place? I noticed you came in very late," smirked Kat.

"*No*," Sam said annoyed. "We closed the pub and he walked me home."

"So, are you seeing him again tonight?" prodded Kat snickering behind her coffee.

"I don't know, if he is at the pub again, maybe," replied Sam putting her nose further down into her cup for a soothing whiff of coffee hoping to escape.

"Well, is he here for a couple of months, years, or just weeks?" asked Lacy.

Sam sighed as the interrogations were getting tedious. "I don't know, and I don't care. Either way he is a short-term visitor passing through. He's a nice guy and I enjoyed talking to him last night, full stop."

"What do you think you are," asked Lyndsey. "Some kind of virgin?"

"Well, I *am* a Virgo, maybe that entitles me to be what *I* want to be."

In her new world of women, if a man found her attractive at a party and she spent time with him having a drink, the *friends* felt she should have gone to bed with him. It was obviously some unwritten code that made her not part of the club and subject to scrutiny by the others.

One evening Kat needed a ride to a pub up the road and Sam volunteered to drive her there. They got into her new used white four door Toyota Corolla that she had just purchased from a fellow teacher. On the way Kat began divulging bits of private conversations she had with the others that she felt Sam might find beneficial.

"You know they have all labeled you a cock teaser," said Kat. Sam had heard the term before but wasn't sure what it meant.

"So . . . what does that mean?"

"It means you just like the attention, will take the drinks, and lead men on," said Kat.

"Obviously you feel that same way too or you wouldn't have shared that little tidbit of information with me," suggested Sam.

"Well, this is what you seem to do."

"Listen," said Sam, "I don't judge any of you on how you target and take down men in bars. I'm wired differently, intimacy happens only when I care for someone. Perhaps having one too many drinks blinds *all* our judgements sometimes, but don't be judging me on how I enjoy meeting people."

"Ah . . . there *all* just jealous," commented Kat.

"You too?"

"Well, yes, of course. I hated you the moment I saw you on the plane. You were just so perfectly made up and coiffed." There it was out in the open. Jealousy was the root of all evil among women.

It was funny Sam didn't learn how to attract men from her mother, she learned from her father. He was the voice in her head.

"Dressing up isn't a crime, it speaks of confidence," he said. "It takes courage to walk into a crowd sharply dressed." My father was tall, dark, and handsome and could obviously pull this off. Sam remembered reading an article written about him in a military newspaper saying, "The Clark Gable of the platoon has just arrived."

He told me to walk into a room and command a presence. "Look tall and proud, fix your shoulders like they are hanging from a clothes hanger. Walk into the room heading toward the back and smile like you recognize someone, and watch the eyes follow you."

"The Bondi Beach Hotel Pub was the first opportunity she had to practice these moves, especially the looking straight and tall part. Her dad had her practice for hours walking across rooms with three books on her head as a young girl, *but* he never let her leave the house, not once.

Her dad's final words were always, "Remember I brought you up to be a lady." It was an expectation that echoed louder than the crashing of waves or lions roaring in cages.

Her presence must have been somewhat successful because it was annoying people. But they were just going to have to get used to it. Sam needed the expat family and so did the others.

Sam was observing their behaviors as well. There wasn't a whole lot of trust in that flat. You could cut the air of jealousy like a knife but it was usually centered around Lacy. Both Lyndsey and Kat vied for her constant attention. Marsha never involved herself with any of it. She floated on an ethereal cloud of natural beauty and charm that radiated from her every pore. She was untouchable.

Sam's view about teaching was another bone of contention. She was never allowed to bring it up in conversation. She was passionate about her work while the rest saw it as a job. So she came home from work each night and threw herself into whatever party was manifesting itself.

The first Christmas Break was coming (a six-week holiday). They had already spent every weekend hanging around the pubs of Bondi; the big question was where to spend the holidays. They all had extra money burning in their pockets. One evening, Lacy and Sam stumbled into their newfound friend, Harry. He ran a tourist agency in Bondi. He told the girls the best adventure for everyone of value was the Island of Bali. That week the five of them booked passage for Indonesia on Garuda Airlines. Sam contacted Robbie, Marsha invited her friend, Lance, and Lacy invited Barry. Before they knew it, they had a large group signed up to embark on this exotic adventure to Indonesia.

There were only four spots on the Saturday flight on Garuda Airlines and another four spots for the day after. Sam picked the Sunday, so did Lyndsey, Robbie and Marsha. On the Sunday of the flight, Garuda Airlines went on strike. Harry, the agent, pulled some strings and by that afternoon they had passage on Singapore Airlines. They arrived in Singapore and quickly decided to spend the week.

They stayed in the world-famous Raffles Hotel, the home of Somerset Maugham and the creation of the Singapore Sling. The hotel was magnificent, filled with old world colonial charm. The girls shopped and Robbie wrote by the pool surrounded by fan palms.

A week later, they were in Bali where the Yank family dynamics began to unfold. The boys nicknamed our group, The Notorious Eight. They all shared a memorable Christmas Eve in Padang Bay where Lacy and Barry unsuccessfully were hoping to jump onto a ship bound for Singapore. Lance was Sam's hero that day. He had followed behind her as she managed to stall out her 100cc motorcycle as she slowly approached every corner.

Everyone looked very relaxed sipping cold beers in the open-air pagoda. Sam desperately needed to find a bathroom. She asked the lady in the back of the café where she might go. She pointed to a fenced-in area out in the back. Sam walked carefully through dozens of chickens and opened the gate. Inside there were a dozen pigs wallowing in muddy patches. Sam came back out and asked again, she shook her head and pointed again to the fence.

"Inside," she said pointing her finger. Sam was desperate so she went back to look again. She walked again through the pigs and saw another smaller four-sided structure surrounding an open pit. *Desperate times call for desperate measures.*

It was late afternoon and they discussed staying the night. They told the owner they would take all six of their rooms. Some would need to share, but after a few cold ones, who the hell cared. It was Christmas Eve.

They ate rice and chicken and drank the village out of all its grog. They began to sing Christmas Carols. Slowly the villagers began to sit on the dirt around the open-air pagoda to listen to the songs. There seemed to be a hundred villagers sitting watching them as if they were performing on a stage. To please the audience, they sang every song they could think of. Finally, they began the "Twelve Days of Christmas". They laughed and struggled over the words but made it through the lyrics. Everyone clapped, the group bowed and headed toward their rooms.

One of the villagers asked if any of them wanted to see a mysterious bay. About five of them followed him up to a large hill filled with rice paddies. They walked in zig-zag steps surrounded by darkness. No one wanted to think what kinds of nocturnal spiders and snakes were living in there. Sam just kept following behind Lance and Robbie who were keeping a brisk pace with several of the village men.

They finally reached the top and took in the most exquisite view below. Dozens of small fishing boats dotted the seascape lit by kerosene lanterns. Someone made the decision to walk down the long dark slope to get to the bay. (One of the villagers described the water being filled with glow worms.)

"I'm not going down this hill," Sam protested.

"Come on, Sam," said Robbie. "What are you going to do, stay up there alone?" She didn't need but a second to decide. Staying up on the cliff alone wasn't an option. The journey down was even harder than going up.

When they reached the beach, they walked to the water's edge. The small waves were full of iridescent critters flipping and turning as if in a dance.

"Let's go skinny dipping," someone yelled. Everyone began peeling off their clothes. Now, Sam had *never* gone skinny dipping in her life, but if there was ever a time or a season, this was it. She slowly took her clothes off hoping the moonlit night wasn't allowing her imperfections to show. She stood alone as the others ran excitedly into the water. It was amazing to see the swirls of luminescence surround each of their bodies and swished around their hands and legs. They each looked like little lit Christmas bulbs decorating a tree. Lance came walking out of the water towards Sam. He looked like a god. His perfectly chiseled body glowed in the moonlight and his blonde hair lit up like a halo. He walked up and took her hand.

"Come on, Sam, it's like bathwater," he said holding out his hand. She took his hand and followed him into the water. As they walked slowly up to their waist, hundreds of luminescent critters followed their bodies. Lance swirled his hands first in front of Sam to show the designs he could make. Then he swirled his hands to the sides and stretched his hands behind her. Sam looked around to find thousands of glow worms hugging each of their curves. His hands slowly moved up Sam's back pulling her closer. They were the last to leave the water holding hands climbing the rice paddies and shared the last available room together.

The next day they all booked into a Hilton Hotel on Kuta Beach. Kat volunteered her American Express card making everyone promise that they would pay her bill as soon as they got back to Sydney. The room alone was over a hundred dollars. What a difference! They were paying only a dollar a night for a cot in a hut in Legian.

Everyone spent the evening taking turns calling their families. Sam wasn't ready to make a call that Christmas. Everyone was filling their family's ears with their adventures. Her family wasn't ready to hear all about this life and she wasn't ready to have a family discussion shared by a dozen ears. She passed.

The nightmare began as they went to leave the penthouse the next morning. They were in the lobby waiting for cabs when the management from the hotel surrounded them accusing them of stealing their towels, ashtrays, and other paraphernalia from the room. Sam had no idea that anything had been taken and began speaking for the group.

"What . . . are you accusing us of, petty theft?" she protested in anger. "Really, you get some young people in a hotel and want to assume we are

a bunch of thieves. Listen, if you want to search us, go ahead, here—"
She pushed her bright orange backpack forward, "Search away." she
protested.

Sharply someone's foot kicked her in the shins. "Shut-up." said one,
"Shhh . . . ," said another. All of a sudden it began to register that as a
group they weren't so innocent.

Since Sam started this messy conversation, she asked the management how much it would take to settle the bill. The manager came up
with some absurd sum and they settled on twenty dollars.

Just then the cabs pulled up front. Sam jumped in with Kat and Lacy.
On the way back, they asked what she had lifted.

"Obviously, nothing or I wouldn't have told them to search us. What
did you girls take?"

Lacy admitted to taking sheets and towels.

"What if they know where we are staying?" asked Kat, who said
someone put towels in her backpack.

"How would they know that?" Sam asked.

"One of us might have placed it on the register," said Kat.

"Weren't you the only one who signed the register for all of us?"

"Maybe, and maybe I put down where we were staying," she
blurted back.

Lacy began to agree with Kat. "They may have authorities waiting at
the huts for us," Lacy stated. The nervousness became a fevered pitch.

"So, what is the worst thing they can do to you," Sam asked.

"Who knows, this is Indonesia. They arrest people who are caught
smuggling drugs and imprison them for life here," said Lacy.

"But you just took towels and some sheets and they settled on
a payment."

"What are we going to do?" Kat asked Lacy.

The two began whispering in the back of the cab so the driver
couldn't hear.

Lacy asked the driver, "How far away are we from our village?"

"About a kilometer, Miss."

"Good, could you let us out here? Thanks, here is five dollars, keep the change," said Lacy indicating it was hush money. They all stood out in the middle of a large empty dirt-filled paddock.

Lacy and Kat began unpacking their back packs. Out came several towels, sheets, and an ash tray.

"So, now what," Sam asked. "Are you planning to leave it here for the locals?"

"No, we should bury it," Lacy said. "We need to bury the evidence."

"*Seriously,* are we going to really dig a hole for all this bloody crap," Sam said in frustration. It was deliriously hot and humid.

"Yup we are, and I suggest you help if you don't want to be linked as an accessory. I'm not spending one day in an Indonesian prison," Lacy shouted.

So, they found twigs and rocks to scratch and dig a hole in the hot, humid midday sun. When the deed was done, they shuffled their heavy backpacks down the road another kilometer, trudging with exhaustion.

When they got to the huts in Legian, the gang was there sipping drinks and happily high on Thai sticks.

"Where have you guys been," questioned Lyndsey, "We were worried you got picked up by the police or something."

Sam shook her head, "I'm not going to answer this one; I'll let Lacy tell you." Sam picked up her backpack and began walking down the winding path to her hut. Suddenly she heard the entire group roaring with laughter. Obviously the others had kept their bed sheets and towels. Kat and Lacy would never outlive their decision to bury their treasure.

Somehow they all survived the twenty-eight days together in Bali. The very next day, Sam traded her motorcycle for a motor scooter with an electric start. She took off and traveled alone for the rest of the trip up to the volcano and then later through Indonesia and Malaysia.

6

Moving On

After Bali, the Bondi flat became party central. The three girls had moved in permanently. Inevitably, everybody from the group at some time or another brought back more people to return to the flat in the evenings. Just because Sam was one of two who paid the rent on the flat didn't necessarily make it a place where she could find room to sleep.

One Friday night, Sam came home to six people sleeping in her bed. There was nowhere to go except the wooden floor or the course wicker couch. Sam had had it! She broke the news to everyone the next day that she would be looking for another flat. (It was far less complicated for her to go than to try to get them to leave.)

Lacy also used the opportunity to move from Bondi into a shared house with her boyfriend Rick, the cab driver in Paddington. The remaining group began to look for another flat.

It didn't take them long to find a large four-bedroom flat in Potts Point next to Kings Cross. Two moves later, Sam found a very nice situation with a businesswoman from New Zealand. She held the lease on a beautiful three-bedroom penthouse on top of a small high-rise in Neutral Bay. It looked like something you might rent in Japan. It was pretty dear (expensive). It cost forty dollars a week, but how often do you get the opportunity to experience a penthouse?

Rice paper screen sliders divided rooms. Large glass walls that scaled floor to ceiling surrounded the entire apartment overlooking the bay bordered by 180 degrees of balcony. It had breathtaking views from every room. If you could tilt your head far to the left, you could see the Opera House across the harbor. The flat was just above the ferry stop that took daily commuters to the Sydney Quay. *This is it, I'm never moving again.*

Barbie, Sam's new flatmate, loved the fact that she was an American. Sam was her conversational piece for parties. Barbie was big at putting dinner parties together. Sam found it easier just visiting her expat friends than living with them.

Lacy and Rick bought a car, a Mini. Rick and his good buddy, Andy, had a side business rebuilding and fixing up old Minis. They were also buying a 420 sailboat to sail on Sydney Harbor. They were looking for a third partner in the boat. Sam had mentioned that she would like to learn more about sailing. The mates needed someone to share the expenses for the fourteen-foot sailboat. They invited her to share the expenses but Sam felt she never got her money's worth. The small sloop design was only a two-man vessel and Rick and Andy always sailed together.

Barbie also used Sam's owning part of a sailboat as a great conversation piece. Not only was her flatmate a Yank but she owned a yacht. Sam felt sure with Barbie's connections, she might find that sailor who would travel with her around the world. However, her luck didn't work that way.

Sam and Barbie were invited to crew on some beautiful sailboats from time to time. One perfect spring Saturday, they were invited to sail on an eighty-foot Yawl named Anaconda II. The wind was up. It was a perfect day for sailing a split-rig. The owner, Josco Helgesen, was a handsome middle-aged man. He had blonde hair, a fit bronze body, and a confident stride. As the girls walked up the gangplank, he shook their hands, "Welcome aboard ladies, make yourself at home. We are heading out as soon as you are comfortable."

No sooner did he say the words when the sails caught wind and they were heading down the bay passing smaller boats with spinnakers. They quickly moved past the heads and headed north to Manly and Middle Harbor. Anaconda II pulled up majestically to a long wooden pier just before the Split and Josco stepped off the yacht like the Prince of Wales himself. Sam was feeling a bit important pulling up on such an impressive yacht. People poured out of the Yacht Club to take in the sight of the Yawl.

The girls had all brought lunch and they set up a brunch table for the captain and crew. Josco grabbed some food and sat down next to Sam. "Are you enjoying yourself," he asked.

"This is an amazing yawl" she said. "I'm trying to imagine how she would perform out at sea."

"Oh, she can handle any sea. I sailed her here from Sweden. Would you like to see below?" Sam followed him on a lovely tour of the boat and hoped he'd invite her back for a moonlight sail but it never happened.

One Sunday morning, Lacy got this bright idea—"C'mon, Sam, let's show the boys we don't need them." She pressured Sam to take out the 420 sailboat.

"Lacy, I really don't know how to rig that boat myself. There is a lot to it," Sam said. Lacy waved it off.

"Sam, we are two attractive women under thirty, we'll have no trouble finding someone to help with the boat." *Lacy Logic.*

Lacy had no trouble attracting crowds to her. Sam, on the other hand, lacked that particular skill set. Timing was not their friend. Sam was still a novice at sailing and didn't realize that the local wind picks up around eleven in the morning. It was after noon and anyone who had a sailing vessel was already out on the bay. Seeing that they had no one to dazzle with their charms to help with the boat, Sam said. "Okay, Lacy, what'll we do now? I'm game to try to rig this boat but I'm not promising anything and we haven't a set of directions."

"Oh well," she said, casually as always. "We've come this far. Let's just give it a go. If we fail, we have reason to go to the nearest pub and see what kind of trouble we can get into there."

Sam was pretty easy-going and her lack of disagreement in those days often got her into trouble. They actually got the mast set and the main rigged, except Sam had major problems with how the backstay should be attached. One kind older gentleman came by and helped.

Lacy was petrified from the moment they caught the wind. She now realized that her outing could end up disastrously. Sam was trying to get her to understand that both of them needed to work the boat. The boat zoomed out hitting ten knot winds instantly. Being such a light boat, it slanted over with water splashing into the hull. Lacy was on the down side and was catching most of the spray against her face.

She began screaming at the top of her lungs. "Oh . . . I know we took a long time to get out here, but you need to stop this thing, Sam, let's go back."

Sam tried to reason with her. "Listen, it took us over an hour to rig this boat. Be reasonable, let's keep it out just an hour." But there was no reasoning with her. "Lacy, we're really in no danger".

She screamed at the top of her lungs. "I just saw the movie *Jaws* and I had to walk out of the theater. This is a country whose waters are full of great whites."

"Yes, and you haven't heard of a single person being attacked by a great white in this harbor, have ya?"

"They have shark nets surrounding all of Bondi and Manly Beaches for a reason, Sam. I'm scared to death out here. I didn't realize these boats would be *so* small. Please, let's go back, *please.*"

She was relentless. Sam gave in.

"Okay . . . but we have to go on a little further so I can shift the sails and turn the boat around. You just stay holding this line for me in the middle of the boat."

The turn went smoothly but the vessel was fast. She had them into Rose Bay in minutes.

A couple of blokes helped them stow the boat. They didn't hang around and Lacy suggested they should go visit the group at their new flat in Potts Point.

This was Sam's first official visit to the flat. It was huge. Marsha must have had first dibs on rooms. She had a large sunny turret bedroom just off the kitchen. Barry had also moved in as well. He and Lacy were just friends now. He got the middle room with the fireplace. Jersey City Kat had the back bedroom nearest to the bathroom.

Kat pulled Lacy aside. She was *so* excited to talk with her about the guy she and Marsha had met from the deli downstairs. "Oh, my God, Lacy, you have to meet this guy! He looks like Mel Gibson. Wyatt is

Texan. He insists he's a Texan, not a Yank. He's definitely different though. He says he just came in from years of collecting artifacts up the rivers of New Guinea."

They spent over an hour talking about this Hollywood-like artifact gatherer named Wyatt Stetson. Since many of the group hadn't met him yet, the two schemed to throw one of their many Friday night parties hoping they could get him to come.

Wyatt came and he quickly became part of the expat crowd. He appeared at most parties when he got off work. He usually cuddled up on floor with Lacy. Rick and Lacy were still very much together, but Lacy was far from settled down. Wyatt was a player for sure. He would occasionally bring a trendy model as a date to grace their bohemian parties.

Without a doubt, Wyatt enchanted people with his eccentricities. People said they loved him or hated him; most of the women loved him because he was so handsome and he knew it. He was definitely colorful, arrogant, strongly opinionated, and snorted loudly when he laughed. He also brought into the group other men from Texas who wanted to party. Jersey City Kat fell hard for one. Sam didn't care to keep track. She lived her life somewhere else and her life at school grounded her. To walk 'King's Cross' was definitely a walk on the wild side.

7

Beware of the Pit Falls

When one wanders far from home for the first time, there is a syndrome that occurs around gaining weight. Sam had heard that somewhere. This was shocking to her and she wished she had been aware of it before putting it on in her first two years.

Sam actually had taken weight off before her adventure to Australia. She was looking and feeling so good about herself. Then suddenly, just coming into a new culture, trying new foods, the parties, and of course the munchies, the weight returned.

By the time Sam moved into Barbie's penthouse, she had to buy larger clothes. She resorted to wrap around skirts and peasant shirts synched with a large belt at the waist. She felt like a happy little Buddha. *Maybe not so happy*. She missed her long hair and began growing it back.

Soon, Sam became a product of roller coaster diets. Cleanses, fasts, and the infamous Israeli Army Diet. She would lose ten pounds quickly, mostly water, and within a month it would all be back. It drove her and everyone around her insane. So she simply decided that she was no longer dateable material.

Wyatt had become the golden boy of Sydney. He sold his share in the deli, got investors, mostly friends, to back him in a restaurant deal in Bondi Junction.

The Village restaurant was located on top of a high rise. It was reachable only by elevator. Panoramic views of the lights of Sydney could be seen from every window. It had become the new "in" spot for many young local couples and of course the expats.

Wyatt approached Sam about investing in his restaurant, but Lacy quickly talked her out of it saying he suggested it to everyone. "You would be stupid to part with your hard earned money," Lacy said, "You'll never get it back."

Lacy loved exploring Australia as much as Sam did. The first Easter break she talked Rick, his mate, Andy, and Sam into renting a caravan together for a week to explore the southern island of Tasmania. Sam was more conscious of her added weight on this trip. Lacy was always able to keep her girlish figure eating the same things Sam did. *It just wasn't fair.*

After a week they returned to Sydney. Sam met Clementine, Andy's Australian flatmate. Clementine began to date a tall, curly brown-haired Aussie named Todd. He was musical and funny. Todd liked Sam's crowd and began to bring more Aussies to their parties. He introduced them to people all over the city. One weekend they found themselves at a party in North Sydney. Everyone there was over thirty and well-off business types. This was definitely not their usual kind of crowd. It was all couples but as was the Aussie fashion, the women were all gathered in the kitchen. Sam was bored and began drinking too much wine early. It was her strategy for getting over shyness.

Sam went out to the living room and began to talk to the men. It was probably taboo to cross that line, but she didn't care. Sam didn't know how she got home that night. The following morning, she awoke on a makeshift couch in Marsha's bedroom. She got up early and made some instant coffee in the kitchen.

Jersey City Kat walked in shaking her head. "You need to lay off the wine. Drink Scotch instead."

"You're probably right. I can't remember a thing. I must have blacked out."

"Well, it is probably a good thing you don't remember," she said.

"Was I *that* bad?" Sam asked looking up over her coffee mug.

"Ooh, yah. Do you want to know how bad?"

"No, not really, but I suppose you are going to tell me anyway."

"Well, to be frank, I probably *saved* your life."

"What," Sam said. She had zero memory of anything after talking with all the men in the living room.

"Yes, you were stirring trouble flirting with all the men. Not just some of the men—*all* of them. You had them mesmerized. The women were ready to kill you. Finally, you took a break and found your way to a bathroom. I saw one bloke follow you in. I knocked and then shoved the door open. I could see he was all over you. I grabbed you and screamed at him, "If you want to be with her, make a date. You don't follow inebriated women into bathrooms and take advantage of them. He got a good taste from me what Yanks won't put up with."

"Christ," Sam said. "Sorry, I don't have a single morsel of memory of any of this. How did we get home?"

"We got a taxi and I dragged you up two flights of steps and threw you in Marsha's room. Now they have signs posted all over North Sydney. Yanks are not welcome to any more of their house parties."

"Hmm . . . just as well, they were a stuffy lot."

"I'm going to give you one word of advice. You are blacking out because you are drinking wine. When your alcohol has sugar in it, that happens. Believe me, I'm a *pro* at drinking. Find yourself something else, some type of distilled liquor, scotch or something."

Sam actually tried her advice once by bringing whiskey to a party. The bottle vanished from the table in seconds. Kat shared with her more than once that she hated Sam from the first minute she saw her on the plane, but her guess was at times she considered her family. Well at least she did for one night.

New South Wales

- Hebel
- Goodooga
- Angledool
- Coff Harbor
- Gold coast
- Bourke
- Lightning Ridge
- Broken Hill
- Armidale
- Tamworth
- Forster
- Quirindi
- Newcastle
- Dubbo
- Maitland
- Midura
- Sydney
- Wagga Wagga
- Finley
- Canberra
- Albury

Victoria

- Melbourne

Tasmania

Author's Drawing
Not to scale

8

Lightning Ridge

As the year went on, life became more about work and less about adventure. Sam knew she was in Australia for the long run. She was investing her energy in her friendships with different groups of people. Nonetheless, she would rarely turn away from anything that smelled like an adventure.

One Friday evening while sitting around the Chalis Street flat, Lyndsey and Jersey City Kat were trying to put together a trip. Kat had found a flyer in Kings Cross about a place called Lightning Ridge in Northern New South Wales where people mined opals.

Lyndsey and Kat spent the past few months exploring all the Kings Cross Taverns and were yearning to get a little Outback action. They tried to get Marsha to join them, but Marsha was beginning to pack it up and was saving her money to head back to the States. She was finished with her adventures in Oz and was looking forward to planning an overland trip through Asia that would lead her back to the East Coast.

The trip to Lightning Ridge would be a bus tour that would take place over the four days of the Queen's Weekend. They also knew that their friend, Lance, had been placed in nearby Goodooga. From the map, it looked like it was pretty close in proximity to Lightning Ridge.

Lyndsey, who became the great communicator among them, wrote Lance a letter describing where they would be in the hopes they could run into him while they were there.

This bus tour was described as a camping trip. So, they brought their backpacks and got on the long twelve-hour bus haul.

When they awoke, the driver was saying it was six the next morning and for everyone to take a look outside to view the sunrise and moon setting over the vast horizon, both at the same time.

Everyone got off the bus about nine in Lightning Ridge. They were told to pitch tents and stow away their gear. Sam wasn't impressed by the surroundings. The spot where they were parked to pitch the tents just looked like a vacant gravel parking lot. There was a large concrete wall surrounding the perimeter. *This has no feel of the Outback.* Sam wondered what kind of adventure they would have going down Opal Mines when she heard Lyndsey yelling, "Oh my God, look who it is!"

"Lance, oh my God. You are a sight for sore eyes," Sam screamed running up to him.

"Hey, Sam, good to see you, too. As soon as Lyndsey wrote me you were all coming, I set about looking to see who I could borrow a car from for the weekend."

"Who would possibly let you borrow their car for the whole weekend," Sam asked.

"Oh, that was easy. The girls I teach with lent it to me."

"Well of course they did."

"Sorry Marsha isn't with us. She's getting ready to leave Australia after this year."

"Yeah, I wrote to her. Australia doesn't seem to be her cup of tea. I'll probably head back after my two-year term is up myself. I'll cash in on that free return flight home."

"Well," Sam challenged, "That means we need to have as much fun as we can while everyone is still here."

"Righty-Oh," Lance exclaimed. "That's what I'm hoping we'll do."

By now Kat joined them. Kat's low sexy voice always came out around men and her personality definitely changed. She had a way of twinkling her eyes when she flirted.

"Hey . . . Lance," she mused. "So, what are we doing? Are you staying for brekky or are we getting to see the Outback? I haven't been able to get out of King's Cross since I moved here."

"Well, if it is all right with you gals, we can all jump into this handsome vehicle over here." He walked up to a beat-up whitish car covered with layers on layers of red dirt. "We'll just travel up some twenty miles of red clay road to meet some of my friends who've invited us to tea."

"Beauty, mate. Let's go," screamed Kat.

"Wait just a minute. I need to run back and get some things," Sam said excitedly.

She ran to the tent and got her camera gear and purse. She felt everything of any value was now in her possession. She told the tour manager they were going off with a friend on a day trip. Kat and Sam got in the back seat and Lyndsey rode shot gun up front with Lance.

Sam listened to the conversation with Lance and Lyndsey catching up. What was Lacy doing and how was Barry? Then Lance shared tales about Robbie. He said he had become a celebrity in Broken Hill. He and Lance became great friends in Bali and stayed in touch. Robbie was a good guitar player and joined a band. He began playing electric guitar. They reminisced back to Bondi, when they all would gather around Robbie's guitar as he played songs from The Eagles, Beatles, and Rolling Stones.

"The community of Broken Hill wants him to stay forever. They've got him singing in the local pub three nights a week. He seems to be loving being a rock star. He is even talking about writing some of his own music."

They rode along the bumpy, rutted Outback roads. Several times they almost lost their transmission. Plumes of red dust from the clay roads filled the car. They began to cough and tried to close the windows, but the air was so stuffy inside forcing them to reopen them and let some of the billowing clouds come back in.

Lance began to shift down the gears and yelled excitedly, "Look right, ladies. There are a few big reds hopping around out there now." They jumped forward sitting on the edge of their seats. They had been in

Australia over eight months and had never seen a roo in the wild. It was electrifying. They also saw wallabies and a few emus on the ride north.

This is far more exciting than crawling down some opal mines. Sam was always trying to visualize the type of towns the guys were sent to and now she was catching a glimpse. It was rough out here. Eucalyptus trees were scattered around scrub bush but not much else, just flat dry red earth.

"Is it always this dusty and dry out here?" Sam asked.

"It depends on the season. During the rainy season in mid-summer, you can't drive these roads without a four-wheel drive. A lot of the locals own British Land Rovers."

"Really, why's that?"

"Because that red clay you see out there turns to paste. It clogs up the vehicles from underneath and nothing can go anywhere. Even in a four-wheel drive, it's dicey. In Goodooga, we stay close to town. Believe me, walking can be a chore."

"Boy, I'm glad the rains are done," Sam said.

"Pretty much," said Lance. "But we have an occasional rainstorm that still mucks everything up. Funny, the weather service was half threatening some showers over this weekend."

"Really? Well, we'll just have to make the most of it."

They finally turned right, down a road that actually had a sign saying New Angledool.

"So, New Angledool is actually a town?" Sam asked.

"Yes . . . well, it is mostly the property of James and Annie Taylor. There is one store in the town, which also houses the post office. Annie is a teacher in my school. That's why we are invited to tea."

When they arrived, two blue healer dogs ran to the car barking excitedly. Lance jumped out as Annie came down the road to greet them. After they exchanged a big hug, she said, "Let's meet your mates, shall we?"

Introductions went around and they began their ascent into the small ranch-styled house with its large bullnose tin roof. It had a screened-in porch that went around three sides of the house.

Annie was lovely. She served a pot of tea and Australian styled sandwiches. They were thin little things made with white bread, a single piece of devon (bologna) a slice of hard-boiled egg, and a slice of beet root. The sandwiches were cut in quarters. The group quickly devoured the lot of them as they had not had breakfast.

James walked in through the squeaky screen door. He was the perfect picture image of an Outback rancher. He had on brown Carhartt overalls, torn and worn in appropriate places, work boots, and a brimmed hat. The hat was torn in every place imaginable, drooping from wear, defining no shape, sweaty and soiled, like it had been part of his life since the day he was born.

"So, what do you bloody sheilas want to see first?" he questioned in his raw Aussie twang. They all looked at each other. *James must be here to provide the entertainment.*

Lyndsey used her soft easygoing voice and answered, "Well, actually anything you care to show us."

They were finishing up their tea when James suggested, "Well, there is a wild boar loose nearby and I've promised these dogs some tucker tonight if you care to join me track him down."

"Really, oh my God, *yes*. I want to go," Sam screamed, raising her hand like a schoolgirl jumping up and down. The others stared at her wide-eyed and then shot a glance over to Lance.

Lance turned to James, "Is that all right if we come along. I know the girls will probably need to get back to Lightning Ridge before dark, and then I'll still have to drive the car back to Goodooga."

"Ah," said James, "We'll only be a few ticks on the old clock."

They all went. Sam was *so* excited she could barely contain herself. She remarked, "I remember Brad describing his boar hunting trips in the staff room. He went out often and described it in such detail that I thought I just have to have a go someday."

James grabbed a rifle and three of his dogs set off in hot pursuit of the beast.

"My God, we are all on a true dinky-dy walkabout," Kat shouted. They jabbered on a bit 'till James signaled. "Shush, no talking from this point on."

James cocked the rifle and moved up behind a tree where he could listen and watch for the dogs to get a sight on the pig. They all stood

watching barely breathing, not a sound, not a breath. The moments
moved to minutes. The dogs kept barking off in the distance. Then they
heard the yelping of a dog. It sounded hurt. James took off and began
running toward the sound of the dogs.

Bang! Bang! the rifle shot two rounds. "He's down," shouted James.
"Come Look."

They ran to where they could hear his voice and there lying before
them was a huge dead boar. Steam rose off its blood-soaked body. James
looked over at Sam and handed her the rifle. "Do you want a picture
with the pig?"

"Oh God yes." She took the rifle, stood next to the pig, and struck a pose.

"No, not like that," said James. "This way." He had Sam put one foot
on top of the pig and hoist the rifle up to rest the butt on her knee. Sam
looked like she was a big game hunter who had just brought down some
large charging African lion. *This will be my prized photo for years.* Now
she could brag she went boar hunting in Australia.

"How is your dog?" Sam asked James on the walk back.

"Just a torn ear, that's all."

Sam thanked James saying he just made her whole adventure in Australia. James didn't stop there though. When they got back to the house,
he asked, "Have you ever seen an emu egg?"

"Not that I know of," Sam replied. He went behind a shed and brought
out a large dark greenish egg with bumps all over its surface. He passed
it to Sam and then she passed it around for the others to hold. James
proceeded to carefully punch out two holes, one on each end. He blew
through the one hole and the contents of the egg began to drip out the
other side into a bowl he had beneath it on the table.

When he was finished he handed the egg to Sam and said, "Here you
go miss, now that's a prize!" When James had left the room, the girls
asked if they could see it again. Sam passed it around. Kat got it last
fondled it and carefully placed it in her bag. "You got the boar hunting
picture, this is mine."

Lyndsey and Sam looked at each other. There was no arguing with
this behavior. It was the justifiable position of possession being nine-
tenths of the law. *Sam guessed she had once again received too much*

male attention that day. Lyndsey reminded Kat of the warning that James had mentioned when he handed Sam the egg.

"You better take good care of it, Miss. It's good luck until you break it, then it's bad luck."

Sam thought perhaps Kat saved her from a lifetime of bad luck. She didn't want to overthink it. Sam said nothing and neither did Lyndsey. It was late and Lance was struggling to figure out what to do.

"How far is it from here to Goodooga?" Sam asked.

"Maybe twenty more minutes each way for me to do those twenty miles on these roads."

"Well, I don't want to be presumptuous but is there any place we can stay for the night in Goodooga? I don't believe there is any way you can drive us back to Lightning Ridge now and get back to your place before dark."

"Well, you all can crash at my place, my flatmates are gone for the weekend. There are couches and sleeping bags around."

For all practical purposes they decided to go on to Goodooga. For Sam, it was an added treat to see the town Lance called home for the past year.

9

Goodooga

Around eight, they rolled up to Lance's humble quarters. It was a small shack-like house that had three rooms and a kitchen. The dunny, like most in the Outback, was located in a small broken down shed in the backyard. They spent the evening getting to know the locals at the only pub where there was one large pool table, a dart board, and a long bar full of local rough and ready swagmen.

Sam slept on the couch and, as usual, was up first. She washed up and did what she could do to help herself look better with some sample make-up she had tucked away in her purse for emergencies. After some toast and coffee, Lance showed them around the tiny country town. A dozen other like houses lined the main street. The school was at the end of the road.

The schoolhouse had only four rooms. Lance said that most of his students were aborigines. The classroom was adorned with all the students' artwork on the wall. There was a photo of Lance with his students grinning from ear to ear. They were adorable. You could tell they loved their teacher.

By afternoon, all the locals were talking about a large party on the river planned for the evening, right after dark. It was Sunday and they had off until Tuesday because of the Queen's birthday. The girls told

Lance they would relax and stay for the party and followed Lance to a shearing shed at the end of town. Sam found a ram's skull behind the shed. For a science teacher, this was a great find and almost made up for the loss of the emu egg.

They made it back to Lance's flat, freshened up, and then headed back to the pub to get a bite to eat before the party. Sam used their pay phone to try to contact the travel agency that had all their gear and let them know they would be returning in the morning. The man on the phone was quite irritated. "Why the bloody hell didn't you let us know you were leaving the tour," he screamed. "You had us worried sick."

"I truly apologize, sir, for the inconvenience," Sam said. "A friend of ours came to take us to a property for lunch on Saturday. We had no idea it was so far away. However, it is our plan to get back to Lightning Ridge in the morning."

"Well, unless you are planning to be here at seven, you will need to meet us before noon in Dubbo. That is the next large town we stop at."

"Okay," Sam replied. "We'll plan to meet you in Dubbo by midday. Would it be possible for you to arrange for someone to put our backpacks back on the bus to Sydney?" The man muttered some words under his breath and then said yes and Sam thanked him for all his help. She called together Lance and the girls to give them the update.

"Bad news, mates," said Lance, "It's been raining south of here. There is no way I can drive you south to Dubbo now or in the morning. In fact, we might not be able to get us out of Goodooga, full stop."

The girls looked at Sam and she turned to Lance.

"What do you suggest we do now," she asked.

"If we plan to meet up with the bus that will take us back to Sydney, we are going to need to find some other way to get to Dubbo. Does anyone have a suggestion?"

One of the locals overheard the conversation. "Listen, one of me mates flies a small plane. He might be able to take ya sheilas to Dubbo in the morning, but it'll cost ya."

"Great," Sam said. "Does anyone know how to contact him?"

"I do," said one. "He's got posters on the walls. I'll grab one and get a call in." Within a few minutes, the pilot, Edward, had them on the line.

"Hi, Edward, we're hoping you can help us. We need to meet a bus in Dubbo about noon tomorrow. Is it possible to meet up somewhere around Goodooga to fly us there?"

Edward described an airfield on the outskirts of town. He suggested they meet him about nine in the morning. He told Sam to bring a hundred dollars in cash for the ride. She assured him they would have it.

Sam turned to the girls and gave them the update. They were shocked by the price tag.

"We don't have much of a choice. We could be here for days if we don't get out of Goodooga now. Let's see what we have if we pool all our money together," Sam said. "Between us we might have a few bob left over. Listen, once we get to the bus in Dubbo, we'll have a free ride into Sydney," she said.

With the decision to catch the plane behind them, they enjoyed the pub and planned to join Lance to go to the party by the billabong. Needless to say, they closed the pub. It was now after midnight. At this point Sam didn't care about where they were and where they were going.

They got to Lance's car and Sam really needed a restroom.

"Hold on," she said. "I really need to run back to the Pub and use their loo." She ran back and tried the door; it was locked and everyone was gone. She began looking for the nearest bush to squat behind. She found one by the side of the building. They would be heading to the bush next; who knows when they'd stop again.

Sam ran back to the car and got in. Jersey City Kat turned around sharply.

"Did you really do what I think you did—squat down behind a bush in the middle of Main Street?"

"The pub was locked, it's dark. I went behind a bush. No one else saw me but you."

"But this is the main street of town. Probably the whole town saw you."

"Who cares, Kat, it's after midnight. I'm not Lady Godiva. No one would care to look, but if they did, they probably realized they all may have visited that same bush at one time or another. Let's just go!"

In response, Lance shook his head several times and drove the car rapidly down the dirt road. Now Kat began to berate Sam further about a rip she decided *she* made in the felt pad on the only pool table in town. She was relentless.

"I didn't see a rip. You're making this up."

"Well, you made one and it was a big one. They probably will never be able to replace it."

Sam just loved how Kat somehow became her hip pocket conscience. She was always supervising her inappropriateness. It was her favorite sport these days.

Lance drove the roads even more aggressively. It was pitch black on the country roads that had just experienced rain. They skidded on turns sliding side to side. It took quite a while for him to find the spot on the billabong where the others were having a bonfire party.

Sam began to feel woozy from the turns. As she got out of the car she felt overwhelmingly nauseous.

"Go on without me," she signaled with her arm. "I think I'm going to be sick." No sooner did she say the words, she proceeded to throw up. *Sam, this is not your proudest moment.*

She slid into the back seat of the car and fell asleep. After an undetermined amount of time, she noticed the bonfire still glowing in the distance in the pitch black night. Against her better judgement, she began to pick her way to the fire.

When she arrived, she saw about twelve bodies asleep nestled around what was now a small bonfire. Many had sleeping bags; bodies were next to other bodies. She couldn't make out who was who. She just thought she'd better find a spot—there was no way she would be able to walk back through the darkness and find the car again. She proceeded to walk around a wide perimeter and found a small vacant spot. It had a piece of someone's blanket on the ground with a foot to spare. She squished in and fell asleep again.

When Sam awoke, Kat was standing over her laughing. "Do you want to know why no one else was sleeping on that spot?"

"No, not really." Sam said sitting up holding her head.

"That's where all the pig guts are," she yelled out with an excited look in her eye. "They killed a pig for dinner, roasted it and you, my friend, are lying on all the guts!"

Sam got up and faced her gloating smile. "It could be worse, Kat. You could tell me I was sleeping on a croc or a poisonous snake. Listen, I had a hard night, will you *please* lighten up!"

They found Lance and piled in the car. Lance said they needed to go back to town to pick up some gear before they headed to the airfield on the other side of town. As they began to spin off, he said, "Now *this* isn't good."

Sam looked at him intently in the driver's mirror from the backseat. "What isn't good?" she asked.

"We never get fog in Goodooga. Look at this. It is getting foggier by the second, it's like soup. I can't see a thing."

"Well, I suppose the rain had something to with it," Sam said.

"Maybe," Lance replied. "Not only are we going to have trouble finding the airfield, but how the bloody hell is the plane going to find us?"

The car got suddenly quiet. The kind of quiet that sobers you up right away. They didn't need to run into any more trouble on this trip.

They drove into town in silence. Lance took a sharp turn on the slick pasty clay road and a wheel went spinning off the car's axle. The car jolted and dragged to a halt. They all starred at each other silently as their slanted bodies hugged the side of the car. *You just couldn't make this shit up.*

Lyndsey broke the silence, "So . . . what are we going to do now?"

"I *don't* know," said Lance, throwing up his arms. "This is insane." He jumped out of the car and yelled back, "I guess I'm going to see if I can borrow another car."

They all sat in the broken-down car realizing it might be days before they could get out of Goodooga. Today was not starting well at all. They were almost out of money and definitely close to being out of time to catch the bus in Dubbo.

Suddenly, Lance drove up in another Holden. Sam dared not to ask him this time where he got it. They jumped ship leaving the disabled vehicle on the side of the road and spun off for the airfield.

The airfield was just a large flat paddock in the middle of nowhere. Lance got out of the car in the dense fog and walked to the middle of the field. Sure enough, they could make out a post with a black callbox attached. Lance called the number on the flyer.

"Hi, is this Edward the pilot who is supposed to pick up 3 girls in Goodooga," asked Lance.

"Righty-oh, mate, but I'm fogged in on my property too. I don't think I'm going to be getting out of here for a least another hour," said the pilot.

"Crap," responded Lance. "What should we do? They are supposed to catch up with a bus in Dubbo before noon." *Lance was desperately trying to find a way to make the girls disappear.*

"We can make it if I get out of here in the hour. Just stay close to the call box, I'll call as soon as I'm leaving," said Edward.

They went back to the car and Lance drove it closer to the post so they could hear the phone ring. They all slid down in the seats and fell asleep for about an hour. Then Lance heard the call and jumped for the phone. "I'm just getting in the cockpit now," said Edward. "I should be there shortly."

They could hear the Bonanza Beechcraft before they could see it. Lance walked them to the plane. Kat was nervous as they were approaching. "I'm not liking this. I've never been in one of these before."

Sam volunteered to get in the front seat next to the pilot. As they all got in, Lance gave a cheery goodbye, "Hate to say this, ladies, but goodbye and farewell. I hope you have a good flight and that you *never* return."

They gave a big wave. "Love you, too, Lance. Thanks for the memories."

The ride over the northern territory of New South Wales was brilliant. It was the best part of the entire trip. Sam wished they could go directly back to Sydney on this four-seater plane. If only money was not an issue. They got to Dubbo before noon and paid the pilot. They found a path and walked the distance from the airfield to the town. They were starving and decided to walk into the local milk bar.

"Are we close to the area where the buses come in and pick up customers," asked Lyndsey.

"Righty-oh, you're a block from there. If you sit at that cross street over there you won't miss anything. Just letting you gals know we are closing at noon for the Queen's birthday." They took the hint and promptly bought a supply of Cadbury chocolates and drinks and went out to sit on the corner. (There was never anything nutritious to eat at a milk bar/candy store except sloppy meat pies.)

They waited for over an hour sitting on the curb of the cross street. "Something is wrong with this picture. The bus should have come by now," Sam said. She knew she was simply saying out loud what the girls were already thinking. They looked around for any place they could ask for information. Someone told them the train station would know. They trudged another six blocks to the station. They were visibly disheveled and exhausted.

The train attendant said, "Yeah . . . I saw those buses come through about eleven this morning. They left a long time ago." They immediately realized they missed the bus by thirty minutes. They looked at each other without saying a word. *"This is a nightmare,"* said Lyndsey.

"Is there any way *at all* we can get back to Sydney tonight," Sam asked pushing her long hair back off her sweaty face in exhaustion.

"Well, there is a slow old wooden passenger train service that comes through here tonight. You can hop on it but I need to warn you it's rough and slow it takes twelve hours to get to Sydney."

"What time does it leave," Sam asked impatiently.

"Not til 7:45 this evening," said the attendant. "It'll get you into Sydney's Central about 7:45 in the morning.

"Oh, God, this day is *never* going to end," Sam sighed.

"How much will it cost?" asked Lyndsey.

"Twenty-two dollars a person," the attendant answered.

Sam turned to the girls. "What do we have left?"

She was amazed—after they counted it all, they had close to a hundred dollars left. They scraped the money together and bought the tickets.

Lyndsey pushed up to the window, "What's there to do in this town for the next six hours?"

He pointed to an arena down the street. "There's only *one* thing you can do on the Queen's birthday—watch the rodeo. It will cost you five quid though. Too bad you'll miss the fireworks tonight. They don't start 'til nine."

"That's quite alright," Lyndsey said. "We can always catch fireworks another time."

They walked another mile down the dirt rode to see their first rodeo. It wasn't anything they would want to do again anytime soon.

The train came on time. They made calls at the station to their staff secretaries to get substitutes. They knew they weren't going to be back in time to go to work the next day. They were told they'd be docked two day's pay each because it was a holiday weekend.

When they got on the train, it appeared as though they had walked onto a century-old train. They opened a glass door that housed a vintage wooden compartment that contained two hard wooden pew-like seats facing each other. The three of them sat on one side and a young couple sat on the other. Sam took off her poncho and used it as a pillow propping herself up against the wooden wall of the car. Kat was offered an extra blanket by the kind couple and Lyndsey and Sam had to beg her to share a part of it as the temperature was dropping by the minute.

"Christ, twelve more bloody hours," Sam moaned. "This is going to be a brutal."

Suddenly, when she thought things couldn't get worse, the unthinkable happened. Sam had been living in these same dirty, smelly clothes for three days and just at this critical moment she began her period. With only bathroom tissue and no one with Tampax she moaned, "Just kill me now!"

10

Love and Relationships

The next day in the staff room the boar hunting adventure caught Brad's full attention.

"So where *exactly* did this take place?" He quickly jumped up and found a map of New South Wales in his classroom and asked Sam to pinpoint where the boar was found. "What calibre rifle did you say your friend was using?"

Sam tried to describe the rifle, but Brad kept insisting that it wasn't an appropriate rifle for hunting boar.

"Brad, I really don't know what calibre rifle it was; he had dogs that actually hunted down the pig. He needed to only get in close range to shoot it." Sam rattled off answers exhausted by the rapid fire of technical questions she obviously was not qualified to answer.

———◦•◦———

As Brad and Sam continued to be the two fifth grade teachers at their little school, they began to open the accordion doors between their classrooms. Their teaching styles were similar and they began to departmentalize their lessons. Sam taught science and language arts. Brad taught math and social studies.

At the end of the second year of working together, they decided the fifth-grade students really needed an adventurous trip to incentivize their work. Brad suggested, "What if we tell them we are going to take them for an overnight trip to Jenolan Caves." On average they shared about fifty-six students between the two classes. The passage would take four hours of travel by bus each way, over the Blue Ridge mountain range.

Brad, of course, did all the research. The Caves House often hosted students for overnight tours. The second floor had dorm rooms and shower rooms for boys and the first floor had the same accommodations for the girls. The biggest attraction was the formal dining room at the facility. The Caves House was a large Victorian-styled hotel with real old-world charm. All the tables had white linen tablecloths, full silver service table settings, with Royal Daulton China embossed with the hotel's monogram—very posh indeed.

They began training the students with etiquette classes every Friday afternoon for a month prior to the trip. It was amazing how little students knew about traditional formal dining. They taught the boys how to escort a lady to the table. They paired them up and showed the boys how to pull a chair out for a lady to sit down. They reminded them all that once they were seated, they remained seated for the duration of the dinner. At the hotel, there were always three full courses to the dinner.

After a full day of hiking in the caves, the girls would shower and spend the majority of their time setting and styling their hair. Then came the time for the boys to join the rest of the group. On this one occasion, Sam and Brad waited twenty minutes for the boys to come down the grand staircase.

Brad was flustered; he was always punctual and Sam could see the visible annoyance on his face. "Bloody hell. Boys are worse than girls."

"Why, what happened," she asked, trying to imagine what could possibly take boys twenty minutes longer than girls.

"They wouldn't go to the bloody showers with just a towel wrapped around them. I kept telling them to leave the clothes in the room and come back and change. Nope, they all needed to carry all their clothes to the shower, change in the shower and then come back to their rooms. Next year, I am going to give them a pep talk before we go," he snarled.

Neither Brad nor Sam had children of their own. But they were certainly the proud parents of fifty or more students. This experience proved to be a passage for many of them. In most cases this was the first time many of them would spend a night away from their parents.

They sang all the way up and all the way back. On the return trip, someone began singing the rhyme "The Quarter Master's Store." It was one of those songs that went for hours. You needed to creatively make-up a verse rhyming with everyone's name on the bus. For a start someone would begin singing, *there was Meg, Meg, sitting on a keg at the store, at the store . . .*

Sam often got caught with the difference between appropriate American lingo and Aussie colloquialisms. Usually, the mishap would occur partying with friends but this one time it was on the bus full with all her students.

One of the sweetest little girls was named Danny. It was Sam's turn to start the next verse and she knew Danny hadn't had her name immortalized. She began singing, *"It was Danny, Danny sitting on her fanny at the store . . .* suddenly, the whole bus jolted to silence and all eyes turned to Sam in the back. She had only thought of the rhyme but had forgotten how rude and crude the term *fanny* was in Australia. It meant a word for a woman's private parts.

It was an innocent mistake but not in the presence of children. She immediately apologized and explained the term meant bum (bottom) in the States. It didn't matter, the damage was done. She knew she couldn't take it back and was mortified. The bus stayed quiet for the remainder of the trip. Sam worried over the mistake for weeks. But somehow the small community forgave her.

Brad began to share his intrinsic love of periods of history, particularly those around great wars, but more importantly he could name all the weapons used in each period. Ever since the brief adventure with boar hunting, they began talking about weapons. Sam knew nothing about weapons but as a cop's daughter, she was always curious to learn more about them. She became a sponge for learning more and absorbed everything that Brad taught her. They even began an archery class for students after school. Brad and Sam were getting close. She recognized that she craved his company and everything of knowledge that came from his lips.

In the mid-seventies there was no problem with a teacher getting permission from the headmistress to bring in a rifle and show the students the weapons of the period. One day, as Sam and Brad talked about colonial times, Brad brought in the most beautiful flintlock rifle. The wood was highly polished and the mechanisms were detailed with shiny high-quality brass.

Later at recess in the staff room, Sam asked, "Where did you get that rifle?"

"I made it." Brad said modestly.

"Are you *kidding* me? You made that beautiful piece of art!"

"Well, that is how I stay out of trouble," he smiled. "I love learning about weapons and I wanted to learn more about how they are made. So, I joined a muzzle-loading club. I began firing them, learned how to make them and set my mind to making the best."

"So how many did you make," she asked.

"Oh, a half dozen or so, some are flintlocks, others are percussion-cap muzzle loaders. I tried to make them all different."

"What makes them all different?" She knew nothing about what makes rifles different.

"Everything," he said. "The stock, the mechanism, but mostly the barrel. You know the old saying lock, stock and barrel, don't you, Rothbauer," he laughed.

"Do you actually practice with these rifles?"

"Well, that's the point. How would I know it will fire properly if I didn't get out there and practice."

"Okay, sorry, stupid question. So . . . do you ever sell them?" Sam asked taking a bite out of her open grilled cheese sandwich smothered with Vegemite, her favorite snack of the day.

"Not yet, but I suppose I should someday. I'm getting to that point. I should part with some. Soon I'll have no place to store them all."

"Well, if you ever want to part with *this* rifle, *I'd* love to buy it." He finished pouring himself another cup of tea from the kettle on the staff room table. Then he walked over and picked up a pikelet, piling it high with jam and whipped cream that the duty ladies had left for them. He walked around behind Sam. Cassie sat on the far end of the table listening to the entire exchange without saying a word. Slowly, he came back and sat down across from her.

"Okay." he said. "I *won't* sell it to you, but I'll trade you for it."

Sam scrunched her nose. "Trade it? What do I possibly own that you would want?" She thought over her entire repertoire of possessions that she brought to Australia. She couldn't imagine anything she owned worth the cost of trading his flintlock.

"Well," he said. "Just last week you commented in the lounge that you had your skis shipped from the States. You said you didn't know when you might use them again."

"My skis?" she said. She remembered Daniel had sent them to her only a couple of weeks ago. She must have mentioned it.

"Well, Sheri and I have an invitation to join some folks in the Snowy Mountains in a fortnight and I have no skis," he said. "Would you be interested in a trade," he grinned at his own suggestion.

Sam looked over at Cassie not sure what to say. "Ah . . . well, if you don't think you'll ever use the skis, it looks like an opportunity to unload them for something you want," Cassie commented never lifting her eyes up from her pikelet. Then they both looked back at Sam for a response.

"Okay, it's a deal. The only thing I want to point out is these skis are only 160 cm long. They may be too short for you." She knew Brad was over six foot tall.

He smiled, "It's a deal, if I don't use them Sheri will."

He gave Sam the rifle to take home that day. The next day she returned with the skis in their case. Several weeks later in the lounge she got around to asking him how the skis performed. He seemed happy.

"They were great. I was able to take every bloody mogul."

Sam smiled and was pleased it all worked out. He had a great ski trip on a slightly used pair of skis and she had a beautiful rifle made by a special friend sitting in the corner of her bedroom in a penthouse. It was far more than a trade; it was something she would cherish always.

"Oh, by the way," Sam said with a wink. "Someday you will need to teach me how to fire that rifle."

———◦•◦———

Sam began to switch her allegiances in the next few months. She was beginning to branch out even more from her American Expat Family. She just wasn't having as much fun going over to Potts Point.

Those who lived there were now at a critical point. It was approaching the end of the first two years. Marsha and Barry were returning to the States. Jersey City Kat was undecided as to whether she was going to stay or return.

Sam's life in Neutral Bay was pleasant. Barbie and Sam had a flatmate who was a pilot. He rented the middle bedroom of the flat but he never used it except for afternoon escapades. She'd came home periodically to find an empty bottle of fine champagne and two empty crystal glasses by the sink. He lived with his girlfriend but explored his world of "Afternoon Delights". After each episode, Barbie and Sam would skip about the flat singing the lyrics made popular by the Starland Vocal Band.

However, over time Barbie and Sam were growing apart and sometimes she found her to be challenging. Barbie had a superior air about her. She reminded people often that she wasn't from Australia, that she was from New Zealand, and that she was from Maori descent. (I guess it gave her royalty status.)

Women are interesting. Barbie was very pampered, displayed high-end goals, hung around with high-end friends and only dated men with money. Sam knew she kept her around as a novelty. Most of the first year went well. Sam had a brief moment of befriending her and seeking her advice when she fell briefly for an American country singer while on one of those short week holidays to Cairns, Queensland.

Sam joined a bus tour with a girl named George, whom she met through someone from school. She was a Yank positioned in a town near Surfer's Paradise. George and Sam hit it off. She played a mean guitar and could sing. They found that they were pretty good at harmonizing. They were staying in a two-story house with a group of Australians in Cairns and gravitated to two Aussie guitar players. The second evening after hours of harmonizing, a girl suddenly burst into the room screaming, "The four of you need to go!" They all looked suddenly to the sound of her shrieking voice. "No, you don't understand," she chanted breathlessly. "There are folk singers from all over the world performing here this weekend."

Just before they went on stage, a soloist who was in his early thirties (who resembled Harrison Ford) got on stage with his Taylor guitar. His smooth voice spoke gently into the microphone.

"My name is Ryan and I'm just a country boy from Modesto, California. I lived all my life on a working cattle ranch. I'm going to sing a song that I wrote about the girl I left behind."

His voice was so mellow and the song so tender, he had Sam mesmerized. However, after a weekend of blending voices at bonfires, she learned he had a girl that he lived with on a ranch in the mountains of Victoria.

"Can I write you sometime," he suggested.

A month later, a letter did come. Sam waited a week before opening it. He wrote how busy work was getting and how he couldn't stop thinking of her.

Sam shared the letter with Barbie. She mused, "Are you going to write him back?"

"There's no point. Why encourage this? He's living with that girl in Victoria."

"Well, if I was really attracted to him, I'd be tempted to write." Sam reflected on her comment, but she didn't write. A month later, a second letter came. She opened it. Ryan informed her he had left the company of the lady he was living with and wondered if there was a chance they could meet up somewhere.

Though tempted, Sam still didn't answer back. He was right the first time, they lived too far apart. She wondered about her inability to reflect backwards. She only seemed to move forward like a sailboat catching the wind and looking for a home port. *Could this be one of my biggest flaws?*

11

Continuing Girl Drama

George and Sam boarded a Qantas 747 together from Sydney to Christchurch for the August holidays. It was a harried departure and they were pretty spent as they headed on their journey to join Lacy and Jersey City Kat in New Zealand.

Lacy and Kat had planned the trip. Kat decided to move back to New Jersey in September and fit in one more adventure before her return. Since Lacy and Kat would be rooming together, they told Sam she needed a roommate and she then threw the idea out to George, who was also excited to see New Zealand before she returned to the States.

The next morning was a damp, rainy winter day. The four of them crammed their backpacks into a Holden station wagon and began their adventure. The scenery was spectacular. Lacy drove, Kat sat shotgun, and George and Sam rode in the back harmonizing to songs they knew. Suddenly the car came to a screeching halt when Kat shouted out, "Look out, there is this hunk of a man hitchhiking ahead."

There was a quick conversation about whether to pick him up. Lacy made the ultimate decision. "Ah, why not?" she suggested, in her distinctive *Lacy logic*, "We outnumber him." To everyone's surprise, Kat took out a large magnum of Johnny Walker Red that she had purchased at the duty free.

"Okay, this is your lucky day. I brought along a bottle to share to keep everyone warm." The bottle went around several times before it got back in the bag. The American hitchhiker divulged that he hoped to do some volunteer work in New Zealand.

Kat turned her head and stared at him fluttering her eyelashes in her signature style as she opened her big baby blues wider. "Really?" As always, Kat's personality softened around men and so did her sultry low voice. You could tell she was hoping to have some involvement with something a little more than kindness. After little or no response from the hitchhiker, she turned around and shot a darting look at Lacy rolling her eyes that said *no,* he's not going to work.

It is funny how one doesn't know what to expect on holidays that are comprised of different groups of people. The trip takes on a personality of its own. George and Sam were getting along fine, but Lacy and Kat were definitely not warming up to George. Kat and Sam still had a strained relationship after Goodooga. *This adventure could get dicey.*

They took off about ten the next morning driving through winding roads and large chasms of snow-covered fairy tale looking peaks, mountains, and babbling brooks. At one point, they ventured through a very narrow bit of road named Lindis Pass. Lacy was having some trouble navigating the narrow rock walls. Suddenly there was a cutting sound and sure enough, when they emerged from the car, they could see a slice into the side door made by a jutting rock which was going to cost them all.

"It's okay, Lacy, you're doing a great job." Sam said. "I vote for you to keep driving."

The Youth Hostel in Queenstown was new and chateau like. George announced that she was heading out to get together with some of the musicians she had just met the night before. *Good for you George, you're going to survive this trip.*

Sam wanted to ski the next day at the neighboring Mt. Hutt ski fields. Kat shared she had never skied before and Lacy said it was too long since she had. Sam ultimately convinced Kat she would regret not taking this once in a lifetime opportunity.

After laundry, they walked to a local pub to get an ounce of courage. Lacy introduced the bartenders to her local Hartford designer drink, the Harbor Light. In a tall cordial glass, the bartender poured the first layer of dark Kahlua, then she instructed him to pour a layer of tequila slowly over a spoon, then topping off the top layer with a dark over-proof rum in the same manner. After the drink was poured, you were able to light up the over-proof rum and blow out the floating flame on top and choose to sip or chug the drink. It was pretty to look at. The density of the liquids created three distinct bands of color, hence the appearance of a lighthouse.

Sam could have easily spent a week in Queenstown, but Kat was determined to find the Caves that featured the glow worms. They headed out to a lake area called Te Anua which was located south of Queenstown. There were no hostels there, but there were heated cabins in a holiday park near the lake. They booked a cabin for four and began to ask about the glow worms. There was an afternoon cruise that would tour the caves where they could view the luminous worms hanging like Christmas lights throughout the caverns.

When the cruise was over, they searched the town for a pub. They found one and marched in and took over a large table. The waiter suggested that they should begin a *shout* (round) with a schooner of New Zealand Beer famous for having 12% alcohol. Sam didn't drink beer but she thought it best just to start with the shout like the rest. Kat and Lacy were on one side of the round table and George and Sam were on the other. They spoke about the caves and began mellowing to the comfort of the beer.

Suddenly, Sam heard an American voice from behind. "Do you girls want company?" The voice came from a tall Norwegian-looking Yank who sported John Lennon glasses. He introduced himself as Lenny. Next to him was a man in his early thirties who looked like a tall James Caan sporting sandy blonde curly hair.

"Sure, come join us," Sam motioned with her right hand.

The two men came over and the tall handsome one sat next to Sam on her left. He turned to her, "Hi, I'm Kirk," he said as he extended his hand. She shook his hand and that of Lenny's and introduced them to the other girls at the table. Lenny began describing his past two years in Australia living on Kirk's ranch and teaching in the small town of Finley.

He must have come over on the same jet as the girls. Sam looked around the table and noticed that no one could take their eyes off Kirk. Not only was he handsome but he was well-spoken and seemed to be a confident man's man, a rugged rancher from the Outback. Sam realized she was infatuated as well. After everyone had eaten their share of hamburgers and fries, Kirk leaned down and whispered in Sam's ear.

"I know a house where there is a party tonight. Do you want to join me?"

"Sounds like fun," she said smiling as they stood up together. She told the girls she'd see them later. It was early but already dark.

She wasn't sure what to expect. They walked for about a mile up a hill to a large mountain-styled wooden 'A' frame house. They could hear the music playing and walked in. They wandered around the party and Kirk said hello to some people who recognized him. They hung in the main room for a while as the music and the crowd grew larger and louder. He guided Sam to a balcony.

"Would you like to go outside for a while?"

"That sounds like a brilliant idea." she said, trying to shout above the noise.

They spoke for what seemed like hours about their lives and failed marriages. About midnight, Kirk suggested they begin walking back.

"What do you and the girls have cooking today," asked Kirk.

"I'm not sure but I think we may be heading out for Fox Glacier."

"You may want to stay just *one* more day. Lenny and I are driving up to Milford Sound. You can't miss it. It is full of fiords. It's a twenty mile ride each way and if we want to make it back before dark, we're going to need to get an early start.

"Well, I can't speak for the others but I don't want to miss it," Sam said.

"We'll come by in the car early to see what you're doing," said Kirk. When the girls awoke they agreed Milford Sound would be an amazing journey and told the lodge management they were staying one more night.

Lenny jumped out of the front seat to let Sam get in, but before anyone could blink, Kat jumped into the passenger seat next to Kirk and waved at Lacy to jump in next to her. Sam was left to sit in the middle of the back seat between George and Lenny. *This day had the rank smell of dead fish.* When they got to the lunch table at Milford Sound, Kat and Lacy immediately sat on either side of Kirk and on the ferry ride out to the Sound, they surrounded him the same way. It was obvious; Kat and Lacy were out to destroy any shroud of intimacy for Kirk and Sam. Sam was sure Kirk could sense the plot. It needed no explanation; he was not a stupid man, he knew to stay out of it and just savor the attention.

When they got back to the cabin, Sam pulled Lacy aside for an explanation.

"What the *hell* is going on here," she asked.

"Oh, Sam, all I can say is that Kat feels you robbed her of her man."

"What the hell are you talking about? We all met Kirk together and he clearly took a liking to me. He specifically asked me to join him. How does anyone see this as *me* taking *her* man? What kind of game is this?"

"Well, before he joined us at the table, Kat pointed over to him and said, 'That's *my* man. He's the Marlboro Man, he's mine.'"

"Well, for one, I never heard that, she just said it to you. You know as well as I do that Kirk had a choice in this matter as well."

"Well, let's just say in her mind it makes perfect sense that today is *her* day with the Marlboro Man." *This felt like the emu egg all over again.*

Sam shook her head. She could see that this was amusing Lacy. "Besides" Lacy said, "This is Kat's last trip and I promised her that she'd have a night with a man."

"Oh, *great,* so I become the sacrificial lamb in this deal? This is not what I call friendship, Lacy. This whole thing stinks. We're not in high school."

"Well, she's my friend, too. Remember, Sam, this is *just* a trip. You are always playing the romantic. You really think these trips could end up with a happily-ever-after story. They are *only* trips to have a good time." Again, Sam was confronted with *Lacy Logic.* She shook her head again and walked away frustrated and alone.

They got back to the pub and Sam clearly wasn't talking to anyone. Lenny and Kirk were not there, thank God. Kat moved over to Sam's side of the table.

"How about we have a drinking contest for who ends up with Kirk tonight," suggested Kat.

"Are you crazy? I can't compete with you, nor do I ever want to. I'm certainly not drinking to win a man."

"I'll tell you what," she said. "I'll drink two full schooners of beer to your one glass of wine and I'll pay for them all. Whoever passes out or gives up first, leaves."

Sam just wanted this day over. "Okay, get the drinks."

Sam was sure Kat rigged this, too. She clearly knew Sam blacked out on wine. After several glasses Sam didn't care anymore. She got up and just left the tavern. She didn't remember walking back to the cabin.

———◦•◦———

The next day Sam barely spoke a sentence to anyone on the ride to Fox Glacier. Three hours into the trip they experienced a flat tire which Kat volunteered to fix, and then they took a bridge too fast and were in big trouble again.

"Oh, shit!" said Lacy. "Let me move us off the bridge and we can take a look." Lacy moved the car off to the shoulder of the road. They all got out and looked over to the left side of the car. It was worse than they thought. They now had two more flat tires. It didn't matter. They had already used their only spare tire. It was cold and the sun was quickly setting in the New Zealand winter sky.

"Now what're we going to do," Lacy asked. Kat reached in front of her seat and pulled out the brown bag of Johnny Walker. Sam went up the road and finally flagged an elderly couple who managed to squeeze them into the back seat up to Fox Glacier. The lady at the hotel said she could help them get the car right away. Sam wasn't following any of her suggestions knowing they had two flat tires, not just one, and no spare. "No worries, my sons can help you right now. You want your luggage tonight, right?"

"So," Sam said staring blankly into her eyes. "I'm still trying to understand. I must be *very* slow today. So how are we going to execute this?"

The lady peered over her glasses. "Well, at least one of you will need to go with the boys and show them where the car is and bring the keys." she said. "You said you have a Holden, right."

Sam nodded.

"Well, my boys will drive you down in *our* Holden, change the two flat tires by taking two tires off our car. Then they'll leave our car out there in the woods tonight and they'll drive yours back. Tomorrow the boys will borrow a car from the garage with our tires with them and put them back on our vehicle and bring it back to the hotel."

Sam looked at her in total disbelief, *How the hell did she ever come up with such a plan?* She couldn't imagine this for a moment ever happening in the States.

"Oh, my God! You are *so kind* and so incredible."

"Well, we're used to being resourceful out here."

Kat got her wish the last night of the trip. She was able to entice some local lads from the hotel back to her room for a party that evening.

Whenever Sam thought about this trip with the girls, it always left her sad. Heaven knows relationships between people can get complicated, but a holiday should leave a happy memory, not scars. She would always develop a sad feeling when she allowed herself to think of one the most beautiful places on earth.

Cockatoo
Island

Sydney Harbour

Balmain

Drummoyne

Wharf Rd

Ballast Pt

Water St

Birchgrove

Monts Bay

Brig
Restaurant

Darling St

Collins

Morts St

East   Balmain

DUKE St

Curtis St

Campbell St

Balmain
Markets

Darling St

Ferry
Stop

SYDNEY

London
Hotel

Clay St

Gladstone
Park

Gladstone St

zolle

Balmain

Carrington St

Author's drawing: not to scale.

12

Getting to Know You

Sam thought she had outgrown her party years after many of the American teachers had returned home. Those first two years in Australia were about finding out where her boundaries were. It was the seventies after all and everywhere you went, people talked of sex, drugs and rock and roll.

Lacy was still unsettled. She and Rick decided they were moving on from their relationship. They split up but managed to stay good friends. Sam's time with Barbie also came to an end. Straightaway Lacy found a flat in East Balmain with a buff water polo player.

Sam found an okay flat in Drummoyne on the bay with an older Englishman. She naively thought she was safe, but when he started sitting around watching soccer in his underwear, she planned to move out quickly.

That Friday night at a party, Sam ran into a friend, a young scuba instructor named Grant. He took pity on her. He had just secured a flat and had a spare room. In a day he moved her into his flat in Birchgrove on Louisa Road. He gave Sam the master bedroom which had a balcony overlooking the bay for thirty-five dollars a week. The three-story terrace house next door was occupied by a group who called themselves "The Little River Band."

Grant was younger, tall, and overweight. They both felt secure there would be no thought of a physical relationship. They began their living arrangement by starting a diet together as a bonding experience. They shared books on fasting.

That April Fool's Day Sam attended Cassie's annual birthday party. The usual suspects were there. All the colorful arty people of Balmain graced her parties. Everyone loved Cassie. There were only two staff members there this time, Kristi and Brad. Sam noticed Brad was alone. *Where was his wife, Sheri?* She talked to people she knew for a while then walked over to Cassie when she was alone.

"Brad is alone. What gives? Where's his wife," she asked.

"I'm not sure. I think there's trouble in paradise," she said. "But have you been watching? He seems to be paying a lot of attention to Kristi." On her cue, Sam began watching them if only for a better understanding of what might be going on. At one point she looked up and they were both gone. Oh well, whatever it was had nothing to do with her.

As far as Cassie and Sam knew, Kristi had a boyfriend from England. It was complicated. Sam didn't pay enough attention to the gossip of the faculty room but it was obviously going to become more interesting. Over the next week, Cassie and Sam became aware that Brad officially separated from his wife, Sheri. Both knew this wasn't a secure situation for anyone to become involved in.

Nonetheless, Sam couldn't deny how she always felt about Brad. The chances of this ending in a happily-ever-after story were pretty slim. She kept a low profile. One school day Brad and she were alone in the play-ground sharing recess duty.

"How's it going," she asked him. She really wasn't wanting to pry into his life. They were still teaching partners and she cherished that particular relationship.

"Ta, thanks for asking. I guess you've heard that Sheri and I split up."

"Yah, Cassie filled me in. Let me know if there is anything you need. I know Cassie and I would be happy to help." He nodded in reply. Cassie was living with a prominent English surgeon who worked for the Royal

Air Force in Australia. The next week Cassie came up to Sam in the faculty room.

"What are you doing Saturday night," she asked.

"Well, nothing really important. I was invited to a party but I don't have to go, why?"

"Well, Jerome and I are having a little dinner party at our Wharf Street House and we would love for you and Brad to join us," she said.

"Me? So, what happened to Kristi?"

"Well, let's just say that'll never work." she commented. "Please come by. It'll be fun."

Sam screwed her face up. "This isn't a set-up, is it?"

"Ooh, come on, no, it'll be interesting," she said.

"Interesting how?"

"It's an evening away from school it'll be fun."

"Okay, perhaps you're right, it *could* be interesting. But I don't want to feel like the next item for the shopping cart."

"This is just casual, Sam. I promise it's not a set-up. We all work together and it'll be just fun. Brad needs a little distraction right now."

Saturday morning, Sam awoke to a nagging guilty thought of what she had agreed to. Here's a man she's been attracted to from the moment she first set eyes on him. He was now separated from his wife. The first conquest may have not ended happily, but now he might be on to the second. Shit, she realized that might be her. There were four single women on the staff and Sam was the most eligible. However, the reality was she was not Australian and Brad was dinky-dy.

She wasn't one for overthinking things. She considered herself spontaneous.

That evening sitting around Cassie's dinner table was homey and familiar. They were all cozy and laughing at the silliest things. They were family. The dinner was exquisite. All the candles and fireplaces were lit. When the evening was over, Brad walked Sam to her car.

"Can I see you home," he asked like a true gentleman.

"Oh, that's okay. I only live a few blocks away," she commented. "I'm pretty sure I'll make it home safely by myself."

"Well, I would love to just make sure you *do*."

"Okay . . . then," she said. He followed her in his car. Over the next two blocks her mind began to race. *What do I do now?* She pulled up to the curb in front of the Louisa Road complex and slowly got out. Without invitation, Brad walked her up the three-story stairwell to the front door of her flat. He moved over to her slowly and whispered softly in her ear. "May I kiss you?"

Sam froze. She was out of her comfort zone. *I could be smart and say it wouldn't be a good idea.* She hesitated then nodded yes and surprised herself by snuggling into his warm embrace. He reached for her face with both his hands and then kissed her tenderly on the lips, then soulfully tightening his embrace. She began swooning and knew she was in trouble. There was no doubt about how she felt about him. *Did he always feel like this too?* She just didn't see that they had any possibility of a relationship under the circumstances of the past few years. Her mind was racing when he asked, "Is there a chance of me coming in?"

"Well . . . yes," again she hesitated . . . "Grant, my roommate *may* be home, but it shouldn't be a problem." This was the first time Sam had ever brought anyone over for any reason. They walked into the living room noticing Grant's door was closed. She asked Brad if he would like a glass of wine?"

"No . . . not really. I don't drink wine. It gives me a headache." He inched closer to her. "Do you really want to drink wine right now?"

"Um . . . not really," she answered. He obviously liked the answer and moved closer surrounding her in a warm embrace. He moved her slowly backwards into her room. He closed the door. She awoke to him wrapped about her as if she were a teddy bear. It felt warm and cozy. Sam didn't want to move a muscle; she didn't want the moment to end. *She smiled to herself. This is a perfect fit.* Brad left early that morning saying he needed to get back home. *I wonder where home is?* She also began wondering how she was going to go back to school on Monday and face him.

As always, being a good Irish Catholic girl, Sam needed to confess her sins to someone to off load the guilt. So, she called Lacy.

"You *what?* But Sam, he's your co-worker. You don't shit in your own backyard."

"I know, I know," she was almost in tears. "So, what do I do now?"

"Ah . . . well if it were me, I'd just pretend it didn't happen." she said. "Best thing is to keep it normal. You're all friends. It was probably just a one-night stand so just don't let it change anything for any of you."

Sam knew Lacy to be the voice of experience. She was usually right about these things. However, the phrase one-night stand seemed to bother her.

She walked into school Monday and just said a cheerful hello to everyone and went about work as usual. Two days went by before Brad caught her on the playground. "We need to talk."

"It's okay Brad, I understand. You don't need to explain."

"No, I do," he said. "Listen, I *care* for you Sam, I care for you a lot, and I don't want to ruin anything between us."

"Well . . . I definitely don't want that either."

"So . . . how about if I take you out to dinner this Saturday night, just you and me?"

She blinked twice as she looked at him. "Are you *sure* this is what you want to do," she asked.

"Bloody hell, Sam, don't make this harder than it already is, just a yes or no will do."

"Well, of course, yes." *I couldn't help myself.* When it feels good you want to keep the feeling going even if your head says it is not the best thing to do.

Saturday came and Brad picked her up about six and drove them to a local ethnic restaurant in Balmain. They sat at a table for the first time as a couple wanting to get to know each other better.

She was intent on listening with all her heart. She had taught beside this man for many years but didn't know a shred about his life except that he was married. "My wife and I met while I was in Teachers college. We married soon after college because that is what people did in those days when they got intimate. When we were edging up to our ten-year anniversary, we realized we had very little in common. We had tried for children but it never happened for us. We decided to end it as friends."

"Well, my story mirrors yours. I married right out of college. A couple of years into our marriage, he shared he didn't want children. Not that I was ready for them then or now but I saw children in my future."

"Why did you see them in your future?" asked Brad searching her eyes.
"Because it is an experience I don't want to miss in my life and I think
I would make a good mother." Brad smiled, he seemed to like the answer.

When they finished dinner, Brad took the scenic route along the harbor on his way back to Louisa Road. He pulled up slowly to the curb. She
wasn't sure if this was going to be goodbye or hello.

"So," he said, "What's next?"

Sam turned to him and stared into his eyes, "I don't know . . . do you
want to come up?"

"Bloody hell, yes." he answered. He was so cute; his enthusiastic
answer was all she wanted to hear. From here on in she didn't care what
happened. She was all in.

Brad and Sam began the interesting journey of staff members by day
and lovers by night. They dated formally only on weekends. Sam never
probed Brad with questions about how things were going at home. It had
to be painful enough, she herself having been there recently. She was just
happy for the gift she had right now.

Cassie would occasionally ask how things were going with Brad.
Sam's answer was always the same. "All's well that ends well."

Sam hated the awkwardness of feeling how she did in those early days.
But each Friday they checked in with each other. There were occasions he
needed to be somewhere else so Sam went on to doing things with Lacy.

Lacy called a few Saturdays later announcing she was moving out of
east Balmain. "Really?" Sam said.

"Do you have a minute? I want you to listen to this ad from the *Herald*," she said. Then she began reading the lengthy description.

*"Come join the group of the wise and interesting. If you are an actor,
architect, lawyer, entrepreneur, model, pilot, doctor, writer, or just an out
of the box thinker, book an interview to live in a progressive Frank Lloyd
Wright styled house in East Balmain."*

"I just called the owner," she shouted with excitement. "He's going to
give me an interview. I'm leaving in thirty minutes. Want to come?"

"Absolutely, you know me, I love an adventure."

They arrived at Duke Street on the east side of Balmain about the
same time. There was a back gate that led through a dreamy backyard.

A brick paved trail led to a small wooden bridge that spanned a running brook. *A little fairy tale world.*

Sam looked at Lacy as they walked up to the door. "Now this is different." She knocked on the open back door.

A voice echoed from within, "Just have a seat at the table. I'll be there in a moment."

Ed then invited them on a tour. This house was truly exciting and Sam found herself feeling jealous of Lacy. They walked into a grand cathedral-styled great room bordered on all sides by heavy logs and rafters. On the left was a large bar and nothing else. Twenty-four feet across the great room on the opposite end was a large open balcony. Surrounding the perimeter of the great room there were a series of large leather couches.

"Boy, this looks like a great place to have a party," Sam chuckled.

Ed turned his head and pointed his finger at her, "That is *exactly* what it's made for, parties, lots of parties." He turned to both of them. "Do you girls like to party?"

Lacy responded, "Well, we have been known to frequent parties." Sam knew Lacy saw herself in Duke Street and she was beginning to pour on the Lacy charm. When she began talking with her hands and waving her arms descriptively, Sam knew she had a captive audience.

"This area of the house feels like a ship, right," commented Ed. "It is designed to be one. Whoever lives in these two rooms share sections of a unique ship's cabin."

The first bedroom to the left had a small built-in closet space followed by a fixed wooden upright ladder that led to a loft. Sam asked Ed if she could climb up and take a look.

"Of course, why don't both of you climb up." When she reached the top, Sam peered over a queen size bed. It was situated under a huge slanted sky light that stretched the entire length of the bed.

"Go on, climb in," suggested Ed. Lacy climbed in behind Sam.

"I would *love* this bed just to look out at the night sky, wouldn't you?" Sam turned to Lacy.

"Not me. I'd be up all night thinking a branch from that large tree would fall and crash through the skylight."

Ed opened the side door and Lacy followed him around a balcony leading to another bedchamber.

"Okay, I could live in this room." Lacy suggested. There was a queen size bed positioned against the wall with added drawers under the bed much like you would see on a ship. Lacy was always good at negotiating contracts; it wasn't Sam's talent.

"What're you asking for these rooms?"

"Well, all of these go for the same price. They are fifty dollars a week.

Lacy and Sam looked at each other, it was pretty dear. She had spent forty a week for the penthouse in Neutral Bay and only thirty-five dollars a week on Birchgrove, both of which were spacious and had water views. *Perhaps the price was set for the value of the experience.*

"So, are both of you ladies thinking of sharing the west end ship cabins?" Ed asked presumptively. Lacy looked at Sam.

"Sam, what do you think?" Before Sam could even answer, Lacy asked, "Now if we were both here sharing this space, could we get a discount?"

"Sorry, I couldn't come down on the weekly price, but maybe we could work with the down payment," he suggested.

Sam cleared her throat. "Well . . . actually, I'm not prepared to move in quite yet. But this place *is* unique. I do love the skylight room. I'm ready to consider it."

"Listen, I have a few more people who are coming to see the place later today," said Ed. "I hope to have the rooms rented out by the end of the weekend."

As Lacy and Sam walked back to the car, Lacy began to chant. "I really want to do this, Sam. I'm pretty sure Grant will let you out of the lease."

"I have a nice situation right now, Lacy. I just would hate to screw it up."

"Oh, come on, Sam, this is a big adventure. You *can't* turn it down." Lacy always had the power of persuasion. "Okay, I'll talk to Grant."

By Sunday they had signed a lease with Ed. Monday at school Cassie and Brad were both visibly shocked that Sam was moving back with Lacy again after the drama that surrounded their flat in Bondi. They both questioned why Sam would leave such a sweet situation on Louisa Road. They probably knew before Sam did that her adventure days were not officially over. Sam was particularly interested in whether this would affect anything Brad and she had going on.

"Are you going to be okay with this new arrangement?" Sam asked Brad when they were sitting alone at the staff room table after school.

"Listen, Sam, I'm not even fully out of my house and marriage yet. You're free to do whatever works best for you. It isn't going to change how I feel about you. Besides, if things continue to move forward for us in the future, you might be glad you got one more adventure out of your system." Sam smiled.

It didn't take long for her to move in. There were just two boxes and the same two suitcases of clothes that she had when she had arrived in Oz. Brad appreciated the architectural uniqueness of Duke Street, but she could sense he wasn't warming up to the idea of communal living. He also recognized the party lay-out in the great room.

"You know I'm not much of a party man." She began to realize this concept of living might create a potential problem for them down the road. *Well, if we were meant to be together, we'd figure it out somehow.*

By the second week in Duke Street, Lacy and Sam pooled all their favorite cassettes together to play each evening. When Fleetwood Mac's *Rumors* album loaded into the cassette high-fi system in the Great Room, the party was on. Dinner at home turned into a party most evenings. Brad would come over maybe once a week. One night he arrived in a tuxedo.

"Are you going to a formal event?" Sam asked.

"No, I'm joining the Masons," he said. "My father was one and I thought I would join. I just needed to buy one of these monkey suits for the occasion."

Lacy actually thought it was awesome. "Now you have a suit for weddings, funerals, and anything else life has to bring," she said, giving her approval. "You know *my* dad was a Mason."

Lacy didn't comment much about Sam's growing relationship with Brad. She was keeping busy growing relationships within the house. But Sam was falling more deeply in love with Brad even though she knew it was a dangerous place to be with his recent separation and pending divorce. She was looking for the anchor in her life.

Sam realized that she and Brad needed to spend more time getting to know each other outside of the classroom. She wanted him to feel comfortable outside of the party house. They went out on weekends, mostly on nature walks. One Saturday she watched him run and compete in Sydney's City to Surf Race.

For Sam, 1977 was becoming the year of return trips. Ever since her unique boar hunting incident in New Angledool, Brad chomped at the bit to get to The Outback. He asked if she could write the property owner in New Angledool and see if they could spend a week up there at the beginning of the Christmas break. James wrote back and said he would welcome Sam and her new friend with open arms. Their first big adventure together was ready to begin.

13

Returning to New Angledool

School let out on a Thursday in mid-December. They were on the road the following Saturday. Brad pulled up to Duke Street in his bush trimmed Holden with spotlights fastened to the racks at the top of the vehicle. There was an enclosed back for a collection of rifles and camping gear. The front of the Holden was equipped with a heavy duty 'Roo' bar. Brad spent an entire week meticulously packing everything he thought they might need.

Their spirits were high, and their excitement could be read through each of their smiles. They kept staring at each other thinking this can't be real. Brad wanted it to be life changing for Sam. After four hours of driving he asked, "Do you want to see where I grew up?"

Sam nodded vigorously, "I want to know everything about you, past, present, and future." The day was very sunny and hot, close to thirty-seven degrees Celsius. They turned down a bumpy dirt road at a sign that said Cessnock.

They descended into the valley of Brad's family farm. The scrub around the area was seared by a recent bush fire.

"Look, Brad, someone's living here," Sam said pointing. There was evidence of life. Shoes on the back porch, a broom, and a hoe against the house.

"Bloody hell, this isn't living. Living is having your tucker from my mum's gigantic garden which used to be over there." He pointed to a barren stretch of dirt.

He had lived such a different life from Sam's. He was born and bred in the country, living off the land, reading books at night by hurricane lamps. Sam grew up fifteen minutes outside of Manhattan. She could see the Empire State Building from her bedroom window. She did feel so lucky to share this time with Brad to be able to experience what it was like to grow up a generation ago in the Outback of Australia. It didn't get better than this.

The western suburb teacher had left, and the country boy was talking a mile a minute about the fights and adventures he had with his brothers. They spent an hour with Brad's eyes sparkling as the memories floated through graphic stories. Then he looked at his watch.

"We better hit the road if we want to set up camp before dark."

They dove back into the car and headed up the road toward the town of Quirindi. This was the town where Sam was first placed to teach kindergarten when she arrived in New South Wales. She always wondered what it would look like. They rode through looking around for the schoolhouse. At the end of a long stretch of road, they found the small wooden building that housed a half dozen rooms. *Oh, I'm so glad I didn't end up here.*

They left facing northwest heading to Tamworth, arriving at five o'clock. There was a cricket match out in an open field on the outskirts of town.

"Do you know much about cricket?" Brad asked.

"Not a thing," Sam answered, "I only know they all wear white and stand in front of a wicket with a flat bat."

"Time for an education, Rothbauer," he said. "Out of the car."

They spent the next half hour going through the basic concepts of cricket. She thought baseball was bloody slow but this game was slower than finishing a race in a pine box.

They returned to the car and found a caravan park and set up a tent in a remote corner. The air was warm and the stars were bright as they sat by the warm light of the campfire and heated up some grub. After dinner she cuddled in his arms. He wrapped his arms and legs around her like a blanket. Then he began rocking her gently back in forth with the dance of the fire. Brad began to kiss her neck then traveling his mouth slowly down her arm. Never separating for a minute, he moved their bodies into the tent as they took off each other's clothing one small piece at a time until every part of each other's bodies touched and caressed to the rhythm of the evening. The next day they awoke to rain. They moved cautiously ahead to New Angledool.

James greeted them as soon as they pulled up to his house. Sam saw Brad's eyes light up as he entered the wrap-around screen porch covered by the tin bull-nosed roof. James was wearing the same grubby clothes she saw him in last.

Brad knew the language of The Outback and got right to the point. He asked about the lay of the land and more precisely where they could find boar. They talked a bit, then James said, "Sorry mates the old farmhouse I was going to rent you for $20 a week is unavailable." However, he quickly made a more appealing offer, "The big woolshed has plenty of room and you can shower here at my farmhouse whenever you want. I've a family staying on one end of the woolshed but you can make good use of the other side. There are beds for the shearers and I'll give it to ya free."

"*Free*, free works for me," said Brad smiling quickly. It was now late afternoon as they made their way to the woolshed. They were greeted by big Tom and his three children who were the occupants of the west wing of the enormous shed. Tom was an avid fisherman, Bush pilot and former postmaster of New Angledool. He introduced his three delightful children, "I'm just taking my bloody grubs for an experience in The Outback. What about you, mates?"

"Boar hunting," offered Brad quickly.

"Bloody hell, S'truth," replied Tom.

"Righty-oh. Have you seen any boar since you have been here," Brad asked?

"Not a one, mate," said Tom, "But we haven't ventured too far from the shed. There's a waterhole down a bit though. If you head east, you'll see a windmill. I would guess the boar will head there at dawn and dusk for a wet one."

"Well, we hope we don't bother you much on the east wing," apologized Brad in advance. "We do have a bit of unpacking to do so we better get to it. Can we catch up with you a bit later?" Tom nodded.

Brad was amazingly efficient with unloading the Holden. All the ammo and guns were in one place, food items in another, clothing etc. He unpacked systematically as he packed them in. They found a makeshift grill and sink area for the shearers and they set up a make-shift kitchen and began to cook pork and beans.

"Even if we kill a boar, we'd never eat it," said Brad.

"Why not?"

"It would be riddled with worms." (Sam was very happy to hear that she wasn't expected to watch skinning, preparing, and the roasting of pigs.) "We're slaying the poor buggers because they've gotten out of hand. There are way too many of them out here in the Bush. The owners feed them mostly to their dogs." *Ugh, poor dogs.*

It was cozy in the shed when the last propane light went out. Brad and Sam nuzzled up and listened to the sounds of the Outback through a large open glassless window that framed their bed. The birds had settled in for the night but deafening tones of chirping crickets, bellowing bull frogs, and occasional yelps from mysterious animals, perhaps dingoes, filled the air.

Before they knew it, the sunrise appeared through the window on Brad's side of their double bed. Sam nuzzled closer into Brad's outstretched arm. He was still asleep but she wanted to watch the sunrise savoring every second thinking how lucky she was to get to see such a view. *The Hiltons of the world could never offer better.* The heat came quickly with the morning light so they got up and made a cereal breakfast and began to put on their gear. Brad handed Sam the .222 bolt-action Bruno with a scope and he took the 3o-3o Winchester and headed out.

Within the hour, James came by and picked them up in his truck to view the property. His dogs went with them. It was a whirlwind of a day. James stopped the car and Brad jumped out preparing his rifle and peering through the Bush for movement. James jumped out and released the dogs. The dogs ran about ten yards forward and Brad ran close behind in hot pursuit. There was a shot, then a squeal and Brad yelling, "Got one."

He shot two in less than thirty minutes. A Land Rover met them back at the house. Steven King, a portly older property owner from up the Hebel Road, greeted them on their return.

"Heard there were some city slickers here trying to kill boar," he said with a smirk.

Sam moved up quickly, "Hi, I'm Sam." She introduced herself extending her hand. "I'm your city slicker. I come from the New York City area; this is Brad," she pointed, "He's a country boy from the Maitland area. He knows a fair bit about boar hunting."

Brad said nothing because James had already begun boasting about Brad's ability to shoot. "He took two out at about twenty meters yonder, Steve," said James.

"Well, there's quite a few out there and they're rooting out my property. What do you think about us getting in the back of the Land Rover and rounding up a few?"

"Yes, Sir." screamed Brad excitedly. *I hope they are going to include me and not just leave me behind.*

"Come on, gal. If you are coming with us, jump in the back," Steve yelled. Sam didn't wait for a second invitation. She threw the rifle over her shoulder and swung it over her back.

They spent the next two hours rough riding up and down gullies, streams and around termite mounds. In two hours, Brad had put down an additional thirteen.

Steve moved up and shook Brad's hand. "You know, mate, that was nice shooting."

"Ah, ta." said, Brad humbly. "I misfired a few and probably could have dropped a few more if I'd been more careful."

"Well, you can come back up to these parts anytime. I guarantee there will be many more waiting for you the next time."

Brad and Sam returned to the woolshed. Brad exclaimed. "You're right, Sam, this is the perfect place to hunt pigs, what a day."

"Well for *you* maybe. I still don't know if I even have it in me to shoot a boar."

"Oh, we have plenty of time, Sam. Tomorrow we'll start before the heat of the day sets in and do a little target practice. You'll definitely have your turn tomorrow, promise."

Bright and early the next day, Brad had them up and out targeting cans. Being the perfect boy scout, Brad began with safety drills first.

"The rifle always faces down. You never aim a rifle unless you are prepared to shoot. Safety catch on at all times. Always pick up the empty shells," he said. "I need to use them again to make new rounds." Despite constant reminding, Sam kept forgetting to pick them up.

They walked for hours through the scrub, hundreds of flies riding on their backs, sweat pouring down under the brim of their hats that were meant to protect them from the intense rays of the sweltering sun. By the end of the second day, they took down twenty more. Sam was proud of her five. On the last day, James picked them up in his truck and took them to a paddock with horses.

"How about we spend today riding the property on horseback," suggested James.

Sam had never been on a horse except at a fair. Her short acquaintance with one made her realize you needed to communicate with them differently than a dog. *They didn't respond to stay and come.* They had a mind of their own and were much bigger than she was and could sense her fear.

"Do you have any horses that are *easy* to ride, something *really* mellow?" Sam asked James in a nervous voice.

"I've just the one for you, she's a sweetheart." He called out for Cindy and she trotted over to him. Brad helped saddle her horse.

"Which one is the feistiest," asked Brad.

"That stallion over there." James pointed to a large horse in the corner of the paddock. "Are you sure you want to try that one?" James asked. Sam was shaking her head.

"Is it okay if I give it a go, mate?" asked Brad.

"We named him Lightning. I'm afraid he hasn't been ridden much," James said.

Sam was mesmerized. Brad walked up to the stallion talking softly. He began to stroke him under his chin, shared breaths with him through his nostrils, then stroked him from the top of his head to his nostrils. *My God he's talking to him.*

Then Brad did the most amazing thing. He walked along side of the horse and ran his hand along its back. He walked about three yards behind the back of the horse and took a running start hopping on the horse bareback as if he was jumping over a small fence. He grabbed the mane of the tall horse and walked him over to James bareback. *If he was trying to impress me, he was successful.* Sam was dumbstruck.

"Well, you know a fair bit about horses then. Are you *sure* you don't want to stay here in these parts and . . . help . . . ?"

"Nah . . . I have a job, Ta. I've been around a few horses in my time."

Sam still had her mouth wide open in amazement. She had been a big western movie fan as a kid, and had only seen a stunt like that done once in a movie.

"It's okay, Sam, it goes along with being a country boy," Brad said sarcastically.

In two days they packed the Holden and said goodbye to their woolshed family. Before leaving, Brad asked James and Steven if they could come back next year. Both enthusiastically agreed.

Sam fell in love with the words *US* and *WE*. She felt like they were becoming more anchored in their relationship. He loved teaching Sam and Sam loved learning. Both of them were always hungry to learn more. They had like hearts and souls. She *was* in love. She didn't want the bubble to burst or her world to collapse. She was beginning to feel that warm secure feeling you get inside embracing a growing relationship.

14

A Quick Trip to the Orient

The long summer school holiday was still ahead of them. The days were getting hotter. Sam was hoping Brad would say he would like to just run away so they could enjoy another adventure together. However, his life was becoming increasingly more complicated. He was going to need time to pack his life up and move his treasured items up to his mum's house near Maitland.

Summer in Sydney is brutal, usually close to forty degrees Celsius (104 Fahrenheit) and often accompanied by a hundred percent humidity. Sam wanted cooler weather and to travel as much as she could while she had the time.

Just the year before, Cassie found a group of teachers who were going to be the first western group allowed to tour China. Mao Zedong, the founder of The People's Republic of China, died on September 9, 1976. Soon after, China was allowing westerners in to see their great Communist Republic. *Sam needed to see it.* She signed up with Cassie to go and then got a phone call from the American Embassy just a few days later.

"Hello, this is the American Embassy in Sydney. We have an application for Samantha Rothbauer to receive a Visitor's Visa to The People's Republic of China."

"Yes, that's right. I'm Samantha Rothbauer," she answered.

"Well, I need to inform you that your Visa is denied."

"What!" she screamed at the phone. "What do you mean it has been denied? I've already paid for the trip!"

"Well, ma'am, I would advise you to get your money back. The United States has no such agreement with China to allow United States citizens to travel through China. Australia may have, but *we* do not."

Sam was very upset at this point. This would have been the first time any westerners went into China, not to mention Sam's first travel experience with Cassie.

"So, what would happen if I went anyway," she asked.

"Simply, you would be blacklisted," the man said.

"What does that mean?" She couldn't even believe she was questioning the United States Government in this tone of voice. She was shaking. Luckily, the man on the other end was patient.

"Well, ma'am, just try getting back into the United States after you've been blacklisted."

"What?" she said, "You can deny me access to my own country? Okay, okay . . . never mind, I get the picture, turn down the Visa."

Three months later, a letter arrived at Duke Street from the United States Embassy stating that she could *now* apply for a Visa to China. She had already missed the trip with Cassie and friends. However, not to be dissuaded, Sam quickly scanned the *Sydney Morning Herald* classified section and found a trip with a group of art teachers who were not only going to China for two weeks, but also spending a third week in Japan over the six-week Christmas break. Sam put down a deposit and talked to Brad to see if he would like to go.

"Sorry Sam, just bad timing," he said. "I'll be busy enough packing up my life. I'm not sure if China is on the top of my list as much as yours. You know Israel would be my first choice for indulging a walk-about outside of this country."

She also asked Lacy if she'd like to join her; she wasn't too keen either. However, as the trip got closer, Lacy booked a flight to Thailand through our travel agent Harry to visit Bangkok. She had received letters from Lyndsey about how beautiful and exotic it was. So, they decided to meet up in Hong Kong on the way back.

China was like nowhere else on earth. Hundreds of thousands of people either walked, rode bikes in droves down city streets, all wearing the same navy blue Mao uniform and the hat with a red star in the middle. The Cultural Revolution was in full swing. The Chinese government showed classrooms, acupuncture operations, manufacturing villages, and communes to their visitors.

When they returned to Japan, the art teachers voted on spending the last two days back in Tokyo visiting all the museums they had missed during the holidays. Sam was itching to get away and was yearning to see Hiroshima. A Russian couple accompanied her and they later joined the group on the flight back to Hong Kong.

When they got to the hotel, Sam spied Lacy waiting in the lobby for her. The following two days were spent in a massive shopping spree. Lacy had already done her homework. Eighteen karat gold and diamonds were abundant and displayed in every store. The cost was about half the price as anything comparable in the States and Australia. They both picked out some beautiful chains. Sam browsed the counters of diamonds with curiosity.

Lacy, however, found a ring with two half carat diamonds that were uniquely arranged in a lotus flower setting. Sam thought for sure she was going to throw the purchase on her traveler checks as she kept circling the counter. She finally told the lady she might be back the next day.

That night in the Hilton Bar, Lacy had the bartender create her infamous Harbor Lights. They had caught up on their trips as they toasted their experiences.

"Sam, I need to ask you a favor," said Lacy.

"Sure," Sam replied, thinking she would ask her to carry some items in her bag as Sam was arriving a day earlier.

"You know that diamond ring I loved so much," she said.

"Yes, it was beautiful."

"Well, I was able to get the shopkeeper to come down another hundred dollars." Sam knew Lacy was frugal with money and better at bartering. *She's hoping I can loan her some money.*

"Okay, so how much are you short," Sam asked.

"No, Sam, I'm not asking for money. I want you to call Wyatt when you get back to Sydney and ask him if he'd buy the ring for me."

Sam just stared at her. "What . . . I didn't know your relationship with Wyatt had gotten so serious?"

"Well, it really hasn't. I'd like to put the question out there and see what he says. You never know, he might surprise me."

"Hmm . . . this is quite the favor, Lacy. I have never talked to Wyatt for more than two minutes and never about anything serious." Sam's reply was met with silence and a stare back from Lacy.

"Okay, I promise to call and I'll leave a message for you at the hotel one way or the other."

"Thanks Sam, I owe you one," she said.

The next morning, Sam flew into Sydney direct and arrived early afternoon. Before she even unpacked, she wanted to get this messy business over. She made her way to the red phone that was located downstairs in the laundry room. It was quiet and no one was around. She was always easy and accommodating to reasonable requests, but this by any means was not reasonable.

She put the call through to Wyatt's restaurant which was the only place she knew to try to contact him. She was nervous. She knew Lacy was seeing Wyatt occasionally. He came by for a few parties at Duke Street and spent some nights with Lacy . . . but a diamond ring . . . this was another matter.

Sam knew she was out of her comfort zone when a male voice answered on the other end. "The Village Restaurant, who's speaking," the voice snapped. She wanted to hang up but stayed on the line.

Sam took a deep breath and cleared her throat. "Hi," she answered, "I'm trying to reach Wyatt Stetson."

"You're speaking to him," he answered abruptly in his Texas drawl. *He's thinking I'm another bill collector.* Without a second's hesitation she said, "Wyatt, it's Sam, Lacy's friend from Duke Street. Listen, I just left Lacy in Hong Kong and she asked me to give you a call."

"Oh . . . hi, Sam, what does she need that's so urgent?"

Sam paused. *This was awkward.* "Well . . . , yesterday she and I were shopping in Hong Kong and she fell in love with this diamond ring."

"Yah," he said.

Sam took another deep breath. "Well, she wants to know if you would buy it for her." There was a *long* unhealthy pause.

"Is she Goddamn out of her cotton-pickin-mind! I mean, has she blown herself away on drugs or something over there?"

"No . . . Wyatt, I just left her at the Hilton last night. She's quite lucid, sane, and is posing this as a serious question."

"Well, call her back and tell her I asked you if she was out of her mother fuckin' mind." He ended the call abruptly and hung up.

Sam sighed a heavy sigh as she rang the Hong Kong Hilton and left the following message. "I called Wyatt and his response was, did you lose your mind? Sorry, I guess that means no. See you when you get home to Duke Street."

15

Fiji by Chance

Lacy arrived back the next day from Hong Kong. They never brought up the incident again. Duke Street continued to be an endless flow of people waltzing in and out.

Lacy and Sam began to get friendly with the next-door neighbors, an Australian couple, Tom and Karee Cousner. Tom was Canadian and Karee was a bubbly Australian blonde who also liked to party. They had two children, a boy and a girl, ages ten and eight. They bought two terrace houses and were renovating both to transform the footprint into one large mansion. Tom was an artist in 3-D motion.

Several nights a week Sam and Lacy visited with the Cousners. The Cousners usually went to Sam and Lacy's for happy hour or Sam and Lacy went to their house for evening tea.

Friday nights, there were always large parties at Duke Street and everyone was curious as to what flavor might walk through the door. Wyatt came over sporadically and so did Brad. However, the environment was not conducive for trying to develop a relationship.

Sam saw early signs that she would need to move out of Duke Street in the coming weeks. The commune systems as designed by the brothers never really worked. You bought food for the week and placed it in your appointed colored bin and it was gone by the next day.

Lacy suspected it was one of the brothers taking the food. She felt they were too lazy to go out and get their own. The only way you could purchase food would be nightly as you made your way home from work. It too was getting old.

Brad and Sam were still trying to figure out the world of *Us*. They worked together each day and never breathed a word to anyone about their relationship except to Cassie.

In February, Brad broke the news to Sam that he and his soon-to-be ex-wife had already purchased tickets to New Zealand the year before and were still planning to do the trip together. They had made the reservations to coincide with Brad's school holiday in May.

Sam was a little disturbed, but not too upset as she and Brad had already moved in together. Grant, Sam's former flatmate from Birchgrove, showed them an efficiency flat across from his. It looked like a good solution for the present and Brad signed papers for a month-to-month lease taking possession on the 1st. He quickly crafted a bed and bought a small TV. Sam needed something to distract her during the time he was away. *She didn't want to dwell on the fact he was spending two weeks with his ex-wife.* When Lacy began talking about exploring New Guinea, Sam told her she might be interested in going as well.

Wyatt had explored the villages up and down the rivers that led to the Coral Sea of Papua, New Guinea. For years he traded the natives for artifacts that he could sell to museums and art galleries, including shrunken heads. In conversations they had around his bar, where the expats would often gather, he described his venturesome life up rivers full of crocodiles.

Lacy continued to spin her happily-ever-after dreams around Wyatt and wanted to know more about the life he lived. Sam and Lacy went to the travel agent, Harry, who spoke about all the shots and the pills for malaria and tropical ulcer-like sores. They also discovered in order to travel up the rivers they would need private planes which would cost a fortune.

One night around the large picnic table that was the center of the Duke Street kitchen, a girl named Sally was visiting one of the brothers. She was a Yank. A beautiful brunette, tall and statuesque. She was also a *wild thing* who enticed millionaires. She shared that she was a borderline alcoholic and told everyone she had begun to clean herself up by caring for this millionaire's island who was developing tourism off the blue lagoon in Northern Fiji.

"So, why don't you girls just cancel that boring trip of yours to New Guinea and come spend a week or so with me on the Island? Come on, don't think twice, I could use some fun company over there. The only friends I really have are the natives."

Lacy and Sam looked at each other. The Island of the Blue Lagoon sounded a lot more appealing than mosquito driven Port Moresby. Okay, *one more adventure for the road before I hope to get into a life-long one with Brad.*

The May school holidays arrived. Brad flew to New Zealand and Lacy and Sam flew to Fiji. When they arrived in the Nadi Airport, they were greeted by a large grinning native named Joe who carried a sign. 'Welcome Lacy and Sam.'

Joe brought them to Roman's new business office. Roman had just purchased a tourist sea plane business to take tourists to the Yasawa Islands located some sixty miles north of the large island of Fiji. Joe said Roman was not going to be around while they were visiting; he was taking possession of a brand new Cessna for his tour business.

The next day, Joe took them to the marketplace. They bought some trinkets while Joe shopped for the staples for the island. Sam spied a pallet filled with cases of beer.

"Joe, who's the beer for?" Sam asked thinking there might be other guests on the island.

"It's for Mamsab Sally, miss."

Sam turned toward Lacy. "It seems that Mamsab Sally isn't really on the wagon. What do you think we should buy for beverages for evening cocktails?" They shopped around and found some vodka and bourbon. Wine was not an option; it was all imported and way too dear.

As they pulled up to the island, a local native puttered up in a small panga equipped with a five horsepower motor to take them to shore. Sally was waving to them and was accompanied by two native children who had made hibiscus leis for them. The greeting was already worth the long six-hour ride.

After everything was unloaded, Joe brought them to cabin number one. None of the other six cabins were finished yet. Sally took them on a quick tour of the island. Roman left nothing out.

That Friday, Sally prepared Sam and Lacy for the party tour boat that was coming through that evening. "Okay, girls, this hundred-foot yacht is taking high-paying customers to the island of the Blue Lagoon. We are invited to come aboard and join the passengers for the evening."

A panga came and picked them up about three in the afternoon. Sally had lent them some colorful sarongs to wear. The Micronesian natives were roasting a pig in an open pit on the island. The female natives sang local songs and danced happily around the fire to the delight of the tourists. About ten, they were shuttled back to the tourist boat. It was dark and the tourists went to their cabins. Sam sat up on deck by the bow of the boat with a young native who wanted to know more about the States. Sally had gone below with the sixty-year-old captain.

Sam didn't know what was going on and she didn't care. Within an hour Sally emerged and was looking for her and Lacy.

"Who's next?" she asked.

"Next for what?" Sam said.

"Well, to go down and entertain the captain."

"What . . . are you suggesting that we owe the captain something for this trip?" she asked.

"Well, nothing is really *free,* Sam. There is always a price to pay."

"Listen, I have money back at our hut if there is payment needed. That's all one gets from me."

"Look, Sam, people pay in different ways on the islands. It is about bartering."

"I'm not judging anyone on how they want to pay people. I'm just communicating how I intend to pay them."

She began to whisper softly knowing how water carries sound. "I'll say it again. I'm definitely *not* visiting the captain's quarters."

Sally shrugged, turned, and disappeared around the corner of the boat. Out of the corner of her eye, Sam noticed a panga approaching the side of the boat. A native came aboard. She approached him and asked him if he knew where their island was and he replied yes. She told him she was very seasick and needed to go back. He was offered ten Australian dollars and he nodded his head. Sam searched for Lacy but couldn't find her, so she decided to make her escape while she could.

She followed the native down the ladder to the skiff. The vessel sliced the water with each stroke of the native's oar making an iridescent foam that followed them in the moon light. The stars reached from horizon to horizon. *This is truly the best part of this whole trip.* Right now, the danger was behind her and a safe silent night's sleep was ahead. She ran to the cabin and got her rescuer his ten dollars and cupped her hands in a prayer motion. She bowed and said, "Many thanks." He nodded back and disappeared from view into the dark waters.

The next morning, the girls arrived. Sally unloaded two large boxes filled with Jack Daniels and had the workers bring them to the kitchen. She shot a Cheshire cat smile at Sam and winked. She was bartering for more than a tour on the captain's boat. Perhaps it was her month's supply of booze. Sam was just grateful she hadn't played into part of the payment scheme.

Sunday was Mother's Day. Mother Sunday, as it was referred to on the Islands. The girls were directed by Sally to wear their Sunday best as they made their way over to the neighboring island. They joined the natives to celebrate the event in the church, which was in the center of Macacawa Levu. They were greeted by hundreds of smiling natives. After the service they were invited to join Joe's family. His father made a ceremony around making Kava from ground piper root.

They returned to the island about seven that evening. Sally said she was going to call her mother for Mother's Day and invited the other girls to do the same. They had to do it by two-way radio and Sam spent some time training her mom to say 'over' after each response. Her mother was happy for the call and she told her she would write a newsy letter about her recent adventure when she returned.

Later that evening, Sally called Roman. She had a strange look on her face as she returned to join the girls. "Hmm . . . ," she said. "It seems Roman is *now* returning Tuesday from his trip and wants to meet you girls. When I mentioned that Lacy and Sam were not a couple but rather two young females, he insisted on meeting you." Sam kept staring at her.

"Girls, he does come with warning labels," she replied. "He is quite kinky sexually. To be honest, I don't even like it when he visits the island."

Sam got that horrible feeling in her stomach again. *The island payment system.* While they were a couple to him, they owed him nothing, but now that they were two young girls they owed him everything. Sam **hated** feeling like this.

Tuesday came and Lacy and Sam were back on the slow coconut trawler. They had a flight set from Fiji to Sydney on Thursday. Roman called their hotel and suggested they meet him in the hotel lobby at noon the next day. She and Lacy sat around the pool early morning trying to figure out their options.

"Listen, Lacy, this is not my cup of tea. I don't feel I owe this man anything."

"Okay, okay, I hear you, but he's coming in two hours and he knows where we're staying," Lacy said.

"Well, we can change hotels or perhaps we can see if there is another flight leaving for Sydney today."

"I'd be up for leaving today if we can get a flight," she said. "I think if we transfer to another hotel, he might still track us down."

Sam quickly grabbed the room key from the table and ran up to the second floor before Lacy could change her mind. She didn't have to fake emergency in her voice as she attempted to plead with the airline attendant that they had to return to Sydney immediately. She said they had stand-by seats and Sam signed them up.

If they wanted to get to the airport and get through customs, they'd have to pack immediately. Lacy looked at Sam somewhat relieved. "Let's go. We can do this."

Sam packed her backpack like a mad woman. In less than thirty minutes they were in a taxi. They hid in the airport's restrooms until boarding time.

Sam took a long, relieved sigh as she entered the front door of Brad's flat. She began to unpack, then all of a sudden she got that sinking feeling. All of her camera gear had been stolen from her backpack. She had sacrificed her usual precaution for packing in a rush to escape.

I guess there was a bigger price to pay for this trip. Her Olympus had been with her since the beginning. Sam left a piece of herself in Fiji after all.

Well, Sam, you're a lucky girl; it's a piece of you that can be replaced.

16

Returning to the Outback

Brad and Sam began to talk about another trip to The Outback before they officially moved onto a bigger project. They had been talking about the next step of renting or buying a house together. They took out the maps of New South Wales and decided they could do one large circle of the entire state and go boar hunting again before they returned. They began to pack boxes for moving from the flat and created other stacks for the trip they would take during the August break.

The day before they were to leave, there was a knock on the door. It was an unfamiliar girl's voice.

"Hello, Sam, are you there? Grant told me if you ever received a phone call to knock on your door." Sam peeked out.

"Oh, hi, I'm so glad you're here," she said. "You have an urgent call from the States."

"Really . . . ?" Sam said, surprised. She had been in Australia almost three years now and this was only the second phone call that she had ever gotten. As she walked into their flat, she just knew something terrible must've happened at home.

"Hello . . . ," she said.

"Sam," a very tired voice said. "It's mom, there was a long pause . . . your brother's dead." Before she could ask any questions her mother added. "He shot himself in the head yesterday with a .44 Magnum."

Sam didn't know what to say or even how to feel. All she knew was that somehow she wasn't shocked by the news. She knew he had been struggling with life for a while. Depression of some kind. However, he had recently gotten remarried and she thought life would be happier for him.

"I'm *SO* sorry, mom," Sam said. (Her brother and mom had a special bond.)

"When would be a good time to call you back? Sydney is currently experiencing a transit strike and a phone strike at the same time. I want to get to a different phone to talk to you for a while longer."

"Anytime, dear, just call me when you can." Her mom's voice sounded vacant, heartbroken.

Brad was not around; he was out shopping for their trip. She left him a note about the circumstances and explained she would contact him later. She was going to try to find some friends who would allow her to make an overseas call. She knocked on the door of her friend Dee, the dancer. Surprisingly, she was home. Sam sat inside exhausted even though she had only walked a couple of miles downhill. She told her everything. She was the best person to talk to.

Dee was petite, sweet, and always cheerful. She was very empathetic.

"So what do you think you'll do?" she asked.

"I really don't know, Dee," Sam answered. "It really makes no sense to try to travel back to the States during a transit strike. You know I would never get there in time for the funeral. It takes a week to get there and a week to get back under good circumstances. I only have two weeks off, but it's just not enough time. I was half thinking I'd take my free one-way ticket back to the States this Christmas holiday and cash it into a round trip ticket. Christmas break is six weeks long. I know my family needs me now, but maybe it'll give them all something to look forward to."

Sam wasn't able to contact Brad to bounce ideas off him. They didn't have a phone in the flat. She decided to stand by Dee's phone for two hours until she got a call back from the States saying the phone was connected to her mother's. They talked for an hour.

Her mother liked the idea of Sam coming home for Christmas. She agreed that it would definitely give everyone something to look forward to. Sam hung up the phone, gave Dee a tight hug, and handed her a check for the phone call. She walked back to Birchgrove before dark.

Brad didn't know how to respond to the news. This was an unsettling situation at best and he made the decision for both of them to move their trip back a day. For the first few days of the trip Sam didn't say much. He respectfully gave her space and they rode along quietly taking in the scenery. They made it to Canberra in one day, and then went on to Mildura.

Sam was dying to see the small little town that was described as being beyond the black stump. It was where Robbie had lived for two years. When they left Broken Hill, they were heading north again for New Angledool. Before they left, Sam received a letter that James was not living on his property. Brad wanted to do some more boar hunting. Sam was ready; she now had her new .3o8 Bruno that Brad helped her purchase for pig hunting.

They got directions at New Angledool to a road that would lead to their old friend Steven King's property near Hebel on the Queensland border. Steven was home and happy to see them. He said he was having more trouble with the Roo than he was with boar this year. He said the kangaroo kept taking down his fences. Sam wasn't enticed by what he was suggesting. *There is no way I'm killing a kangaroo.*

Steven gave them directions to his shearer's quarters where he told them they could stay. They rolled up to their new rustic mansion. The long wooden row of buildings was made of ten individually enclosed bedrooms to lodge shearers. At the end of the row was a large kitchen facility that backed up to shower rooms and toilets. *Very sophisticated.* They had been pretty happy in James' open space shearing shed the year before but this was more than the Hilton; it was by far the Waldorf Astoria. Brad got out of the Holden and stretched.

"So where do we want to park our goodies?" he said.

"I think we have our pick. You choose. I don't care."

Brad carefully opened each cabin door, inspected the rooms, and sat on all the beds. He finally chose one room in the middle of the long row of shearer's quarters. They began filling the room with their backpacks and extra sleeping bags. They moved the two single beds together to make one. They walked around the buildings and brought all the grub into the kitchen. There was a big open hearth. Brad went outside and located a wood pile and began stacking the hearth. He had a fire crackling and in no time warming the large kitchen area with its twenty-foot wooden table glowing and feeling cozy. The year before, they had arrived in the summer and it was hot. Now they had just moved out of winter and it was still damp and chilly.

"Oh, this is absolutely perfect," Sam said. "I can't believe we have this whole place to ourselves!"

"Come here, look at this," Brad said. "This lever here allows the fire to heat up the water system for the showers. In about an hour, you'll have a nice hot one."

Excitedly, he headed toward the door.

"Where are you going?" Sam asked in surprise.

"I'm going for a walkabout. I want to scope out the area before dark and who knows, maybe I'll be lucky enough to ding a pig."

Sam waved goodbye and settled in with a good book. She cozied up near the fire recognizing how lucky she was. For the next three days, they walked about the property looking for boar. They were scarce this trip. "Hunted out," Brad said when he returned. They found some by a riverbank early one morning and some later by the same spot feeding off the dead ones. It was not exciting. This trip felt different. On their walks, Brad pointed out several Gila monsters and some other iguana species. They also found mounds and mounds of termite colonies reaching over ten feet high.

On their last full day, Steven came by to see how the hunting was going for them. Brad was honest but humble stating that Steven was right, the pickings were slim.

"Well, I need some tucker for the dogs. Do you want to join me and my partner here and see what we can rustle up?"

Sam admittedly loved the rush of being on the back of a Land Rover racing through the scrub. She knew she wasn't going to shoot anything but boar but she didn't care. She and Brad hadn't been in the back of the flatbed long when Steven headed the rig through a thicket of trees. They went straight through an immense spider web that stretched two tree lengths. The web was draped all over Sam's hair. She tried not to overreact or look horrified. She looked to Brad who seemed unaffected positioning his rifle over the roof of the Land Rover.

Sam began pulling the sticky web off her hair examining every inch of it. From the size of the web this critter was immense. She was looking down at the wood chunks piled in the lorry when all of a sudden she saw a hand sized tarantula crawl its way to the top. Sam reacted from her gut letting out a *blood*-curdling scream. Steven reacted by slamming on the brakes. Brad and Sam were both flung over the top of the cabin.

Steven immediately jumped out and ran to the back of the truck.

"What the bloody *hell* just happened!" he yelled. Sam had scared everyone to bits. Her heart was still in her throat. She frantically looked back at the wood pile but couldn't see the monster that had scared the life out of her. Sam's eyes kept scanning the back of the bed of the truck and then . . . she spied the long hairy legs again crawling back over the top of the wood. Her body was shaking as she raised her right hand to point to the beast. She was just so happy to be able to show evidence of something that would cause such a scream.

In a single bound, Steven jumped up onto the flatbed. "What . . . you let out that death- defying scream over a bloody spider!" he yelled. "You put our bloody lives in danger screaming like that, miss. Crikey, you bloody sheilas."

Steven proceeded to jump onto a few logs and grabbed the back of the spider with his bare hands. Without a moment's hesitation, he tossed it over the side of the truck. "The lady wishes you G'day," he screamed to the spider. He spun around to face Sam pointing his index finger. "Now, I don't want to hear another bloody scream like that unless someone is truly dying. Got it, mate!" Sam nodded her head vigorously. *Now she was more afraid of Steven than any creature roaming the earth.*

She looked over at Brad who burst out laughing. He knew the Out-back and its men. He knew their bark was worse than their bite. They spent the next three hours racing and rattling over hills and ravines. Both the boar and Roo were scarce today. Steven spied a herd of emu and began chasing them. There must have been a dozen of them running together in a pack. Sam was surprised at how fast they were. They were outrunning the Land Rover. *She was cheering for the emu.*

Steven instructed them to shoot. Brad took careful aim and brought down one. Sam just shot in the air; she *couldn't* shoot an emu. They were beautiful birds, the cousin of the African Ostrich, not to mention highly revered in Australia and immortalized on the government crest. Steven circled the flock and Brad took down three.

"Thanks. That's all we need mate," Steven yelled. Brad responded by resting his rifle on the back of the cabin. Steven circled the Land Rover around the remains of the carcasses left behind. He jumped out of the vehicle and went up to each dead emu and began chopping off their legs at the hip with a machete. There was the deafening crunch of bone followed by large spurts of flying blood.

He threw each leg to the back bed of the lorry where Sam and Brad were standing just as if they were chicken bones. He seemed to have no need for the rest of the emu. He looked at Sam as though to answer her question. "The dogs like the legs," he responded in a flat tone.

They got back to Steven's house and he asked them to come in and meet his wife. Mary had already prepared tea for Steven and asked them to stay. Sam looked over at Brad raising her eyes as she was grubby and looked a sight.

"Well, we certainly would enjoy your hospitality, but it has been a long day and we need to prepare for an early start tomorrow," said Brad.

Mary wouldn't accept the excuse. "*Please*, we would love to have your company. We don't get much company in these parts and the food is already on the table."

Sam and Brad turned to each other and Brad agreed to the offer. They washed up and followed Mary into the parlor and noticed the extensive spread situated on a lace tablecloth set with her finest china. Sam was just very excited not to be feasting on emu.

After tea, Steven took them behind the house to some kennels. He threw the emu legs to a set of dogs chained to posts. *I never want to come back as a dog in the Outback.* The following day they packed and began the long journey back to Sydney.

17

Reaching New Heights

On their return from the Outback, Brad and Sam quickly proceeded to the next stage of their relationship. They had felt the walls closing in around them in their bachelor flat in Birchgrove. It was as if they had been living in a small hotel room for months.

They began looking into buying a house in Balmain. The rundown properties were going pretty cheap. Renovating houses became an investment for many in the small artsy peninsula of Balmain. They knew this would be a large project that would keep them busy for years so they began to look at quite a few small homes.

Brad kept going back to one that was about a thousand square feet. A one bath, two bedroom attached row house that looked like it had been a recent pit stop for the homeless. He said it had good bones. He suggested they could live in it and just gut it one room at a time.

Sam could see the wheels spinning in his head. He needed a project. The Gladstone Street house was situated east of Gladstone Park and in between the two main churches in town. The one downside was that the backyard was adjacent to the back of the noisy London Pub that faced Darling Street.

It took them about a fortnight of going back and forth to revisit the property when Brad suggested they better buy it. They were already seeing prices going up daily. Balmain was going to be the next trendy area. Their offer of $29,000 was accepted. Now they needed to get a loan. The lending institutions were financing at a 14% interest rate for first time buyers.

Brad had just finalized a divorce and was pretty maxed out for cash. Sam, however, had $5000 burning in her pocket. The year before she almost invested it in Wyatt's restaurant and more recently, she had eyed the car of her dreams, a creamy white Morgan.

One afternoon after work, Sam brought Lacy over to see the house. Lacy was still living in Duke Street but was anxious to move out. Within a few weeks she went to a Saturday morning auction that was selling a small clapboard Cape Cod styled house and signed her own paperwork. Her house was situated across Darling Street from Sam and Brad, just two blocks away.

"Sam, I've been thinking we should double the size of the house and put in a large upstairs bedroom," Brad suggested one evening.

"Are we thinking we might create a two bath house, one upstairs and one downstairs?" she said with a smile.

"No, I don't think we should. It will double the cost but we'd better bring in an architect to help us get a rendering of the job. We can get some solid ideas about bearing walls and how much this is going to take to finance as we go along."

Sam agreed; she knew she would defer all decisions on the house to Brad. She respected his knowledge about everything that involved building. Cassie suggested a friend who was an architect and he drew a beautiful set of plans. He gave an estimate on what the job was going to cost. Brad was right—they were looking at doubling the cost of the house.

A lot happened in their lives all at the same time. One Saturday evening Brad and Sam went off to the city to attend the premier of the new movie *Star Wars*. They were so excited by it, they decided to take their entire class to see it and the students loved it so much, they created a play around the plot.

In the meantime, Brad recently joined the Commandos on the weekends. At least once a month, he was going off to play soldier. He always wanted to learn more about modern day weapons and jumping out of airplanes. Sam shared with Brad that jumping out of airplanes was a longtime goal of hers as well. She convinced him to let her join him for a practice jump. "It's on my bucket list too," she said.

"Bucket lists start when you retire," he said.

"Not for me they don't. They started the day I was born, and I have a *very* long list."

Many of her friends stated they would like to join her, but as the days grew nearer to the date, everyone conceded that they had more pressing plans. In the end, Brad, Valentino (Val), his friend from his Commando unit, and Sam were the only ones going. These were static line jumps. You jumped alone and you needed to know what to do if anything went wrong. The most useful part of the training was learning how to break your fall when you hit the ground.

Sam was beginning to lose sleep over her decision to jump out of a perfectly good airplane. Brad and Val already had seven jumps each and were now seasoned jumpers. She took solace in the fact that if they felt it was a grave danger for her, they would stop her from doing it. The next Saturday they got into Brad's Holden. Both Brad and Val agreed it was a perfect day for a jump. It was slightly overcast with no wind. "No wind, no drama," Brad said.

The instructor, Graham, met them on the airfield at nine. He led them to a room where they first needed to pass a four-page test. Luckily, they all passed.

"Okay mates, here we go. The pilot's ready."

Graham was an attractive man in his thirties. He had a calm voice, and seemed even-keeled. He sensed Sam's resistance getting into the plane. She was getting weak at the knees. He arranged them in order at the rear of the plane. There were four of them. He positioned Sam next-to-last before Brad. He knew that Brad could help him encourage Sam if he needed to. She didn't know what she was afraid of more—jumping out of the plane or never being able to live down Brad kidding her for the rest of her life that she was just a chicken. The pilot announced they had reached twenty-five hundred feet. Val moved to the open door and jumped first. From the look on Graham's face, and his remarks to the pilot, he wasn't exactly pleased with that jump.

"Remember everyone do a *hard* arch," Graham said. Words from the song "Only The Good Die Young" by Billy Joel rang in her ears. This was *crazy*. She just wanted to throw up. Fear was plastered all over her face. Graham signaled for her to move up to him by the open doorway.

"Are you ready?" he asked. Sam shook her head.

"Ah, don't worry, they all say that on the first try. Perfectly normal," he said. "Here, come closer I want to whisper something to you." She moved closer to the door hoping there would be some magic words that would give her courage. Suddenly he gave her a wisp of a kiss on her cheek. "Now . . . just go out on the strut and don't look down."

There may have been an ounce of courage in that little kiss. It was enough to get her to move slowly on the strut of the wing. She turned back to Graham.

" I can't, I don't think I can do this," she yelled back to him.

"Well, you can't come back in without endangering everyone in this plane," he said. "Just push off and remember your hard arch." *So this is it, in order to save everyone else I have to jump.*

There was no sense in arguing. Sometimes, you bring yourself to a place and you just keep to your initial decision. She pushed off. She could only hear the swish of the wind and the sensation of her uncontrollable heartbeats attached to her erratic breathing. She was counting one thousand, two thousand . . . she had the strong sensation of falling in a bottomless dream. She was totally unaware that her eyes were closed until she felt her feet kicking uncontrollably.

Oh shit, she thought, *is my chute in a daisy chain? Crap, I am going to die!* Somehow she commanded herself to open her eyes. She was trying to think of all she would need to do to save herself if her lines were twisted. She was instructed to pull out the reserve chute and manually push it out, ONLY if the main chute did not open. She looked up and to her surprise discovered that the canopy was open. *The big round bloody red canopy was perfectly formed. Okay I'm going to live.*

Sam began the process of trying to control her breathing which was totally out of control. Her heart was beating out of her chest. She reached for her toggles, trying to take in the view of what was left of a short ride. She was coming up to some fences in the open field and pulled on the left toggle so the breeze could take her more into the center. She became aware of a forward gliding sensation. She was only about two hundred feet above the ground. She remembered that in order to have a good landing, you needed to face into the wind.

A voice from a loud hailer yelled a command, "More on the right toggle!" Sam did as she was instructed and faced her feet forward to be ready to land. It turned out to be a very undramatic landing. Her feet touched the ground and she landed in a sitting up position. The air was so still the chute came down and dropped over her head. She looked like a walking tent as she tried to pull the canopy off. A ground crewman ran up and helped her gather the chute.

"Listen, if you want to do it again, I would sign up right away. The spots will fill up quickly. You can get two rides in today for the price of one," the instructor suggested. Sam turned to him.

"No . . . that's okay," she said. "I've had enough excitement for one day." She saw Brad walking towards her with a big smile on his face.

"Let me take some pictures of you in that jump suit. Val took some of us on the way down."

She sat back down on the ground alone in the field. She became aware that every inch of her body was drenched. She could have easily been pulled out of a swimming pool. All of her clothing was wringing-wet. She had never experienced this kind of nervous perspiration before. This was the first time she had looked death in the face. It wasn't pretty. For all the experiences we allow in our lives, she was quite sure she wasn't going to choose this one again.

Brad helped her up. Her feet were still like putty. They walked alongside of each other; he turned and said, "So, what do ya think?"

"I don't think I'm going to do it again anytime soon."

"You know, Sam, it really does get easier the more you do it."

"I'm sure that's true," she said surprising herself that she could even talk. "But it won't be today." She handed him the instamatic camera and he took some shots of her in the jumpsuit. They walked off the field together carrying their chutes. *Check that one off your bucket list, Sam.*

———◦•◦———

At the start of the construction phase, they received the unexpected news that the brick wall between them and their neighbor was one shared wall instead of two separate walls. We were listed in the hall of records as a detached house. In order to keep that status and build a second story they were now going to have to construct another load bearing brick wall that would take away a foot of house on the east end.

A quick three thousand went out the door to build a wall that was not in the original cost of the house renovation. Sam began looking through *The Sydney Morning Herald* for a second job. She spent many years as a waitress at the Jersey Shore during the summer months and felt it would be easy for her to pick up some extra income. However, the classifieds were full of jobs calling for barmaids in local pubs. She knew nothing about pouring beer, but felt it was a skill she could probably learn. The Hunters Hill Hotel kept repeating an ad. One day after school she went over to talk to the manager.

"Do you know how to pour a beer, Miss?" questioned the manager.

"No, sir, but I'm a quick study. I'm sure I could learn if you give me a chance." They reviewed the hours he wanted her to work. He agreed to try her out for a week. The rate per hour for a barmaid was twice the pay for a waitress in the States. Australians as a rule didn't leave tips. The year was 1979 and some of the pubs still didn't allow women in the public bar area. The ladies were expected to go to a back lounge room.

The Hunter was pretty upscale compared to most local pubs. However, the bigger challenge was getting the head on the beer perfectly set with a half inch below the rim and a half inch head over the top. It was a skill that left no margin for error.

Sam began throwing out more beer than she was pouring. She told Brad she was sure she would be fired before the week was out. But, fortunately, one week went into another and they began to realize that their project would certainly need an extra sustainable income to keep up with added expenses.

Lacy had bought the easier house. Hers was a free-standing clapboard that only needed some new paint. Brad and Sam's was a building nightmare. However, Sam knew she had the right man for the job.

About two months into the project, Brad felt it was time to travel north and meet the family. Sam was pretty nervous. Brad had only been officially divorced less than a year and Sam knew being accepted so early by his family could pose a challenge.

Brad packed the plans for the house. He wanted his father's input. He had never shared with the family how close he and Sam had become. He could sense Sam's nervousness on the ride north.

"Sam, it'll be okay," he said. "My family are simple country folk. They knew my wife and I weren't happy for years. In the end, people just want to see loved ones happy." Sam turned and nodded in agreement. Within four hours, just outside of Maitland they pulled into an unpaved driveway that led to a yard behind a three-bedroom ranch which had a large screened-in back porch. They got their bags and walked by a large aviary that Brad told her his dad built for a collection of birds that his mum cared for daily.

Brad's mother, Sharon, came out to meet them and hugged her son like she hadn't seen him for years. She turned to Sam and smiled and gave a soft welcome. Sharon was about 5'5" like Sam. She had a full head of white hair, very perky and fit. Gran came to the back door first and gave Sam an instant big hug. She fell in love with Gran immediately.

Sharon gave a call out to Brad's dad who promptly stuck his head out the garage that he converted into a workshop. Bob gave both Brad and Sam a hug.

"Welcome. We're so glad you finally came to visit. Brad has told us all about your big project. I can't wait to see the plans."

They went back to the Holden and carried the bags into the house. Brad followed his mum down the hall. Sam could hear the tone of an argument brewing immediately.

"No, mum," Brad said, "You are not putting Sam in a different bedroom. She is sleeping with me. Yes, I know we're not married but we sleep together every night and that is what we will continue to do." Sam heard some retort.

"Do you *really* want us to stay somewhere else for the night?"

Sam caught a glimpse of Brad's dad who was silently shaking his head in the living room. There was a mutter from mum in the hall and all the bags went into the one bedroom on the left side of the hall. Sam gave a soft sigh. It was the 70's and although the last generation had stiff rules about needing to be married before sleeping together, their own generation did not.

That evening they enjoyed a lovely country meal, fresh greens from the garden, mashed potatoes and roast beef. Mum, Gran, and Sam did the cleanup while Brad and his dad retired to the parlor to look over the plans of the house. Bob brought out a bottle of wine and poured everyone a drop. Sharon, Gran, and Brad skipped the wine which left more for Bob and Sam. Brad's dad and Sam immediately bonded.

She was happy with their first trip to meet the parents. Sharon warmed up to Sam by the end of the weekend. *All's right with the world.*

18

Gladstone Street

Brad and Sam remained busy people. In school they were both very focused on the kids and their work. But after work, she didn't get home most nights 'til nine after working a second job. They fell into bed and started it all over again the next day. Brad worked on projects at the house and made all the calls about what they were doing with a redesign.

The small house was a workman's cottage from the 1870's. After the brick wall was built, Brad began ripping out the rest of the floors. They were gutting everything. Sam's prize was an old gas stove called a Kooku-burra. It had a white enamel front door with a colorful kookaburra embossed on the panel. The rest of the body had a soft green top and legs. It was covered in a century of grease.

Once the floors in the first two rooms were replaced, they needed to move everything they owned back into the front living room: bed, clothes, and groceries. They walked on planks for weeks. Brad kept Sam busy on weekends, hammering the plaster off the convict brick walls. The fireplace was taking shape and looking inviting.

One Friday evening with Brad off to Commandos, Sam was sitting alone on their queen-sized bed in the living room when there was a

knock on the door. She walked cautiously over to the door slowly opening it. Standing at the front door with a freshly-baked pie was the neighbor to the right of them.

"I thought I would introduce myself," she said. Sam looked around as
if to share her situation.

"One bed in a living room, that is all I have to offer you. Come on in if
you dare," Sam said smiling. Rachael came in holding the pie in her right
hand. Sam spied a spot on the nightstand to the right of the bed that
housed the alarm clock and nodded for her to place it there.

"As you can see, we are in a bit of a mess," she said, apologetically.

"Blimey, we were sitting in the same mess a year ago. We've finally
reached the second story. Ours is a small townhouse on Jane Street. We
face the park."

She told Sam their story about getting married and traveling around
the world for a year. "I'm a teacher," she smiled.

"Really, so are Brad and I." She was down to earth and Sam got the
sense they would get much closer.

The summer heat was beginning to drag them down. Although they
certainly loved each other, they never broached what it might mean for
the future. They both survived failed first marriages and the level of
commitment was never spoken past the house project.

This was going to be a test of endurance for any relationship. Brad
would often choose to work on the house rather than join Sam's friends
for a time out Sunday barbeque. They played separately a lot. He didn't
like to drink or hang around those who did. Though she didn't notice it
then, they were beginning to drift apart.

Christmas holidays were coming and Sam had a flight booked to
return to Jersey. She hadn't seen her family in three years. Lacy decided
to head home as well. She hadn't gone home to visit her family since
coming to Australia either. Dee, the dancer, also decided to join them on
the flight. She wanted to look up some friends who were showgirls in
Vegas. They planned a time to meet in Connecticut before their return.
Lacy wanted Sam to look up Kat who had returned to Jersey and entice
her to travel north with Sam to visit her.

Brad seemed to be okay with her leaving for a month. He claimed he had a lot of work to do, especially with framing the back of the house and the upstairs.

Upon returning to the States, Lacy and Sam stopped in Los Angeles to look up Lyndsey. Her letters had indicated that she was staying in a house rented by her brother and sister in Redondo Beach. Lyndsey picked them up at LAX airport in her new bubble car. She had recently purchased a brand new blue and white AMC Pacer. Sam had heard about these funny-looking cars. There were certainly none in Australia. Dee, Lacy, and Sam surfaced from customs loaded with luggage. As she pulled up they all stared at each other. Sam thought, there is no way the three of them could possibly fit all the luggage in this little fishbowl of a car. Sam was shaking her head when Lyndsey said, "G' Day, Mates."

"I don't know, Lyndsey, old girl, we may need two cars for this pick up," Sam said, giving her a hug. All of them had come for a month and had two bags each. They were prepared for winter and were not traveling light.

"Oh, let's give it a go, shall we. It really holds a lot more than you think," she said.

Sam kept shaking her head, "I don't know about this."

The bubble surprisingly opened into a wide hatchback. They engineered suitcases standing up and some on their edge and others flat down. Lyndsey slammed the hood down several times until the latch caught.

"See, there, it fits," she said with a grin.

"I'm speechless," Sam said. "But where will we all fit?"

"Easy, one lucky girl gets to go in the front, the other two snuggle in that little space in the back." Lacy moved as fast as the eye could see into the front seat which left Sam snuggling up to petite Dee.

"Luckily, we don't have far to go to Redondo," Lyndsey said.

Sam had never driven around Los Angeles before. She stared at the flat dated landscape of worn-out ranch houses. She decided quickly it was nowhere she ever saw herself living. To her it was just a sprawling mess of cheaply made houses cloaked by horrendous smog.

On the ride to Redondo, Dee shared that she was heading to Vegas in a day or two. She planned to stop and visit one of her friends who was a

Show Girl at the MGM Grand Hotel. Lacy turned to Lyndsey. "Have you ever been to Vegas?" she asked.

"Nope, I was meaning to do it when I first came out west but never got the chance."

"Would you be up for going now," Lacy prodded.

"Well, I'm supposed to work for the next few days, but I could see if I can get the time off." Then Lacy turned back and looked at Sam. "You up for going, Sam?"

"You don't have to ask me twice. I've never been there either."

Lacy and Sam spent the next day touring Disneyland, which she had only seen on TV. Like most places when you first tour them, they seem much smaller than they appear on the tube. The following day they were packing everyone and some clothes back into the Pacer to drive the five-hour journey to Vegas. They took off late Thursday afternoon and ran into an unexpected blizzard in the high desert.

Who knew it snowed in Vegas? Poor Lyndsey was petrified driving that Pacer and so were all the passengers. It was already dark by five and they had an estimated four more hours of treacherous driving ahead of them. All of them had the duty of peering out the side windows from the bubble-styled car to locate the edge of the road through the driving snow.

There were no lights lining the two-lane highway and they had no chains or snow tires.

It was nerve-wracking, but Lyndsey kept her calm, and after many hours they saw the glow of lights on the horizon. "Oh my God." Lacy shouted, "We're going to make it."

They pulled into the MGM parking lot after eleven. Lacy, Lyndsey, and Sam went straight for the bar. Lacy immediately ordered a round of Harbor Lights. Dee went to the Green Room with a pass to see if she could locate her friend. As Sam looked around, she could see there were Christmas lights everywhere but no people. The hotel was deserted. *It must be the snow or perhaps it was because we were just days away from Christmas.*

For the next two days they walked about Vegas making sure they stepped into every large hotel in town. They just needed to say they'd been there. Sam watched Johnny Carson every evening. Somehow the words, "Here's Johnny," created a cozy warm feeling around her reassuring her that she was actually home in the States. A day after returning from the Vegas marathon, Lyndsey piled Lacy and Sam back in her Pacer and dropped them back at LAX.

Sam felt like a celebrity as her mother and sister screamed her name across the baggage claim area at the airport. They reunited like old friends. It would be a trip for healing. Sam began to contact some friends and those of her brother. She also spent some time catching up with her ex-husband, Daniel, who enjoyed hearing about all that had happened to her since she left. They were truly best friends. It was a heart-warming feeling to reconnect again.

Sam visited New York often and, of course, she and her sister took a ride to the Jersey shore and ended the journey having dinner with their father and his wife, Kate, in Toms River. He may have been happy to see Sam but he overwhelmed her with his fatherly criticism.

"When are you going to cut that hair of yours?" he questioned. "You're almost thirty years old."

Then almost as quickly, the very question Sam had been hoping to avoid came up. "So when are you moving back to Jersey?" he asked. *Never.*

Her father saw the struggle in Sam's eyes. "Of course you *can't* come back and live in Jersey. You probably aren't even a United States citizen anymore."

Now she was getting pissed off. "What makes you think I'm no longer a U.S. citizen?"

"Well, you're not one anymore. You live full-time in another country."

"Do you need to see my passport?" Sam asked in her defense.

"No," he answered. "You just don't belong here anymore."

Sam stopped there. Now she could see he was getting pissed. "Listen, Pop, I know this doesn't answer your question but I'm in a serious relationship with a teacher named Brad. Right now he and I are renovating a hundred-year old house. I have met his family and that is all I am prepared to say at this time."

The dinner did not have a great start, but her father settled down knowing that getting critical wasn't going to bring her back to Jersey anytime soon. He wasn't stupid.

Sam found Jersey City Kat. She was now living in Old Bridge and she was commuting to Newark to teach every day. Good pay but tough schools.

Lacy lived outside of Hartford, so Sam set up a road trip with Kat for the week before she flew back to Sydney.

On the ride to Lacy's house, Kat began an annoying diatribe about how she should have never left Australia and it was all Sam's fault.

"What are you talking about that it was all my fault that you left?" she asked.

"You know that I didn't want to leave," Kat bantered.

"Then *why* did you?" Sam said, getting increasingly annoyed.

"Well our two-year contract was up and everyone in my flat was leaving. When I asked Lacy, she told me to stay and we'd figure it out." Her voice rose to a shout. "But when I asked you, you just answered I needed to do what I felt I needed to do."

"Well, that isn't telling you that you should go back home!"

"Well, I took it that way."

"You heard what you wanted to hear. The truth is we make decisions and then we have to live with our choices."

Kat dropped it a notch, "Well, part of that is true, but I still will *never* forgive you." *What's new.*

"Great . . . thanks, let's go and have a good time and see what Lacy's life was like before she moved to Australia. They let it go and enjoyed their time meeting her family. Sam especially loved meeting Lacy's mother.

Hawaii was a non-event for all of them. Lacy got sick and spent most of her time in the hotel room and Sam laid on the beach with Dee the dancer. Dee was working on an even tan and wore her string bikini each day on her perfect petite body. Sam never felt fatter than lying next to her in the noon day sun like a beached whale, so she walked the beach a lot and went to the markets.

One day, Sam called Brad and told him she had found this unbelievable scrimshaw slate ballast from a whaling boat that she wanted to buy. It was pretty dear but it would be a unique keepsake. Brad spoke back with common sense.

"Listen, buy it if you have to, but we have a lot of expenses coming in for the house. You decide. You're the one working two other jobs. I also need you to know there's a surprise for you when you get home."

When their trip was over, Brad picked up Lacy and Sam at Sydney Airport but refused to talk about the surprise. After they dropped Lacy off at her house, they walked into their little torn up cottage. There behind the door was the biggest German Shepherd Sam had ever seen in her life. She threw herself back against the wall in fright.

Brad smiled, "Say hello to Fritz! He needed a place to live. He's a great guard dog. I found him at a friend's petrol station." You could see he and Brad had already bonded. Sam put her hand down nervously for him to sniff. Fritz began to lick it all over. He was very sweet. "Okay Fritz, I'm home and I guess we're just one big happy family."

19

Man's Best Friend

It was funny how having Fritz made them feel like a complete family. Sam was glad to be back in Oz. Australia was her home now, she had no doubt about it. Brad and she worked feverishly on the house every weekend and Brad most evenings.

Often when she drove home from school in her Toyota Corolla, Sam milled around the streets of the western suburbs. Many of the houses were being renovated by Greek migrants who were kicking out the older beautiful ornate lead-light windows to replace them with what they felt were more modern aluminum windows (pronounced al-loo-min-I-um by Aussies).

Sam found some beauties that were just sitting out by the rubbish waiting to be picked up. Brad would often grab Val after dark and drive out again and pick them up. Before long they had a beautiful collection of them lining the backyard. It had become Sam's task to burn and scrape off all the old paint around the frame, sand the wood, and repaint the frames. It was very time-consuming, but the windows looked magnificent when finished.

The biggest score was a twelve-foot-long window that took up the entire length of the family room. It was gorgeous. It had two casement windows on each side. Although the lead-light was mostly clear, there were colorful vines and flowers that laced through the window carefully framing the view of the garden below.

Brad immediately went about constructing a doggie door for Fritz. Fritz was friendly enough around humans but they had to muzzle him when he went outside. His former vagabond life had left him suspicious of other animals, particularly other large dogs. He was pretty formidable walking along with her at night. Sam had a leash but when they got to Gladstone Park Fritz always wanted to have a run. After ten there was usually no one around, so she would sometimes let him loose.

One Friday night, when Brad was away at Commandos, a bunch of yahoos from the local London Pub began to follow Sam as she was circling the park. They were definitely up to no good. She made a right and they followed.

Normally, she would be nervous walking home with four blokes behind her. She quickly made a left hoping to see Fritz. It was pitch black, no full moon tonight, and no Fritz. Sam walked faster and so did the pub boys. They were gaining on her.

"Fritz," she screamed at the top of her lungs, "Come here, boy." She peered around, still no Fritz. One of the blokes said, "She's bluffing, mates." They stepped up their pace. Sam began to wonder what they thought they would do with her since they were all so bloody sloshed.

She yelled again this time in a firm commanding voice. "Fritz, come HERE, boy!" Suddenly she could see his outline barreling down at full speed; all hundred plus pounds of German Shepherd sporting the large muzzle over his snout.

The next scene was right out of a movie. The lads were less than four feet on her heels. They saw the figure barreling through the trees coming right toward them. Sam wished she could have seen their faces, but her back was to them. They must have spied him all at once as they screamed, "Bloody hell. What's that, a bear?" Just as quick, Sam turned and they were gone.

Fritz sensed her anxiety as he nuzzled her leg. Sam went to the nearest park bench and took deep breaths as she sat trying to bring down her heart rate.

"Good boy, Fritz. You're the best," she said as she threw her arms around his neck and nuzzled her chin into his deep fluffy fur. "You're my hero, mate," she said the words over and over. Fritz knew he was her hero and he liked it. A few minutes later her heart rate down, they strolled down the dimly lit narrow lane that led to their house.

Every couple of months Brad and Sam would take a break and go up to visit Brad's folks. Fritz always went with them. Sam enjoyed getting out of town and grew fond of his family. On this occasion, it was the four day Anzac Holiday. Brad's older brother, Doug, coaxed them into celebrating the event in a local pub. Everyone was getting hammered on grog, as they would probably celebrate on most weekends, but the focus on today's activity by tradition was the game of Two Up. Brad turned to Doug. "Sam wants to play Two Up, don't you, Sam?" She turned to Brad. "I do?"

"Bloody hell yes. Beginners luck." Brad looked coyly at his brother.

"How much do you want to wager, mate?"

"Okay, I'll wager a quid," said Doug.

Sam had no idea what that meant and she had already had two glasses of the pub's finest Riesling. She turned to them both. "Are you *sure* I can play this game?"

Doug laughed, "*Anybody* can play this game." In seconds he explained the rules.

"Look, you stand in the middle of the circle of blokes over there. See that bloke," he pointed to a large burly man in the middle. "He will hand you a small wooden paddle with two coins on it. When he says *Go*, you then throw the two coins high in the air, if they land on the ground with two heads up we all win. Got it?"

"Got it." Sam winked back to Brad. She sauntered over to the large circle. The wine had given her the boost of courage she needed. One man cleared the way.

"Let the sheila through, mates. She's going to make us a wager."

"Done this before, Miss?" asked the man holding the paddles.

"Nope," she answered. "This is all new to me."

"You're a bloody Yank!" screamed out one.

"Yup, and proud of it," she said lifting her head even higher and tossing her hair. All of them laughed and reached into their pockets and began peeling out notes from their britches. Sam didn't know what Brad and Doug wagered on her but she was just hoping to make them proud.

She steadied herself and threw the coins as high as she could. All eyes raced to the ground as the coins hit the floor. Men moved in from every direction as the call came out.

"It's two heads!" one man screamed. The crowd roared. *Yea, I did it.* Sam began to leave the circle.

"No way, Miss. You're not going anywhere. You need to keep throwing 'till you miss." She looked over at Brad with a pleading look, but he shook his head.

"Throw it up again Sam," he shouted.

She centered herself in the circle as the blokes made their bets.

"Bloody hell, she ain't going to do it again," screamed a voice from the crowd.

"Not true, mate. It's beginner's luck. She has a lot more in her, just look."

Sam took a deep breath and threw it as high as she did the last time. The coins came rushing down. Again she couldn't see a thing as the lads jumped in for a look.

"She did it again, mates. The Yank tossed two heads in a row, imagine that."

"Okay, mates. Fix your wagers. You know she can't do three."

Money was stacked high. Brad was beaming. Sam was hoping he wasn't going to bet the farm on this one. The paddle began to sweat in her hand. "Ready, Go," yelled the man. The coins soared high and spun and again they came down and hit the wooden floorboards stained with grog.

"Oh," echoed the crowd. "Two tails." The crowd gave a sigh.

Sam's brief moment in the sun was over and so was her beginner's luck. She walked head down back to their table. Brad threw his arms around her. "We won twenty bucks," he shouted. Later that night Brad bragged about their lucky day to his dad.

"You should have seen her. She was a beauty. She had them all wagging their tails."

"Really, Sam, you went into the circle and took on the pub? Well, I'm proud of you. You're a true dinky-dy Aussie now," he bolstered with his award-winning smile. "You know, not many women folk in these parts would go in that circle. It wasn't that long ago they even let women go in the public part of the pub."

"I know," she said. "I guess you best know that I'm moonlighting as a barmaid most nights in a local pub to off-set the bills on the house."

"S'truth", Brad's dad said, "You are dinky-dy."

She smiled back. Sam really loved his dad.

Brad and Sam continued to skirt the issue of what this all meant for *THEM*. She often wore a silver ring that was given to her by an old boy-friend which began to irritate the hell out of Brad.

"Why do you continue to wear that ring," he questioned. She looked at him and laughed, "It doesn't mean anything, I just like it. Besides, I don't have any other ring to wear."

"Well, I'm not too keen about you wearing that one," he stated one night when they were heading to bed.

"Listen," Sam said. "I'll be very happy to take it off if I could replace it with another ring." So, one Thursday evening, just before Sam's birthday, they cruised casually down George Street for a bit of Thursday night shopping. (Australia was funny about their shopping days. You could only shop past six on Thursday nights.) They found a jewelry store and went through all the rings. They both walked past the diamond rings. Sam selected a sweetheart shaped ruby ring with two diamond chips on the sides. Brad was always pretty frugal with money. The ring was dear but he paid for the ring to make her happy.

Lyndsey had just returned from her trip around the world and moved into Lacy's house. She got her job back substituting as a casual teacher.

Sam's usual routine on most Saturday mornings was to go up to the church bazaar on Darling Street. She always found little treasures there. She usually swung by Lacy's afterwards to share her goodies with her over a cup of coffee at her kitchen table as they'd catch up on the week before.

On this particular Saturday, Sam managed to tear Brad away from working on the house straight away. They walked up to the bazaar and browsed around. She fixed her eye on some old jewelry and Brad went right for the tools.

They paid for their purchases and walked down to the newly-painted burgundy clapboard house on Campbell Street. It looked darling. Lyndsey greeted them at the door and gave Sam a big hug. Then she grabbed her left hand and looked at Sam's ring finger.

"What the fuck!" she screamed, "What have you done?" Sam was so embarrassed. How could she have spotted the ring so quick? *She must have had radar vision.*

"It's okay. This isn't what you think, nothing that serious." Sam answered her faster than she could take a breath. Sam glanced over at Brad who didn't seem to notice. They all sat down around Lacy's kitchen table and ate her award-winning banana bread and caught up on Lyndsey's travels.

One evening not long after, while Brad and Sam were cuddled up, she finally asked her burning question, "So, do you *ever* think about us ever getting married someday?"

He grew silent and answered, "Ahh . . ." he chuckled. "Be serious. You're a bloody Yank. If I were to marry you, you'd just take off and leave me and go home to the States. You know I'm never leaving Australia. Bloody hell, this is God's country."

Sam knew he was kidding and pushing any plans of moving forward away, but it made her wonder over and over if he did *fear* that about her. Had he already decided it wouldn't work? *Then why buy a ring?* It made her second guess everything.

We could think this thing to death and our fears could strangle us. It was best just to enjoy every day and push the question aside, and so they did. Occasionally they talked about one day selling their properties and building a bigger house together on the water up north. Sam told him she needed a place for boats. These conversations were somehow safer than marriage. She still felt pretty secure in how they felt about each other. She wasn't mentally ready for marriage and all the fixings yet either. The heart-shaped ruby ring was just going to have to do. It was a symbol of love. *Things have a way of working themselves out.*

Lacy was turning thirty and they all felt her personal turmoil. Loose Lacy was depressed. They were all beginning to miss her. She was visibly absent. She must have felt her wild days were coming to an end.

Brad and Sam began their third year of remodeling the house. They started the upstairs. Their project was coming to a close. The question remained where were things going from here? They argued more about little things, especially the house. Sam didn't want to lose the house. She had no ability to build another house on her own if he forced the sale of the house. She was determined to spend the rest of her life in Australia, even if they weren't ready to settle down. She didn't want to push the question of marriage any further. The unexpected unrest came from not having a plan.

One weekend after Commandos, Brad took Fritz for a quick Sunday night walk. He didn't have Fritz on the leash thinking it was pretty safe to walk around the neighborhood at that time of the evening. Out of nowhere, a jeep came barreling down the street and struck Fritz. Brad said Fritz got up right away and began running for home.

When they got back to the house, Brad and Sam looked Fritz over. He seemed okay; no external cuts that they could see, no broken bones. The next morning Fritz was lying sadly on the carpet in the living room.

"Maybe you should stay with Fritz today," Sam suggested.

"No, he'll be okay, there's nothing anyone can really do," said Brad.

Brad needed to go to Lacy's house after school to do some work. By the time Sam came home, Fritz was lying in a pool of blood on the floor. She ran over to Lacy's not wanting to trust that her fingers could dial a phone.

"Brad, come quick, it's Fritz." As he walked in, he was immediately struck by the same devastation. *This wasn't good.* Brad picked up Fritz in his arms and loaded him in the Holden to take him to the vet. Brad returned within the hour without Fritz.

"He has peritonitis. He must have broken a rib and punctured a lung when the Jeep struck him and he was bleeding from the inside. The vet said he had lost a lot of blood and gave him something to stop the bleeding and something to make him rest."

The next morning, they received the dreaded phone call. Fritz had passed that night. Brad took the day off. Sam knew he wished he had taken the day before off. He picked up Fritz while Sam was at work and buried him in the yard. When she got back, he was making a plaque for Fritz. She put her arms around Brad who was sadly hunched over the plaque. He pushed her away.

"Don't touch me."

"Sorry," she said stepping back, shocked and heartbroken. "I know you are really sad and wish none of this happened. But I loved Fritz, too. I was just hoping we could both comfort each other during this sad time."

Now Sam was doubly sad. Before they went to bed, Brad gave her a little hug and a short sorry. Sadness lingered over the house like an approaching storm. The end was nearing and Sam could feel it. She needed to get some context for what was happening.

That Saturday she began the tough conversation. "So, do you *still* feel you love me?' she asked directly.

"You know I do, but that's all I am prepared to say."

"Well, are you thinking of selling this house now that this project is almost finished?" she asked directly.

"I'm thinking of a lot of things right now," he replied.

"Well . . . if you're thinking of selling, I would like the option of buying you out. We both know *I* could never take on another house project alone," she said. *There I said it out loud, fishing to where his thoughts were going.*

Sam wasn't a controlling person and she was glad that he wasn't either. She wanted their lives to be organic and authentic. There was a lingering pause defining the *elephant in the room.*

"Listen, Sam, I put a lifetime of toil into this house. I understand that you would never be able to build another house alone, but if we were to separate this title, I would at least want another house in Balmain in my name." *Her worst fears were realized. He was thinking of selling and he saw them apart.*

It sounded as though he already decided that he was moving forward on his own in the very near future. One day he came home after work and sat down heavily on the kitchen stool.

"I went into the city to visit the Department of Education and discovered that there are overseas exchanges with Canadian teachers. I've never been to Canada. It would be a break for us and an adventure for me for a year. I need one. You've had many."

"What kind of a break," Sam asked sadly fighting back tears.

"Well, the kind where you do *your* thing and I'll do *my* thing for a year, no ties."

She just stared at him. "Is that what you really want?"

"Sam, we *need* a break. We have been together 24/7 for years now. Right now, it isn't feeling good for anyone and I'm not ready for anything else. Who knows, it might draw us closer together. I put in an application. It's only for a year. You know I'd never live permanently anywhere else but Australia."

She tried not to get defensive or overreact to the news that he had not only explored leaving but single-mindedly submitted an application. They say if you let butterflies fly free, they will return to you. Sam shared these feelings with Brad.

So, the moving on process began to unfold even before Brad's official acceptance to be an exchange teacher.

20

Life is but a Dream

Sam hadn't dared to talk to anyone about Brad and where things seemed to be going. One evening, Lyndsey, Lacy and two of their friends came over to have a girls' happy hour at Gladstone Street. They were sitting around Sam's round dining room table next to the huge leadlight picture window. Brad was out playing Commandos. Sam was now going on thirty-one and her relationship with her forever man was in question.

"Sam, are you ready to have babies," asked Lacy who was sitting directly across from her sipping a glass of wine from her Riesling box.

"What, **no** . . . not even remotely," she blurted out looking up from her glass. Sam looked around at them blankly trying to understand the motivation for this very direct question. She was always on guard with her friends. It was like swimming with sharks sometimes. *Where was this going?*

"Well, we've all been talking about the prospect among ourselves. You know, the questions of when to have babies," suggested Lacy.

"That's an interesting question," Sam said. "I understand that I'm the oldest by a year and the one you might want to ask first. However, none of us is in a permanent relationship and I think that's probably when one should think about those kinds of questions."

"Yah, *you* are," said Lacy.

"Well, I'm really not bit by the 'time is a ticking clock' yet. Are . . . *any* of you?" she asked as her eyes searched the faces in the room.

These questions hit women in general when they turn thirty, but Sam really wasn't in a hurry to have children yet. She was still trying to find herself.

"Okay," Sam said. "I guess it is a good time to share with all of you that Brad has applied to go overseas alone next year. He feels we need a break," she said slowly.

All eyes looked blankly in Sam's direction. "So where does that leave you?" asked Lacy.

"Well, obviously, alone. It's a break. He'll do what he wants. I'm free to do what I want and if we are meant to get back together, we'll see what happens after a year, I guess."

"Hey listen, Sam, Brad isn't really the right man for you anyway," suggested Lyndsey.

"Why do you say that?" she asked, hurt.

"It's obvious, he just isn't," Lacy concurred. "He's a dinky-dy Aussie and you're a Yank from the New York City area, for crying out loud. You couldn't be any more different. We could all see it would *never* work."

Sam was devastated. *Was it true that people could really sense and feel things better than the people who were actually in relationships?* Could others from the outside reduce it to statements as simple as, "He isn't for you." Sam felt betrayed and tried by her peers in the court of public opinion.

"You've all missed so much of what is important to me. I have more in common with that man than anyone." She didn't let on that their words affected her in any way. She never wanted to show her cards to the girls. She smiled and the conversations went on as before. Everyone was lost in their worlds of trying to see where life was going after thirty and the safety net of sharing them among women.

A week later, Brad came home with the news that he had been offered a teaching position in a small town outside of Ontario, Canada.

He would start at his new school soon after the New Year. Almost immediately, they began hunting for houses for Brad that were available in Balmain.

"I think I found one," Brad said one afternoon. "It is smaller than ours. Want to come over and take a look?" They went together to see the house. It was a one bedroom, narrow eight hundred square foot detached house with a small front porch and yard.

They went to their solicitor and he drew up the paperwork in Brad's name, removed his name from the Gladstone Street's title, and placed his name on the Carrington Street title. The contingency clause stated that if Sam ever sold Gladstone Street, she would owe him a percentage of the house as a buy-out. There they had it; they were apart on paper. The river was widening.

Brad went over to inspect the house after the title was finalized and came home with a dog. It was a giant white Alsatian wolf dog, a type of white German Shepherd that loved to fetch anything. He would pick up rocks from the back yard and drop them on your foot to entice you to play. They ended up finding lots of balls and piling them in the yard.

Life is complicated. It was a chess game, at least for Sam. She wanted circumstances to be mutual, but you can't always get what you want. She hoped the new dog, whose tag said Ben, would help them feel more like family again, but Brad definitely didn't feel the same connection to Ben as he did to Fritz. Neither of them could understand why anyone would just abandon a dog at a home when they officially moved out of a house. It was like Ben came with the title.

One spring weekend they were invited to Brad's sister's wedding. They packed up to spend the weekend with his parents along with Ben in the back of the Holden. They recently heard the news that Princess Di was going to marry Prince Charles in a month's time. The world, especially Australia, was focused on every detail of the wedding.

The Newcastle wedding was a typical country wedding. Everyone in Brad's family was there. Sam felt nervous knowing she had overdressed. Brad's mother whispered, "You look gorgeous, dear. I can't thank you enough for going to such effort for my daughter's wedding." Her words were kind and showed a sweet acceptance of Sam.

Sam began to realize that this might be the last time she would ever see Brad's family again. Brad's dad got on well with the dog, so Ben would stay with his parents. You could see that Ben liked men better than woman.

On the last day, Bob took Sam and Brad into his garage and unveiled his newest masterpiece. He surprised them with a beautiful black spiral staircase elegantly finished with rosewood steps. Sam wanted to cry. She realized how close she had grown to Brad's family.

"Listen," Bob said, "I'm going to load the truck up and bring down the staircase next weekend and help Brad retrofit it. Brad will be back in a year, I know him. We'd be pleased for you to come up and visit us anytime." *Those words meant so much.*

The situation around the house grew awkward. Sam spent more time with Lyndsey. She recently had a disagreement with Lacy and moved out of Lacy's house. Brad was spending more time with Commandos.

One weekend while Brad was away, there was a knock on the door at two in the morning. It took Sam a while to maneuver her way down the spiral staircase in the dark. By the time she reached the front door, the knock had turned to pounding.

She had no way to see who was on the other side. So she just opened the door and was shocked to see Wyatt.

"Are you okay?" she asked. He was swaying. *Had he been in a fight?*

"I'm drunk and I can't make it home," he managed to say. "Can I stay here?"

"Well . . . sure," Sam stuttered. She let him in and opened the door to the unoccupied downstairs bedroom. *This was awkward.*

She went upstairs and mulled over what to do. Lacy must be home and she was only two blocks away. Did they have an argument and that was why he landed here? Sam wanted to do the right thing but wondered if she should call Lacy and let her know he was at her house now or just wait till the morning?

Sam kept tossing and turning. She couldn't sleep so she called Lacy and woke her.

"Listen, Lacy, I don't know if you and Wyatt are even together anymore, but for some reason he knocked on my door saying he was too drunk to get home and asked if he could stay the night. I showed him to the downstairs bedroom. What would you like me to do?"

"Is Brad there?"

"No, he's at Commandos."

The answer was short, "I'll be right over." Lacy knocked within minutes. She walked in and Sam directed her to the small bedroom. The conversation was loud enough for Sam to hear.

"Wyatt, wake up. You can't stay here. Get up and come home with me." You could hear him moan incoherently. Sam could hear her repeat her plea several times without any response. She came out of the room frustrated.

"Okay Sam, you need to call the police."

"**What** . . ." she screamed. "Listen, Lacy, I'm not calling the police to come to my house."

"You have to," she commanded. "Someone needs to teach him a lesson. He can't keep doing this."

"Well, this is the first time he has done it to me and I did the right thing and called you. That was the last call I'm making this evening."

"Call the *police,* Sam. I'm serious," Lacy repeated.

"So am I. Wyatt is a friend and I'm definitely not calling the police. If he wants to stay here, he is welcome to and so are you," she offered.

"Is there something going on with you two?"

"No!" Sam answered. She knew Lacy was aware that Brad and she were moving apart.

"Seriously, think about it . . . would I have called you if there *was* anything?"

"Then *call* the police. You owe Wyatt nothing."

Sam looked up at her. It was Saturday night. She had just worked eight hours at the Oxford Tavern in downtown Sydney. It was a bar full of Czechs and Spaniards who had fist fights every night over pool games. Sometimes she had to walk around passed-out bodies in the alley to get to her car. She was tired. She walked over and picked up the phone. "If you want the police here so bad and you want to teach him a lesson, call them yourself," she commanded.

To her shock, Lacy called the Balmain Police Department. "Yes, we have a man who forced himself into a house on Gladstone Street and we need him removed," she said resolutely.

"I can't believe you just did that," Sam said. Almost instantly a knock came on the front door.

"Okay. Then go answer it," she said as she waved her hand in disgust.

"Hi, officer, he's in that room." She pointed to the guest bedroom. Lacy was now pointing at Sam. "She answered the door and he just forced his way in."

The officer went into the bedroom and tried to rouse Wyatt who displayed no sign of life. He finally got Wyatt to his feet, grabbed his clothes, and dragged him out to the living room.

"Is that his car down the street?" the officer asked. Sam looked out but had no idea if it was or wasn't.

"I don't know, Officer. I can only tell you it's not mine," she answered.

He was grappling with how to charge him. Driving under the influence in 1980 was a serious offense. Australia had just brought down the alcohol level to .5.

The officer turned to both Sam and Lacy and asked, "Who owns this house?"

Sam answered, "I do, sir."

"Well," he said, "In order for me to remove him from your premises you need to charge him with trespassing."

Sam looked at Lacy feeling sick about how she put her in this situation. She looked back resolutely. "You heard the officer; you need to charge him."

Sam turned to the officer meekly. "I can't charge him. Sorry, Officer, for wasting your time. He's a friend."

The officer turned to go but then turned to Wyatt and asked him what car he drove to get to the house. Wyatt came alive with rage and began flicking the rim of the officer's hat.

"Listen, you son of a bitch. I was dropped off here and you have no reason to even think you can pull me in for anything." Wyatt yelled viciously into the officer's face.

The officer made his way to the door and let himself out. He must have thought he had one too many dramas for the night. Sam felt the same way.

Wyatt turned and made his way back to the guest bedroom.

Lacy turned to Sam and said, "Now what?"

"I don't know, Lacy, and I don't care," she said waving her arms in the air. "I'm going to bed. You can stay tonight with him or go home, your choice." She turned and made her way up the spiral staircase.

When she got up about eight in the morning, they were both gone.

She poured some coffee and hoped that she would be able to explain the evening's drama to Brad. *It will probably give him just one more reason to feel he needs to move on.*

Sam was working three extra jobs besides teaching to support the funds needed to close the deal on Brad's house. Weekdays right after school she drove across town to run a health food restaurant for some friends in Kings Cross, after which she was a barmaid at a pub called The Honest Irishman from seven to ten four nights a week. On Saturday nights, there was the combat pay she earned at the Oxford Inn on Queen Street. Sam didn't really mind working; it kept her out of trouble.

21

Times Square, New Year's Eve

Sam always imagined life as a roller coaster ride. You reach a high point and you are just hoping that on the next turn, you are not plummeting to the ground. With the Carrington Street property purchased for Brad, they only needed to figure out details for his trip to Canada.

"Listen," she suggested one day to Brad. "I think I'm going to take this opportunity to travel back to the States as well this Christmas. It'll give me something to look forward to. I don't want to sit around moping with this vacant feeling in my gut. Here's a suggestion, why don't you plan on spending some time with me and my family before your big trip north to Canada? My mom and sister live just outside of the City. It'll be a chance for us to see New York City together. It might be good for you to meet my side of the family. I've met all of yours."

Brad stared for a minute and said, "Ta." "That might be something *I can* do the week before I start teaching." Over the next few weeks, Brad and Sam began to plan a stay with her mother and sister for the week after Christmas through New Year's Day. She broke the news to her mother, who was so excited for the company.

"You know I have only two bedrooms and a pull-out couch in the living room, but we'll make do."

159

Sam wanted so much for Brad to meet her family. The next door neighbors, Bob and Rachael, decided to join them on the trip and so did their friend, Clementine. Sam broke the news to her mother that there may be more people visiting.

"Well, as long as everyone makes it their home and does not expect me to cook or clean up after them, they're welcome to stay."

"I'll pass the message along, Mom, thanks."

They had a quick dinner meeting one evening about what everyone was hoping to see while in New York. Brad added to the top of his list that he wanted to see West Point, the Military Academy that graduated famous generals as far back as George Washington. The group was also hoping that they could visit Times Square and be there for the ball dropping for New Year's Eve. This had been on Sam's bucket list for years and she was delighted she would have such a fun group to share this experience.

Sam flew to New Jersey a week before Brad arrived at Newark Airport. The sad news that John Lennon had been shot and killed outside of his Dakota apartment had just surfaced. People killing other people for fame, hate, or notoriety didn't exist in Australia. It would be difficult to explain to the others what prompts people to do this in the States, not that she could even explain it to herself.

She also thought she'd better give everyone a brief education about traveling in and out of the streets of New York. In the seventies, crime was rampant on the streets of *Gotham City*. As a rule, Sam never wore any jewelry in the city. She always kept extra money in her boot and placed a small purse under her long winter coat.

In spite of the risks, NYC was immersed in an energy. You walked quickly in sync with everyone else. Streetlights on corners meant you paused but you never stopped for traffic. People, like molecules, flowed around each other, making no eye contact, rarely pleasantries. She wasn't sure how to prepare everyone for the perpetual insults the native New Yorkers hurled at each other daily. "Get out of my way, you greasy Wop," a truck driver would yell at a car blocking his way.

"No, why don't you just move that piece of crap vehicle, you Irish Mick." If it was a good day, only the words flew. "Fuck you" and ethnic slurs graced the landscape of the City. Perhaps their resentments came from living in their separate neighborhoods. When they all came together in the back allies of the Big Apple, the words just flew back and forth like spit in the wind. God forbid someone offered someone a compliment like, "Nice coat." The response might be, "Yeah, fuck you!"

However, during the holiday season, people sometimes struck a chord of kindness and occasionally one might open a door for another or offer a polite Please and Thank You to strangers. Sam could only hope that on this occasion, New York City might shine for her foreign guests.

When Brad arrived, Sam and her family went together to pick him up. They had a delightful evening getting acquainted. The next day, Rachael and Bob flew in and the following day, Clementine. Brad and Sam took her sister's room; Rachael and Bob took the pull-out couch in the living room, and Clementine slept on a cot they managed to borrow. It was like staying with the Walton family. Everyone would take turns saying, "Good Night Rachael, Good Night Bob, Good Night Clementine." Sam tucked the feeling of coziness around her like a down comforter. The reality was it was going to be pulled off in January when she took Brad to the airport.

They spent every day organizing destinations from people's bucket list. West Point was first for Brad. Rachael wanted to see everything on Fifth Avenue, so they made sure Rockefeller Center, the Theater District, NBC Studios and Saint Patrick's Cathedral were all visited in the same day. They would sit after dinner in the living room and process their days together.

"I'm chockers," said Brad after filling up on the delicious spaghetti dinner Rachael and Bob had prepared. What's on the agenda for tomorrow, mates?"

"Well, I'm not leaving until we see the Empire State Building. Bloody King Kong may still be up there," laughed Bob.

"Ripper, mate," said Brad. "On to the Empire State tomorrow."

"Has anyone heard from Lacy yet?" asked Clementine walking into the living room. "Wasn't she going to try to meet us in New York City while we're here?"

"Yeah," Sam said. "I need to make a call by tomorrow. We're running low on clock. Before you know it, New Year's Eve will be here and everyone will be scattering to the four winds after that."

"No, just Brad will scatter to the arctic winds. The rest of us will head south for the tropical breezes," Bob said. Everyone looked at Brad and laughed.

"I know you're concerned that I'll continue to wear my bloody work shorts to school while in Canada, but I did bring a pair of jeans."

"A pair of jeans, really," Sam said. "And I'm sure several pairs of shorts. I don't ever remember you wearing anything but your grey dress shorts to work every day."

"Fair dinkum and when I wear out these jeans and the warm weather comes, I'll be wearing that lovely grey pair once again. I'll show these Canucks how real Aussie men dress."

Rachael walked in the room and so did Sam's mother. "Thanks for the tucker. It was bloody beautiful," said Brad.

"Ta," said Rachael. She wanted to make sure they are still on for New Year's Eve in Times Square. "I've not come halfway around the globe *not* to see the ball drop for 1981."

"Okay, that's my cue." Sam said. "I think I better see if I have a number for Lacy's mum in Hartford." She left the room and let her sister Dina stay and soak in the Aussie accents.

Sam returned to the living room. "Well, I just talked with Lacy who said she had been in touch with Kat. Her thoughts were that she and Kat would meet us in New York on New Year's Eve sometime early evening in the bar at the Hilton on 54th and Sixth. We better start looking for a place in the City ourselves or we'll be left standing upright in a crowd of millions for the entire evening."

Sam's sister brought out a New York City phone book and they jumped to the Yellow Pages where a section marked *hotels* was listed in alphabetical order. When Sam got to the Biltmore, she booked it straight away.

"We're in luck. We have a room at the Biltmore on 47th and Eighth. It's only eight blocks from Lacy and Kat and only two blocks from Times Square."

"How many beds?" Rachael asked.

"Two queen size beds but we'll all fit. We just need a room to crash for the evening."

"I'll probably come over with my fiancé, Robbie," Dina said. "But we'll be heading back to Jersey after the ball drops. Don't worry about us."

New Year's Eve came too fast. Sam's time with everyone, especially Brad, was ticking, marking the end of 1980. It was a very cold evening, but because they threatened snow on the weather report, the wind wasn't bitter. They booked into the Biltmore and then walked to Broadway first and noticed that the streets were all cordoned off, marked by tape and poles. Police officers blocked each street access. *We'll be trapped if we go to Times Square first.*

"Let's head over and find the Hilton Bar where Lacy and Kat are supposed to be," Sam suggested.

"Bloody right, I'm snookered and it's cold as tits out here," Bob said.

They found Lacy and Kat in the bar fairly easily. From the evidence, they had been there for hours. Lacy ordered Harbor Lights when she saw Sam and she was the only one from her group who had a go at one. The boys ordered a brew and the girls a Manhattan to mark the occasion. They ordered some appetizers and some more drinks then left to get their place on Broadway before they were backed up as far as Central Park. Lacy wouldn't budge.

"What do you mean you're not going," Sam said dumbfounded. "You came all the way to New York City to witness the ball drop and now you are not going out to experience a little cold air?"

"I'm way too cozy and I really don't think once I slide off this stool that I'll even be able to stand. Kat and I have a lot to catch up on. Just go without us."

Sam reluctantly left the bar shaking her head. "This is a big one for a bucket list, Lacy. I don't get it."

They walked down ten city blocks in order to get to Broadway along with thousands who rushed in behind them. Only fifteen minutes to go. As the clock came closer to 1981, Sam wondered how life would change for Brad and her over the next year. *An eeriness crept over her.* She knew it would mean change but had to wonder just how much. She closed her eyes and made a big wish—*I only hope there is still an US.* "Five, four, three, two, one . . . HAPPY NEW YEAR!"

Brad turned to Sam and gave her a big long kiss and hug, "Happy New Year, Sam."

He was so excited for the change of the upcoming year. Sam looked down at the ground with tears in her eyes. "Happy New Year, Brad."

✈ 22

1981

Sam arrived back in Sydney wondering how she would get along with her new flatmate, Patty Maple. Patty planned to live with her, and Brad went to live with Patty's mother as part of the exchange program.

Sam had lived a pretty colorful life in Sydney up to this point. She wondered how a librarian from a small rural Canadian town, who lived with her mother alone in a large farmhouse, would manage living with the likes of her.

When she arrived at Gladstone Street, Sam knocked on her own front door to see if anyone was there. The door flew open and a cheerful bubbly blonde yelled, "Welcome home," and handed her all her mail. It was difficult not to like Patty straight away. She was always cheerful, happy, and funny.

The first evening of her arrival back, Sam received a call from some neighbors down the street to come join them for dinner. Sam thought, well, if Patty can get through the first night with her friends, she might be able to adjust to the rest of the year. She fit right in.

———◦•◦———

Soon after Sam's arrival, the word got out that she was single again. Since she was known for throwing a Fourth of July party each year, it allowed her to network with all of the other weekend parties that Sydney had to offer. Sydney *was* a party city.

Most nights the phone rang off the hook. Patty always answered the phone, "Sam's answering service." She loved parties. They got dressed to the music of Billy Joel's "Scenes From An Italian Restaurant", and always sang the lyrics to Queen's "Another One Bites the Dust" as they flew out the front door. Sam was quite happy to be experiencing a whole new Sydney crowd and taking in the warmth of its people.

Each weekend they received a half a dozen invitations - their pick of Friday night parties and barbeque lawn parties on weekends. Their calendars were full. Patty repeatedly commented, "One day I'm going to write a book, 'Is There Life After Sam'," said Patty. Sam smiled with amusement as she wondered how life would be after Patty. But for now it was pure fun.

Brad kept true to his promise of writing often. Every fortnight a letter came from him and at the same time, Patty's mum composed a letter to Patty. Sam imagined them both living together in that big farmhouse saying together, let's write the girls. Sam visualized Brad posting the letters in the mailbox the next day on his way to school. He was a great writer. It was amazing how much detail he used to describe the frigid cold snowbound winters in Ontario.

Patty's mother quickly adopted Brad as her own son. She clearly spoiled him. She made lunch for him every day and had hot meals waiting for him when he came home at night. Patty joked that she had been replaced and surmised her mum would have a hard time adjusting to her return.

Sam and Patty stood in the kitchen at the woodblock peninsula on those evenings in the family room at Gladstone Street and they read out loud their recent letters to one another. Patty would read her newsy letters about her family, her uncles, aunts, and her sister. Most of their events were hosting family dinners for Brad. They all loved Brad as a new member of the family. It was easy to do, Brad got along with most people. He, too, had a cheeky sense of humor and had grown up as a country boy. So, he fit right in.

"Oh, I just have to meet Brad someday," she mused. "Everyone loves him so much and I might *never* get the chance to meet him. We might just be ships in the night."

"Oh, you'll definitely meet him, don't worry about that."

Brad's letters to Sam always ended on a tender note. "I get up every morning missing you, Sam, and you are forever in my dreams when I go to sleep at night. Love Always, Brad." Sam was always filled with a warm afterglow and she delighted to read the letters out loud to Patty to assure herself that she really did hear tenderness in his words. And so, Sam became more confident things would end up just fine as the months slid by.

When Patty and her friend, Holly, went out of town, Sam accepted a date or two just to assure herself she was not in any way interested in anyone else. Her acceptance of dates with Frank or Ron just enlarged their party pool. She had no desire to be intimate with anyone.

Sam hadn't spent much time with Lacy or Lyndsey since the Canadians arrived. She heard a rumor that Lacy was taking a leave of absence from school and she and Lyndsey were planning a trip through South America. Sam saw them both before they left. They were heading to Machu Picchu, traveling through parts of the Amazon and planning to end up in Rio for Mardi Gras. She was a little envious but was happy enough with life in Balmain at the moment.

One day, a month after they left, Sam got a phone call from Wyatt.

"How's life without Brad," he asked.

"Well, it's been quite the party. The Canadians are sure enjoying life in Sydney."

"What is your roommate like?" he asked.

"Personally, Wyatt, she's not *your* type. She is a librarian from rural Canada."

"Well, let me be the judge of that. Why don't you girls come over to the Brig tonight. I have a friend in town from the Outback. You girls may enjoy meeting him."

Sam told him she would share the invite with Patty, but if she didn't want to come, Sam might try to make it.

Patty was more than interested in meeting Wyatt as she had heard so many stories about him. When they arrived at the restaurant, a waiter led them up to the Captain's Quarters on the top level of the three-tiered restaurant overlooking Sydney Harbor. The Brig was created to look like a Brigantine ship. Sam did play a small part in its design. Wyatt had asked her to draw some sketches to illustrate how it might look when he talked to some investors. He won the bid.

When they made it to the corner table at the top of the restaurant, there was a man about six-foot-two. His name was Tim and was handsome in a rugged kind of Outback way. He wore a tailored western shirt, pressed blue jeans, and cowboy boots just like Wyatt. They sat down to dinner and Wyatt began setting up a situation for Tim and Patty to become better acquainted.

Tim began sharing stories about his horse ranch in Tamsworth. He declared he was a breeder of horses and had one that he was racing in Randwick that weekend. *Wyatt had a way of attracting the rich and famous.* Sam became interested in getting to know Tim better herself. She also became suspicious that if Patty was to go off with Tim, she would be left alone with Wyatt and she didn't need any more drama happening between them while Lacy was away.

After dinner, when the others were excused, Sam leaned over to Wyatt. "Your friend seems quite nice," she whispered.

"You think so?"

"He seems like a gentleman and very attractive."

"I thought Patty might be interested in him," Wyatt said.

"Well . . . so am I, maybe you could let him know I'm interested too."

Wyatt nodded in agreement and Tim passed Sam his phone number before he left. He was staying in Double Bay. She did call him after a respectable few days. Tim said he wanted to see her again and had tickets to a concert to see the Willie Nelson Concert in Sydney in five days. He asked if she would like to go. He also had purchased two extra tickets for Wyatt and a friend.

A few days later, a fellow Sam had met at a party, a writer, contacted her and said he'd been invited to a party at Willie Nelson's suite at The Sebel Town House. He asked if she wanted to go - and she did.

When they arrived, Willie wasn't there but his band was. The room was soaked in dense noxious fumes produced from cigarettes and weed. Empty liquor bottles graced every table along with the damp rancid smell of stale alcohol. Her friend interviewed a few of the band members and they left. Sam was pretty excited by the events of the evening and spontaneously called Wyatt at the Brig. She just needed to brag a little to someone.

"Guess where *I* spent the evening," she asked playfully. When he heard that it was with Willie Nelson's Band, he muttered.

"Well, pretty lady, if you want to *meet* Willie himself, he's coming as my special guest Friday night to *MY* restaurant."

"Oh my God, really? I'll be there." Wyatt one-upped her once again.

After work Friday, she raced over to the Brig. She ordered her usual catch-up drink, a Rusty Nail. Wyatt was up at his table in the Captain's Quarters. He introduced her to members of Willie's sound crew. After a few drinks, one of the members of the crew took Wyatt outside for a joint.

During dinner, the pianist played his polished black baby grand and always finished his set with the long version of Billy Joel's song "Piano Man". (On Friday evenings after ten o'clock, Wyatt's restaurant venue turned from a fine dining experience into a disco with a hefty cover charge.) This evening, Sam could see a bunch of 'yahoos' from the nearest footy (soccer) club had pushed their way into the bar.

Suddenly, she heard some unusual noise and peered down to where she saw some disruption on the bottom level. A man took a chair to someone's head! Wyatt was sitting facing Sam and she yelled, "There's a fight!" She looked over at Wyatt who was clearly stoned. She yelled again and shook him a second time, "Wyatt, there's a fight!"

He stared up at her blankly and then registered her words.

"Where?" Sam turned his body and pointed below so he could not miss the mayhem. By now there were waves of people punching each other. Wyatt jumped off the seat and grabbed some of his waiters flying down the steps. He literally threw himself on top of the group of men who were fighting.

Harvey, one of the members of Willie's sound crew turned to Sam and asked, "Is there a back entrance to this restaurant. We need to get out of here quickly. We have a concert tomorrow. Willie never wants any of us getting involved in incidents in cities where we perform." She thought for a minute and remembered there was a back entrance to the alley below from the kitchen.

They followed her through the kitchen. When she got to the underground parking, Harvey asked where they might go next. "Well," she mused. "I'm not sure, but there are plenty of restaurants and bars in the Cross that are open all night."

"Oh, we've done that scene," said Harvey, "Isn't there anything more local?"

"Well, I'm heading home to my house in Balmain. It's on the way back to the Cross. The pubs of Balmain usually close by ten though. However, if you want to visit a small century-old workman's cottage, you can always come back to my place. I can make breakfast and I *do* have alcohol."

"Perfect. Sounds good to me," Harvey said, "We've been dying to see how the locals live."

Somehow, Sam managed to fit three grown men in her little Toyota Corolla and Harvey sat shot gun in the passenger seat. He threw his guitar case in the boot of the car. She walked into her humble Gladstone Street House with three beautiful long-haired men and knocked on Patty's bedroom door.

"Hi dear, try to wake up. I have another chapter for you to write in your book."

The evening was so much fun. Harvey played guitar all night as they sat around Sam's dining room table. They sang the words to Eric Clapton's "Cocaine" at the top of their lungs. Patty made omelets and toast as Sam emptied and shared every ounce of alcohol. Everyone crashed all over couches and beds and the crew ordered a cab first thing in the morning to return to the Cross. The concert was scheduled for seven in the evening and Sam planned to meet up with Wyatt and Tim back at the Brig at two in the afternoon.

She called Wyatt around one just to make sure he was actually going to be there. God only knows how everything ended up at the restaurant last night. One of the bartenders answered on the first ring. "Hi, this is Sam. Is Wyatt there?" she asked.

"Yeah, he crashed here at the restaurant last night. I'll get him." Wyatt got on the phone.

"How's the restaurant?" she asked.

"It's a little battered and bruised just like me. By the way, where the *hell* did you go?"

"I rescued Willie's sound crew out the back door. They ended up coming back to my place to party and crash."

"Well, you didn't bloody well care what happened to me, did ya?"

"I knew you'd be okay. We all know you have nine lives."

As a consolation prize, she told him that Harvey had invited her and her guests to the sound platform to watch the concert.

"Okay, then let's first see how good the seats are that Tim purchased."

They got to the concert and although the designated seats in the fairgrounds were good, Sam could see that the sound booth was far better situated directly in front of the stage. She waited until the opening act was through and told Tim and Wyatt that she was going to check out the sound stage. She was given access to the platform immediately when she said she was a friend of Harvey's. She went up and found him behind a large instrument panel filled with controls.

He gave her a big hug. "Great time last night, Sam. Pull up a chair." She explained she had three other guests with her. "No problem. You can bring them all up here," he said.

They felt pretty special until a dozen Hells Angels worked their way on the sound stage standing in front of them. Sam looked at Harvey. "Willie gives unlimited access to the Angels at all his concerts. One time he was attacked by some skin heads and the Angels gave them a dose of their own medicine. The Angels are now Willie's Angels." Sam felt a little sad that she never got to meet Willie, but if his band and sound crew were any indication about the company he kept, he must live a wonderful life.

After the show, the group went to dinner and Tim escorted Sam home.

"It's not going to work with us, is it," he asked.

"No, probably not," she replied softly, "For many reasons, geography being the biggest one. We live three hundred miles apart. I hope you understand." Tim was a gentleman. He gave her a big hug and off he rode into the Australian sunset.

A couple of weeks later, around two in the morning, there was a knock on the front door. Patty answered the pounding and she called for Sam upstairs from the living room. Sam came down the stairs and once again found Wyatt at the front door.

"I wondered if I could pull up a couch for the night?" Sam looked at Patty and then at Wyatt not sure what to say.

"Sure . . . . I guess." She showed him the couch that was in the family room. She went upstairs and got some blankets and a pillow and brought them down. She said good night and returned upstairs.

The next day, Sam shared with Patty the incident that had happened the year before with Lacy. "Maybe you should talk to him about what position this puts you in," she suggested. Sam knew that Patty was right and sure enough the next Friday, Wyatt was at the front door again. She waited till the next morning and stayed around until he was ready to get up and leave.

"Listen, Wyatt, we need to talk," she said handing him a mug of coffee. You know I'm always good for helping a friend out, but you staying here definitely poses a problem. I'd just appreciate it if you could find another spot to place your boots. I have Patty living here now."

He looked at her, saying, "You sure about that?"

"Yes, I'm sure, please."

Sam thought everything was resolved until the next Friday night when there was another knock on the door. Patty didn't get out of bed. Wyatt was again at the door.

"I *need* to stay," he said. Without waiting for an answer, he proceeded to walk through the door. However, instead of going to the couch where he had gone before, he walked up the spiral staircase to Sam's bedroom. *What the hell?*

She took out some blankets and immediately went to the family room couch to sleep. She tossed and turned wondering what she would do if he came down in the middle of night. What was he doing? What did he want?

The next morning, Sam waited for Wyatt to come downstairs. Sometime late morning, when Wyatt had not come down, she crept her way up the spiral staircase. She had to get her clothes from her closet for work.

Suddenly from behind she felt his right arm wrap around her waist as he lifted her off her feet as though she weighed nothing, throwing her on the bed. She tried to push him off saying, "Wyatt, don't, you can't," but both his arms held her down and he began kissing her lips over and over devouring her. His naked body slid over hers and she could feel her body rising to its rhythm. The passion was consuming her. She knew she should continue to resist but she couldn't. *She had never felt passion like this before.*

Sam lay across her bed staring at the ceiling dazed, overwhelmed with mixed emotions.

She didn't know how to feel about what had just happened. All she knew was the chemistry was undeniable. It had hit her like a thunderbolt. Chemistry *was* her Achilles heel. It was like a shot of heroin intensely taking over her brain. They both knew it and laid silently. Sam was torn, confused, and just kept staring at the large beams that Brad had positioned to create the beautiful pitch ceilings above the bed. Unable to talk, she waited for some words from Wyatt. Finally, he felt for her hand.

"Sorry, I had to," he uttered.

"Why?"

"Because I *always* wanted you. I had a feeling it would be like this. I also knew you would never betray your friend. I had to find a way to get you over your guilt."

"Well, I guess you achieved your goal. Maybe you should leave."

"No, I don't think I should." He nuzzled closer and looked over at her. "Do you really want me to," he asked as he leaned over and stretched her arms again above her head moving his fingers tips slowly down the inside of her arms. *I'm in trouble.*

She knew all the girls were attracted to Wyatt. Although she had been too, she wasn't attracted to his behaviors. She saw him only as a friend. Now, she was instantly hit by lightning, such unleashed passion. They made love for hours not surfacing until the sun was setting. Both needed to call work. Sam missed her shift. Wyatt said he still needed to appear at his restaurant.

"I need to go, but I don't want to," he said.

"Well, I'm relieved this moment is over," she said. "Your curiosity must be more than satisfied . . . it has to be over."

"No, it's not over, it's just beginning," he replied buttoning up his shirt. Sam looked at him, trying to understand his meaning as she stared into his large crystal blue eyes. "Really, Wyatt, we can't continue to do this. Too many people will get hurt. This was a moment, nothing more."

"Well," he said, "Let them get hurt. We are two free consenting adults."

What he said was true. Sam fought hard for it not to happen but when it did, she was gripped by its power. For weeks, they never left her bed. Their passion consumed them and the endorphins created a constant need for more. Every waking minute they were not working, they were exploring each other's bodies. Somewhere the tangled mess of them became one.

He began to suggest that Sam come to work with him. She didn't want to leave him either, so she tagged along to the Brig as he went about his business of running the restaurant.

He came back and forth to the mid-deck bar where Sam usually situated herself and sat himself across from her sliding his hand slowly and sensuously over and under her hand in erotic ways as if their hands were silently making love without anyone knowing. This passion went on for months. She knew it had to end, but her mind, body, and soul didn't want to give it up. She was addicted. Wyatt had somehow unleashed her addictive personality, but their needs were mutual as they couldn't let each other go.

One Saturday evening, Wyatt decided to stay and play hooky from work. He made dinner, putting together one of his famous Scotch omelets. He also poured a couple of single malts on the rocks. He began to bring home bottles of his finest liquor from the restaurant. He pulled Sam closer into his arms. They were relaxed and not limited to the power of the bed. Sam knew she needed to bring up the topic of the inevitable splitting off of their relationship while she still had her senses about her.

"Wyatt, I need to talk to you," she said with a shaky voice.

"About what?"

"Listen, Lacy and Brad will be returning very soon."

"Fuck them," he said. "This is about *us*, not about them."

She looked into his eyes pleading. "Okay . . . I thought you might say that, so I just need to hear one thing from you."

"What's that?"

"You have always bragged to me and everyone else for years that you tell *every* woman you meet that you will *never* marry them."

"Soo . . . ?"

"So . . . I *need* for you to say that to me. You haven't said it in these past few months and I just need to hear it." He stared at her for a very long silent moment. She could sense that he could understand how hard it was to ask for this. He looked deliberately into her eyes.

"Sam, I'd *never* say that to you."

Something grabbed her heart and she gasped. She could feel a large gulp in her throat. She didn't know if she was ready to hear anything else. She had prepared herself for the inevitable end, nothing more. She just stared up at him.

"Why not?"

"Because I have watched you for years and I wouldn't say that to you."

"And . . ." she said, "What does that mean?"

Without hesitation he replied, "It means *you* are the woman I want to be the mother of my children."

"*What*?" She gulped again. She couldn't believe what she was hearing.

"Do you understand *now* why I wouldn't say those words to you?"

Sam nodded weakly. She knew in her heart that Wyatt hadn't made any such suggestions to any other woman that *she* was aware of.

He scooped her up and said, "Let's go upstairs." Within a week, they were naming their children. They picked out a girl's name and a boy's name, since in his mind, he visualized two babies, one of each gender.

He began to talk about his family and the ranch in Texas. He drew pictures of the ranch house on a serviette (napkin) one evening to show Sam how the river rock house created a cross design around a large center fireplace that had four hearth openings to keep the entire ranch house warm.

He shared that his family raised cattle and that he raised pigs as a side business while in high school. Sam was being introduced to his family and the world she might see in their future. The more he talked, the more real their relationship became. One day he said, "I'd like to call my father." He went on to explain that he and his father had grown up more like friends. His father had him at the age of nineteen and when his dad divorced his mother, they would go out to bars and pick up women together.

Wyatt brought Sam up to speed about the plan with his father to open the restaurant in Sydney. His father guaranteed that he would front him the money based on an undivided Trust that a third of the ranch belonged to Wyatt as stated in his grandfather's will.

However, Wyatt's father had defaulted on the money, never giving Wyatt an explanation and caused the Brig to struggle over the past few years to stay alive. He felt the restaurant's evening disco had become lucrative enough to pull the restaurant back into the black.

"Can I use your phone to make a long-distance call? I want to let him know I'm in a serious relationship, but also to put all of this bad business between him and me behind us."

"Sure," she said, "Go for it. Do you want to be alone?"

"No, I want you beside me. I want you to hear all of this."

Sam could hear the phone ring several times and a man's voice answered. "Howdy!"

Wyatt said "Howdy" back. She was finding it hard to follow the conversation, so she lay back on the pillows and just listened to Wyatt's responses. She could tell this was a difficult conversation for him. His father left him in a desperate situation. Wyatt made deals based on the fact he was going to pay his restaurant investors back their money on short-term loans. With little remorse, his father just seemed to explain that business had gone bad for him and he was not going to be able to make good on the money promised. Wyatt was visibly sad and frustrated.

When Wyatt placed the receiver on the cradle, he began to sob. Sam held him close and didn't say a word. She knew life with family could be challenging.

"I'm never going to be like him, I promise," he said. "This is why I have waited so long to have children."

23

The Drama Begins

Wyatt confided in Sam that over the past year, he had also dated another girl who owned a shop in Double Bay. "You met her. She was my date when we went to the Willie Nelson Concert." She remembered a tall confident brunette hanging all over Wyatt. Sam was more interested in the fact he had been seeing her for over a year and what he was hoping to do about it with their present commitment.

"So, how do things stand right now?" she asked.

"We have not seen each other in three months because you and I have been together every waking minute. Well, now she knows about you. It didn't take her long to track down some of my staff and find out she'd been replaced. She isn't taking it lightly. I met with her today. She's not one to move on, she's a fighter and a shrewd business woman."

"So, what does this mean? Do I need to worry about her? Is she a stalker?"

"I *know* she isn't giving up easily. I recently introduced her to a prominent naval artist from Sydney in hopes they would hit it off. She likes him but she isn't giving up on me."

"Did you let her know you are in a serious relationship?"

"Yeah. Well, I alluded to it, but she isn't hearing it. To her it's a challenge."

"Well, does that mean you're going to be dating both of us? I can't do that, Wyatt. I'm very worried about Lacy coming home as well. I'm trying to prepare myself for how I'm going to handle that whole scenario."

"I told her that she and I aren't going to be seeing each other again. She walked off and said, "We'll see about that.""

Wyatt's restaurant partner, Otto, was getting married in two weeks on a yacht in Sydney harbor. Wyatt had asked Sam to go with him. Two days before the wedding, Wyatt broke the news to her that Eileen invited herself. He said that he forgot he mentioned the wedding to her months before and she insisted that Wyatt had invited her first to go with him.

"Maybe I shouldn't go," Sam said. She wasn't a fighter. She was like her father. Even though he was a police officer he would always say, "I'm a lover, not a fighter." *Sure, I wanted to go. This was a big coming out party for us.* However, it seemed ridiculous to invite confrontation. especially to a couple's wedding.

"No, you're *my* date. I told her she can go to the wedding, but I was with you."

"So, what did she say when you said that?"

She said good, she was going and she insisted on picking us both up in her Jaguar to go to the yacht for the ceremony.

"Oh, God," Sam said. "This can turn out to be disastrous."

———◦•◦———

Another situation was occurring on the homefront. Patty's sister and uncle were flying to Sydney together to visit her from Toronto. Sam told Patty weeks before that they could stay at the house and she would head over to Wyatt's apartment in Pott's Point for that week. She was shameless by now. Her passion and commitment to Wyatt were leading her into uncharted waters and she was in well over her head. She knew the moment Patty's relatives came to Sydney, her relationship with Wyatt was going to go global.

She also knew the time had come to write Brad a letter. She tried to sit down several times when life gave her a quiet moment, but the words just wouldn't come. All she could do respectfully was tell him how she felt and that she wanted him to hear the news from her first and not someone else. Her plan was to have Patty's sister deliver the letter to him when she returned to Canada. Sam wasn't ready for any of this. *I'll never be ready.*

Sam went to dinner with Patty and her family on the second night after they arrived in Sydney. Patty wanted her family to have a first-class experience and she asked Wyatt if she could bring them to the Brig. Wyatt was honored and treated them royally. He led them to the finest table in the Captain Quarter's. He lavished Patty and her family with anything an exclusive restaurant could give them. He gifted them bottles of champagne and fine French wine. He sat next to Sam every moment he could and held and stroked her hand visibly in front of them.

Patty's sister took a picture of Wyatt and Sam holding hands and staring longingly into each other's eyes. The evidence was tangible and the secret was out. Patty's family already accepted their relationship. But Sam wondered if Patty's sister would be sharing the photo with Brad and their mother?

Saturday arrived and so did Otto's wedding. Sam paced the family room nervously talking to the four walls in the presence of Patty and her sister.

"This is insane. I can't allow this to happen with Wyatt escorting both Eileen and me to this wedding. She is *so* unpredictable, anything could happen," she stated in desperation.

"Do you *want* to go?" Patty asked.

She nodded.

"Then just go, Sam. If things get out of hand, take a cab back here. My sister and I will set up the pull-out couch in the family room to sleep tonight. We'll be entirely comfortable."

Sam was thankful that Patty was being so easy on her. She had stayed at Wyatt's apartment the past two evenings, but who knew how this evening would end up.

Wyatt came to the door smiling and gave his signature snorting laugh to everyone and off they went. Sam turned to the girls. "Pray for me."

The wedding was absolutely gorgeous, the day was brilliant and by early evening Sam was ready to return home. She sought out Wyatt who was talking to the groom, Otto.

"Look, I'm going to leave," she said.

"Why, where are you going?" he asked.

"I'm going back to my house for the evening. Just let Eileen drive you home."

"Like hell." he said. "Listen, tell her you are heading home, but have the cabbie take you to my flat." He handed Sam his keys. "If she follows me to the restaurant, I'll lose her somehow."

"Are you sure? I'm not certain she is going to be that easily deceived."

He was getting impatient with her.

"Okay, then, I'll meet you back at your place." Sam took the keys.

Wyatt said goodbye to everyone and left for the Brig and she began the walk up the hill to Darling Street to catch a cab. Suddenly, Eileen pulled up behind her in her Jaguar.

"Where are you going?" she asked sweetly.

"I'm heading home."

"Don't you dare do that, it's way *too* early. I'll drive you home later," she promised. "I have special keys to the Playboy Club in Sydney. Have you ever been there?"

"No, but I better not go, maybe another time. I have company in from Canada and I better get back."

She glared at her. Sam began to realize this was no dumb broad. She was cunning. She knew Wyatt didn't make plans with her for later and if she kept Sam in protective custody, she had half a shot.

Finally, she insisted that Sam jump in and she would just take her home. Sam gave up and jumped into the Jaguar which suddenly changed course on the road and headed up the alternate route toward the City. Sam knew this could get really ugly. It was just so amazing how she kept the pretense up.

"I must have taken the wrong turn. We might as well just have a cocktail at the Playboy Club." There was no arguing with her. Sam knew she was her captive. *Why did I do this, I just knew this would happen.*

After a drink or two at the Club, Sam slipped away pretending she was going to the bathroom. She found a phone booth and called Wyatt. "Where are you?" he asked.

"Hi, baby, she isn't going to let me go. She pretended to take me home and took us to the other side of town to the Playboy Club. I'm going to try to get a cab home. That is if I can ever break away from her."

"Well, thanks for the update, but promise me you'll try to make it back to my place. Call me when you get somewhere."

"I promise." Sam tried to cover her tracks by coming out of the restroom where Eileen stood waiting for her.

"You've been gone awhile," she stated inquisitively.

"I know. I'm sorry. My tummy isn't well. Too much drinking today, I think. I'm just going to get a cab and go home."

"Don't be silly, I'll take you home. It's on my way. I'm heading back to the Brig."

Sam showed no reaction as Eileen searched her eyes. How coy she was. How conniving, it made her feel *very* uncomfortable. Sam already resolved herself to understand that Eileen was going to win at this game tonight. Besides, Wyatt needed to sever this relationship somehow for them to ever move forward.

When they got back into the Jaguar, they made light conversation about how pretty the wedding was when Eileen again missed the Balmain exit.

"You missed the exit to Balmain again, Eileen. You're going to have to turn around somewhere at the next stop," Sam said as she pointed to the street sign.

"No . . . it's still early and we're almost there. Let's just go to the Brig and surprise Wyatt, shall we?"

My God, what is she up to now. It became increasingly clear that this woman's game was ridiculously embarrassing and there was no end in sight. Wyatt met his match. She parked the Jag under the restaurant. It was now one in the morning. The restaurant closed at two. Sam was just hoping for this night to end. How far could this woman go. She was clearly obsessed and Sam wanted to try to keep the drama down.

They walked into the restaurant together. All the waiters looked at both of them and then back at Wyatt. Eileen excused herself to go to the restroom and Wyatt walked up to Sam.

"What's going on?" he asked as he moved closer to her.

"She won't let me go. Her plot is to get you one way or the other and she won't let me out of her sight."

Wyatt walked slowly behind the bar and poured himself a stiff drink switching the music to Bob Seger's song "You'll Accomp'ny Me." He walked over to Sam and put out his two hands. "Dance with me," he said. Sam looked at him sadly but willingly and they began to dance as they did so often at the house. He twirled her around the dance floor and they danced like they made love, in perfect unison.

Wyatt wasn't a writer or poet, but he knew his lyrics and the words would say it all for him. Sam knew *now* she could take whatever tonight was going to offer. Eileen may win a battle, but she would never win the war. They had pledged each other their hearts.

Eileen walked towards them. "Okay, you two, make room for me." The music changed to the Eagles singing, "Desperado." They all danced individually to the music. Then Wyatt said, "I have to close up."

When he finished, Eileen turned to Sam. "We'll drive you home, it's on our way."

How nice. Sam sat in the back seat of the Jag and Wyatt sat in the passenger seat. They finally pulled up to Sam's house in Balmain. Wyatt got out and pulled the back seat up. He gave Sam a kiss and then turned to Eileen.

"I have to go to the bathroom."

She was not to be deceived and answered, "I guess I better go, too."

Wyatt had a key to the house and opened the door. Then he slammed the door shut in both their faces. Eileen tried the door which was clearly locked from the inside.

"What the *hell* is going on here!" she exclaimed louder than Sam was hoping she would.

"Eileen, please, I have a house full of guests. Don't shout."

"What's he doing," she attempted to whisper.

Sam looked at her, "Damned if I know."

"Well, open this damn door. You *must* have a key!" she demanded in a hostile tone.

God, I'm so done with this. "Eileen, I think you better go home."

"Like hell I am," she yelled. It was a stand-off. She wasn't going to leave and Sam was so done with this drama. *This is no lady. She's an embarrassment to women.*

It was probably going to get worse before it got better. Slowly, Sam reached into her purse, found her keys and opened the door. *Big mistake!*

Eileen had never been in Sam's house and she quickly demanded to know where he had gone. Sam went through the living room to the kitchen, then the family room. Patty and her sister were pretending to be asleep in the double couch bed. Wyatt wasn't in the kitchen or bathroom. So pointing to the spiral staircase, she said he must be upstairs.

"What is he doing up there?" *This was truly getting exhausting.*

"Well, he probably was tired and went to sleep," Sam answered.

"Well, go up there and get him down," she commanded.

"I'm not doing that, Eileen. Nothing will get him up when he goes to sleep."

"Oh, yeah, you want to bet," she said. At that she marched up the stairs. Both Patty and her sister now had their eyes wide open. Sam turned to them both, "Do you mind if I crawl in with you girls for a moment. I'm *so tired* of this drama."

They moved over and let her snuggle in between them. All three lay on their backs looking up at the ceiling listening intently for the continued drama to unfold. Sam hoped nothing would wake up Patty's uncle who was in the front bedroom.

You could hear her whispering at first.

"Wyatt, get up. You're coming home with me," she commanded. He must have rolled over and ignored her and now her demands were getting louder and louder.

Patty turned to Sam and said, "What do you think will happen?"

"I don't know. She might just hop in bed with him," she said. "I don't think there is any way she's going to get him down the stairs."

"Wyatt" she screamed, "You know I'm not going to leave without you." There was a scuffle and then a large thump. *This is ridiculous . . . should I call the police?*

Finally, after a few more thumps, there were footsteps. Wyatt walked down the stairs first followed by Eileen. She turned to Sam in disgust.

"I lost a very valuable pair of diamond earrings up there. I would appreciate it when you find them, return them to me."

She opened the front door and walked out with her prize. Sam went over to dead bolt the door shut. She went up to her bedroom and began to think of all the drama that was still ahead. Within a week's time, Sam's letter about her involvement with Wyatt would be in Brad's hands.

This evening was just the first test of whether Wyatt and Sam could rise "Against the Wind". The wind from the north was heading south.

24

The News is Out!

When Patty's sister prepared to leave for Toronto, Sam pulled her aside and handed her the letter she had finally finished to Brad.

"I know this is a lot to ask, but could you personally hand this letter to Brad?" she asked. "Please let him know I still love him dearly and that I cannot in my wildest dreams explain what has happened to me. I just need to send this to him in a timely manner." She handed her a white envelope.

"Is this a Dear John letter?" asked Patty's sister, examining the exterior.

"I suppose it is. I'm clearly not in my right mind to call it anything else."

"So . . . I want to be clear," she questioned. "You want ME to hand this to him? Are you sure about that?"

"I know this is a great imposition and I understand if you feel uncomfortable. I just know you will know when the time is right. I respect him too much to mail this kind of letter. This isn't the flu. I'm not going to get over this in a week," Sam explained. "You've seen a lot in the past few days and you have a sense how this controls me. I don't want information to get to him through other people. *Please*, I would just be *so* grateful."

She took the letter gently in her hands and put it in her purse. "I'll do my best," she said. "Good luck, Sam," she smiled. "I have a feeling you are going to need it."

Over the next few weeks, Sam kept a careful watch for a return letter from Brad. She kept asking Patty if she had received anything from her mum, but it was all quiet on the northern front. A fortnight later, the letter came. Sam read it slowly, shaking, trying to take in every word of its content. When she finished it, she handed it to Patty to read for herself. She couldn't read the words out loud.

Brad's letter began friendly enough but slowly turned to a flavor of disgust. He demanded that she help him understand how this could happen with someone like Wyatt?

"You're aware of his reputation all over Sydney, Sam. You have always shared with me how you pitied the women he dated and for the way he treated them. Why? How did this even happen? I could understand you falling into a relationship with another man. I left you alone. I would have understood that, but you are too smart for this. I just don't get it."

He was absolutely right. Sam knew she was a smart woman who allowed passion to take over her life and like any addict, it controlled her, she didn't control it. She had to admit she couldn't explain any of this to someone who had never experienced this. Any explanation to defend herself seemed frivolous.

He ended the letter with the news he was going to be spending his summer break of July and August traveling to the West coast across Canada and then the United States. He added he was going to be traveling with a female companion. This was a sting for Sam as well. She guessed he had to be dating other women while he was in Canada, but traveling two months with someone through all the places she would have loved to travel with him was hard to take. She knew she deserved it. *But truth is, he never asked me to join him.*

Patty and Sam were both terribly sad for a while. She spent more time away from the house with Holly filling her life with parties and more travel knowing they would be leaving in December. Within a week, Sam received another very short note from Brad. "School just got out and

Lacy has invited me to come visit her in Connecticut for a week." It was a heads up. He found a way to share the news with Lacy.

Holy shit, she thought. *How did they link up? Did he call her? He must have.* He needed to know if she knew already. And . . . Sam wondered . . . how did he get her number in Connecticut?

It was a Saturday night. Sam had just fallen asleep; it was well after two in the morning and for some reason Wyatt was not back yet. The phone rang on the nightstand beside the bed waking her. *Who could it be?*

The voice on the other end was that of an American female.

"Hi, Sam." said the calm familiar voice. "How are things?" she asked. Sam was dazed for a second and then identified the voice.

"Lacy," she shouted sitting straight up in bed. "Where are you?" She feared for a minute that she was back and calling her from two blocks away.

"I'm still with my family in Connecticut," she said.

Whew! "When will you be back?"

"I have a flight set for two weeks from now."

"How was South America?" Sam asked, diverting the conversation.

"It was pretty good. Lots of poverty but a lot of rich experiences. We will have to catch up sometime after I get back. By the way, Brad paid me a visit last week. He, of course, wanted to visit every historical site attached to the Revolutionary War."

"Of course he did," Sam answered softly.

"So, how's Wyatt?" she asked.

"Listen, Lacy, before we ended our phone conversation, I was going to tell you about Wyatt."

"I'm just *struggling* to understand how this happened," she said.

"I'm not sure. Nothing was deliberate or intentional. I can't explain how any of it happened either, it just did," Sam's voice began to tremble. *I wasn't prepared to tell anyone about the details.*

"All I can say, Lacy, is that *I'm in love.*" There was a long silence.

They both knew that if she had written a letter to Brad, it had to be very serious. It didn't need to be explained. It also had to be so serious for Brad to personally want to visit her as one of the victims.

"So," she said matter-of-factly. "Does he say he *loves* you back?" she asked.

This was a hard one. Wyatt never used the word love out loud, but Sam knew he did. He whispered it often in her ear.

"Listen, Lacy, all I can say is I believe he does, but that would be something you'll need to ask him."

"Sam, I just got off the phone with Wyatt. I called him at the restaurant."

"So, what did he say?" Sam asked.

"Not much, you know him; he just did his snorting laugh when I tried to get a serious answer from him. So, I asked him the same question I'm going to ask you. How the hell is this going to work when I get back? Is this going to be a lovers' triangle?" she questioned with a pang of sharp disgust.

"I can't predict anything about the outcome of where it's going." Sam was not about to quantify it by sharing intimate conversations about him asking her to be the mother of his children. She knew that sharing too much would destroy everything. People would whittle it away as they did with her relationship to Brad. The less said the better.

"I'm just so sorry this happened. I didn't want to cause anyone pain. All I can say honestly is I'm *hopelessly* in love with him."

Sam thought to herself about the famous saying, "All is fair in love and war." Things start and end with paths of destruction in between. She truly meant for no one to get hurt but it was inevitable. She knew it from the start. Who would experience the worst of it was the question that lingered in her mind—perhaps it would be her.

"Okay, Sam, I guess there's no more to say. I'll be back in two weeks."

Sam sat silently in the dark. She feared she lost one of her closest friends. Lacy knew Sam better than anyone else. Lacy knew this wasn't a frivolous fling. She also knew Sam would never deliberately hurt her.

After Wyatt came home, they began to discuss Lacy's arrival.

"Lacy asked me point blank if you ever said to me that you loved me. I know in my heart that you do, but you seem to have a hard time admitting it to others."

"Well, my daddy always said when you are in lust, it's lust. If after three years you feel the same lust, it's love."

"Well, that sounds like something your daddy would say to his son sitting in a bar in Texas ready to pick up women. This can't possibly be the explanation of how you feel after these past three months of this relationship where we've named our children. This is a critical point. Simple question needs a simple answer. Do you love me?"

"Yes, you know I love you." *How could it be so hard?* Sam didn't need to push further. He said the words, now his actions had to prove them. Lacy would be home shortly.

The weekend after Lacy arrived, Wyatt broke the news to Sam he was going to spend the night with Lacy. "What! Why would you do that?" she asked.

"She wants to see me and try to understand things," he said. "I owe her that much."

Sam realized this was probably the only way things would resolve themselves. She just nodded. "Do what you need to."

They spent the next Friday night at his place. It was hard for Sam to imagine them together, but she knew it was probably very difficult for Lacy as well. Saturday he came back.

"So how did it go?" she asked.

"It was harder than I thought," he commented, "I felt like I was cheating on you the whole time."

"Under the circumstances, that was probably a healthy feeling, don't you think?"

"Yup," he said.

"So, what's going to happen from here?"

"She ended it and said she wasn't going to see either of us anymore from this point on."

Well, that was inevitable. Sam had lost a long-time friend. It seemed reasonable, but she was already experiencing a great sense of loss. Good or bad, Lacy, too, was so often the voice in Sam's head. However, love was something you didn't argue with.

<hr />

The next week Wyatt came home concerned. "A new business group has taken over all the leases in our business complex. It is a new insurance group that recently bought the entire complex and they were giving every occupant thirty days' notice to establish new leases."

"Well, is that going to be a problem?" Sam asked.

"Yes."

"Why?"

"Well, for one, I'm behind in my rent."

"If you don't mind me asking, how far behind are you?"

"About a year."

Sam gasped, "*A year*!"

"I needed to keep things afloat until my father came through with the money and we now know that's not happening."

"So, what *is* going to happen?"

"Well, I'm not vacating if that's what you're asking. I've put three long, hard years into making that place work. I'll be dammed if they hand me a notice and I just leave without a fight."

"What are you planning to do?" she asked.

"I'm going to fight it out. I heard they've begun moving into some of the businesses and are changing the locks at night. Starting tonight, I'm going to camp out at the restaurant. They're not changing my locks."

"Do you want me to come with you?"

"No," he said. "I have some of my friends who are Vietnam badass Marines; they are going to camp out with me. I'll keep you posted. I promise."

On the second evening that he stayed at the Brig, the shit hit the fan. Two men came to the front door of the restaurant and began jimmying the lock. The war was on. As told by Wyatt, he and his friends screamed and yelled and threw bottles of liquor at the men as they tried to get inside the door.

The next morning, Wyatt called Sam at school.

"Here's the phone number of my solicitor," he said. "Call him and tell him to come and meet with me tomorrow morning at the restaurant. They turned the power off to the Brig and we're losing thousands of dollars on thawing fish. Also, call *The Sydney Morning Herald* and tell them

I have a front-page story for them *Little Man Fights the Big Insurance Conglomerates.*"

Sam got right on it. It was hard for her to make calls during a teaching day, not to mention that she was too distracted to do any real teaching. It was a Thursday and she told the office she had some appointments on Friday.

That evening she went to the Brig. Wyatt was happy to see her. They spent the night cuddling up side by side in one of the large booths in the captain's quarters.

About two a.m., there were voices at the front door of the Brig. *Really, these guys aren't going to try this again? Oh my God, what is this going to turn into, a real life scene out of The Alamo.*

One of Wyatt's buddies pulled out something from his pocket and yelled through the door, "Stop what you are doing. I have a weapon. We have solicitors (lawyers) dealing with this right now, back off. You don't get paid enough to get injured. The owner is in here with me."

Wyatt had now gotten to the door, "Get the fuck out of here, you bastards. You're outnumbered." The two men who were jimmying the locks paused and then left without further incident. Sam sighed, this was definitely a Texas cowboy story.

The next morning at the Brig, Sam put on a pot of coffee for everyone. About ten, Wyatt met with his solicitor.

"Well, here's the plan," said Bradley in his Aussie twang. "We're going to apply for an injunction for the insurance company to Cease and Desist until this matter is heard in a court of law."

Bradley asked Wyatt for a check to begin proceedings. It was actually sounding quite civilized right now. No more scenes from the Wild West.

"Wyatt, I'm sure you might want to go home and have a shower at some point. This will happen today, and all parties will be notified," said Bradley. "Make sure you can give us written estimates on the damages to all your frozen fish due to the power shut-off." Wyatt nodded.

Soon a reporter and a photographer from *The Sydney Morning Herald* came and took pictures of Wyatt looking out from the restaurant and holding the large brass front door handles which signified possession.

The next morning, Wyatt's picture was splashed all over the front page of *The Herald*. He was building an army of interest around his situation. All the other businesses in the complex were also being forced out. At least Wyatt's actions halted further shops from being taken over. *The Herald* now claimed Wyatt as officially notorious, *Little Man Takes on Large Insurance Company*.

In thirty days, the case was pushed up for a decision by the high court. Sam took the week off from school to support Wyatt through the hard days ahead in the courtroom. It was quite an experience. There was Wyatt, with his barrister and his solicitor on one side of the courtroom, and there was the Singapore Insurance Group with a dozen barristers on the other side.

When you walked into the courtroom, you had to bow to the judge who wore a white wig and black robes and then take a seat in the back gallery. It was impressive to see scenes that reached back to colonial times.

During the first break of the first day, Wyatt sat next to Sam and held her hand. He took off the ring on his right hand. It was the gold one with the single diamond inlay that his mother had given him when he graduated college. She knew it was very dear to him.

"Sam," he said, as he placed it on her ring finger of her right hand. "Will you wear this for me for good luck throughout the trial?"

Sam nodded. She was deeply moved by this gesture and hugged him. She was the closest thing to family he had on this side of the world. She was praying and holding good thoughts that she was going to bring him nothing but good luck. They didn't talk much about how the arguments in the court were developing each day. They were just hoping against hope the outcome would be in his favor. It did seem rather hopeless though. A dozen barristers against one. Dozens of books were opened to challenge every argument.

The verdict was handed down on the following Friday morning. The Brig had ninety days to remain open. That was when Wyatt had to hand over the keys to the insurance group. This was the same for all the other small business owners in the complex.

It seemed that the decision of the court came down to a simple matter of the signing of the original leases. The solicitor who had set up all the leases had never paid the Stamp Tax for each lease. A clear oversight, but a vulnerable one. Everyone in the complex now needed to leave or be granted a new lease. *The Little Man Lost* was the follow-up article on a back page of *The Herald.*

Wyatt was livid and was not going to take the decision lying down.

"What're you planning to do?" Sam asked.

"I'm going to operate the Brig at full volume and no one is going to be the wiser that I need to hand over the keys in ninety days. I have a lot of friends who helped me open this place who I need to try to pay back."

Evening after evening, Wyatt brought home mementos from the restaurant. First, bottles of opened fine liquor, then pictures from the walls and the big brass ship's bell engraved BRIG.

It was sad times. The roller coaster of highs was now heading into the valleys of lows. For the next ninety days, they were living a life with an inevitable end. There were nights Wyatt didn't come home stating he was saying goodbye to long-time friends. One day he broached the dreaded topic around his future.

"I'm probably going to have to return to the States, Sam. Sydney is dead for me now."

"What are you going to do over there?" she asked.

"I don't know. Probably try to open another restaurant."

"What shall I do?" she dared to ask.

"Well, I think you should just stay here with your house and your job and I will call you when I get set up with something."

"I know you don't really know, but do you have an idea about how *long* it might take?"

"A while, Sam, maybe even a year."

"Where do you think you'll be heading?" *Could I visualize a future in places he was describing? Was I really prepared to follow him anywhere?*

"I'll probably go back to one of the prettiest places on earth."

"Where is that?"

"Ruidoso, New Mexico."

25

A Knock on the Door

Life went on for the next few months, but it wasn't business as usual. Wyatt arranged to buy a ticket for Los Angeles from their travel agent, Harry, for three weeks after the restaurant closed.

Lacy was true to her word to never see Sam again, but Lyndsey kept in touch. She came over often for Saturday visits. She kept up on the news of the restaurant and even went to the Brig with Sam once or twice.

One Saturday afternoon, she wanted to get into the details of how Wyatt and she started their relationship. "Come on, how did it start? Think for a minute. What makes you think you are *any* different from all the other girls he dated?"

"Listen, Lyndsey. I can't and won't talk about the nitty gritty details. It's not going to help any one of us to dissect this. I love him and that's all I'm going to say. It's passion, it can't be described; it controls you. Just call it chemistry, dopamine, heroin - it's all that. It is what it is," she threw up both arms.

"Well, I can't relate to that," she said.

"Well . . . if you haven't experienced it, you probably wouldn't."

However, she wouldn't let it go. "I know you've said that, but what has he *ever* said that makes you believe that he truly loves YOU."

Sam sighed. This was exhausting. Lyndsey was back living with Lacy on Campbell Street. Lacy probably still needed answers or maybe Lyndsey was just trying to be a good friend to Sam.

"Lyndsey, I know people are trying to be my friend, but you all were the same friends who told me straight out that Brad and I would never work. I'm not asking for input this time. I want you to simply understand that Wyatt and I have had conversations that have been way deeper than anything I know he has had with other women. Please don't mind if I want to believe them."

Lyndsey stared at Sam blankly. Her eyes softened. "Okay, Sam, it's YOUR life. No one can tell you how to live it. As your friend, I just hope it ends well for you."

"Thanks, Lyndsey, so do I." They never brought up the topic again.

Wyatt and Sam continued to take one day at a time. One morning while they were still in bed, he said something weird. "Listen, if anyone knocks on the door and is looking for me, you need to just say you haven't seen me," he said.

"What?" she said a little disturbed, "Who'll be looking for you?"

"I don't know, people, the law, who knows," he said quickly. "Listen, I'm not paying my bills right now and people are pissed. I keep promising the money next week, but I have other people I owe restitution to, good friends who trusted me."

"Okay, so, if the law knocks on the door, what should I do?"

"Well, you ask them if they have a search warrant. I'll hear you ask and I'll jump over the neighbor's wall. Don't worry, I have been in rougher spots than this. Just stay cool. You can do this. It'll be okay. I'm leaving the end of September and this part of our journey will be over."

"Okay," Sam said. *This isn't really okay.* This wasn't the tour she signed up for. She had to sit down and have a pretty hard talk with herself. She realized her addiction to her passion was now getting her into unimaginable trouble. She thought of all those women who marry Mafia hit men in Jersey. Were they as addicted as she was? Did they decide, like she had, that even questionable men have children? She was beginning to torture herself with questions.

She warned Patty that if there were any knocks at the door in the future not to answer them. She didn't share why. She'd answer them all from this point on. One August morning about seven, there was a loud knock.

Patty was finishing her coffee in the family room before they took off for school. She looked over at Sam as she stood in the kitchen. Wyatt was upstairs asleep and she had no chance to warn him. She slowly approached the front windows to see if she could peek at the person at the door, but the angle didn't permit her to see. She took a deep breath and opened the door a crack to peek out. She gasped . . . . *"Oh my God,* what are you doing here?" she screamed in shock. It was Brad.

"Is that all you can say . . . what am I doing here?" he asked, somewhat hurt.

"Sorry, I apologize, it just . . . came out."

"Are you deliberately blocking the door from me coming in?" he asked.

"Not really . . . well, maybe. Wyatt is upstairs and I don't think I can handle the two of you in one space right at this moment. Would it be possible for you to come back in about an hour?

I'll call school and get a sub and then we can visit and talk more comfortably," she asked, her eyes pleading.

"Sure, I understand," he said. "I'll head over to Campbell Street."

"Okay, no . . . just wait a minute, please," she said putting her index finger up. Please come in for a quick moment." She pointed to the living room and ran back to the family room.

"Patty, come quick. Here's another chapter for your book. There's someone at the door I want you to meet before I call for a substitute."

She looked up from her coffee confused. "Just come," Sam instructed, waving her arms. She walked her to the front door and made introductions.

"Patty, this is Brad. Brad, this is Patty. I know you both have a lot to talk about. I need to call Miss. Find for a sub." She left the two of them hugging in the doorway. They were ecstatic to finally be meeting.

Patty made a comment to Brad, "You know you ruined this whole scenario that I've been playing in my head about meeting you in an airport for the first time."

Sam told Miss. Find that she had an unexpected situation come up that needed to be dealt with right away.

"Yes," Sam answered, "Patty will be coming." I knew she hoped she wouldn't need to find two substitutes. She was beginning to doubt Sam's sanity. She had never asked for subs before this year.

Sam turned to Brad and said, "Here are the keys to my car. Would you be so kind to drive Patty to school. I know you have a lot to talk about. Listen, I *am* very excited to see you. I promise Wyatt will be gone by the time you get back." They both got in Sam's car.

"S'truth, Rothbauer, I hate these little cars," he yelled over to her.

"Well, yours is all the way up in Newcastle," she said. "Beggars can't be choosers." They all laughed, and drove off down the street for the western suburbs.

Sam went up to the room and woke Wyatt. She was still reeling in a state of shock and wasn't sure how to approach Wyatt with the news. She walked over and sat on the side of the bed.

"Listen, do you remember when Lacy came back and you needed the night to sort things out with her? Well, I sort of have the same situation."

"What do you mean," he looked up half asleep.

"There was a knock at the front door this morning. I was half expecting the police, but it wasn't . . . it was Brad."

Wyatt looked confused. "Isn't he in Canada and not due back 'til January?"

"Yup." she said with a nod, "But he's here right now and I'm not sure why. We didn't have a chance to talk. I told him you were upstairs."

"Okay, I get it. Let me shower and get dressed and I'll head to the restaurant. Call me later when you have time to talk." Sam paced the floor hoping Brad wouldn't get back before Wyatt left. "By the way, where is he now?" Wyatt asked.

"He's driving Patty to school in my car and then stopping in to see Lacy and Lyndsey."

"Well, that should be interesting," he said with his famous snort. Sam didn't feel much like smiling today. She sat in the family room nervously drumming the walnut table waiting for Brad to knock on the door. Why was he here? Did he just miss Australia? He was supposed to be traveling through Canada and the States with some girl. Was the girl here as well? Did they come together to visit his homeland?

Sam's stomach was in knots trying to anticipate why he came back. It also dawned on her he came to Gladstone Street first. He must have surmised that Wyatt was here and that didn't stop him.

An hour passed when she heard the car pull up. *I don't think I ever had a reason for Brad to drive my car before.* He knocked on the door. "Is he gone?" he asked now hesitating to enter.

"Yes. Thank you for allowing me not to have a scene."

"No worries, Sam. I didn't want a scene either. So . . . you two are still together I take it."

She nodded.

"I hear from Lacy that he's losing his restaurant," Brad said.

Sam couldn't even imagine what Lacy and Brad might have discussed. "That's true," she answered nodding again.

"So, what're you going to do?" he asked.

"Seriously, I don't know. He's heading back to the States after September. He says he's going to try to open another restaurant somewhere in New Mexico."

"Are you planning to go with him?" he asked directly.

"These are all good questions, Brad. All I can answer is not right away or perhaps never, depending on how people feel in the future and what happens along the way."

He made his way over to the walnut dining table. "May I sit?"

"Certainly, please. Where are my manners."

He sat across from her as she sat on the couch in the family room. "What about you," she asked him trying to change the topic. "How were your travels through the States?"

"Honestly," he said, "I couldn't imagine in my wildest dreams how vast and empty the States are. I drove through five western states and barely saw people. I expected low populations driving through Canada but there are 250 million of you Yanks living in America. Where are they all living?"

"They're all hiding in Los Angeles and New York City."

He laughed, and the mood got lighter.

"So, how about your girlfriend, is she here with you?" Sam asked.

"No, she isn't here, and she isn't my girlfriend," he said. "We're just friends teaching in Ontario. She wanted to see Canada. When I told her I was heading to Sydney for a while she went back to Toronto.

"I was just wondering. I thought maybe the poor girl was standing outside or something." Sam didn't know why, but she was somewhat relieved to hear he wasn't with her anymore.

He looked around and asked if he could take a look at the backyard. He wandered around admiring his handiwork and came in smiling. He carried Sam's newest stray dog in his arms.

"Who's this?"

"Oh, meet Toby. He was hanging in our school's playground for weeks. The staff finally talked me into taking him home. The only problem is Toby knows how to escape this house everyday faster than I can get out the door."

"S'truth," Brad said. "How?"

"I believe he crawls under floorboards under the back deck and resurfaces at the area of the front door. He waits for Patty and me to leave and takes off. He's up to his old tricks hanging out in school yards. He's homing in on the private Catholic school up by Gladstone Park. I got a note put in my post box just this week saying he is begging food and humping the legs of the students. The nuns are giving me a week to stop him or they're calling the pound. I guess I should be thankful they gave me a heads up."

"Listen, if it's okay with you, I'll come by tomorrow and see how he gets out. It should be simple to solve. I can put up some screen mesh at the foot of the floor boards under the front area of the house to prevent him from making future escapes."

"Will you? That would be so wonderful. I've been at a loss as to what to do about him." Brad knew every square inch of the house. If there was a crawl space, he would know where to find it.

Toby was a terrier-mix. He was a clever little character. He would jump up on your lap, roll over on his back and want you to stroke his belly until he fell into a deep sleep. Patty adored him.

Brad and Sam talked a little more about his life in Canada. She was telling him how much she and Patty had loved his descriptive letters. "When are you coming back?" she asked innocently.

"December. I'll stay for a week after school lets out and then plan to head back to be with my family for the Christmas holidays."

"So, what's your plan?" he asked.

"I told you I don't have plans, Brad. Life is a little upside down right now. Wyatt is leaving at the end of September and he's suggesting that he wants me to follow sometime in the distant future. There's no structure to any of this. This is all day by day. Very simply, I've stopped making plans."

He stood up from the dining room chair and walked toward her inching closer. She peered up at him with a sad look.

"Let me ask you something, then."

He got down to look her in the eye. She noticed with a side glance he was kneeling on one knee. He raised her left hand which still had his ring on it. She could feel her body produce heat from her toes to her head. *This really isn't happening to me, not right now. This is surreal . . . I must be imagining this.*

Then he spoke softly. "I never really asked you . . ."

Please don't let this be the moment that I wished for so long, not now.

"What," she shifted nervously.

"Will you marry me?" he asked quickly.

She felt like she must have looked like the Edvard Munch painting, "The Scream". She was in shock. She couldn't digest this. *So this was the reason he was here.* The unexpected proposal that she had wanted for years. *Is this how my luck goes?*

"**What**?" was all she could reply as her eyes were blurring with water.

"Sam, I just flew ten thousand miles to ask you to marry me. I've spent the last month traveling empty corners of the world trying to figure out what I want. I want you. I want to spend the rest of my life with YOU." It was the perfect proposal at exactly the wrong time.

He continued to kneel in front of her holding her hand waiting for a response, but she said nothing. There was nothing she could say. She could feel herself shaking.

"Sam," he said softly, "Tell me it isn't too late. *Please* tell me it isn't too late."

She began sobbing. She was speechless. All she could whisper was, "I think it is . . . "

Brad instantly got up to his feet. He was now visibly angry, obviously humiliated, and hurt. He began yelling.

"I flew over the Pacific Ocean to propose to you, Sam. Maybe you need to think long and hard on this. I'm just so mad right now." He looked up at the staircase and yelled, "I rebuilt this house with you. My father made that staircase for *US*." He pointed to the left of her. "I just want to rip it out right now," he yelled. "I'm renting a truck this afternoon and ripping it out," he screamed.

"Brad, come on, remember, *you* left *me*. I didn't know where things were going with us. I know you are upset. Demolishing the staircase isn't the solution to your feelings right now. Remember the house *is* in my name."

"I spent hours on the road thinking about all the time I put into rebuilding this house feeling used and never properly compensated. We need to sell this house and divide this properly if we're not going to be together." Sam knew he was hurt, but was this really more about money? Was that the real reason for the visit?

"Brad," she said slowly, "We talked about this before you left. I don't want to sell the house. If you need some more compensation, let's talk about that before you leave. Maybe this is not the best time to discuss it."

"I'm literally sick. I'm leaving. I can't believe you'd throw away your life with this guy." He threw her car keys on the woodblock peninsula and stormed out the front door.

Sam went up the stairs and threw herself on the bed. She was frightened and heartbroken. Why did life always throw in these barbs? Men always wanted her when it was too late. Didn't they understand that all she could do at this point was follow her heart? After a few hours of sobbing, she collected her emotions and called Wyatt at the restaurant.

"Well, how did it go?" he asked.

"It was a hard day," she answered. "He proposed to me." There was a long silence.

"So . . . what was your answer?" he asked.

"I told him it might be too late."

"Okay . . . well," he said. "So, is it still okay that I come back to the house when the restaurant closes tonight?"

"Sure, I was hoping you would." *I wondered how would he have handled the loss of his restaurant and the future mother of his children all at the same time? Either decision would've hurt someone.*

Patty came back from school. Cassie dropped her off and she announced that they were all having dinner that night with Brad. She told Sam that Brad was going to spend the next few weeks staying at Cassie's house before his return to Ontario. He was putting a new coat of paint on the interior walls of her house.

Brad was a treasure and Sam kept thinking over and over to herself his question about what she was doing with her life? Wyatt had never gotten down on his knee to propose; in fact, to be honest, he had only been suggesting that he wanted her to be the mother of his children. She anxiously began to pull herself apart with self-doubt. *What* was real? Who really loved whom enough?

As usual, she put off hard questions avoiding the answers. She began to take small refuge in the thought that Brad would probably never trust her again after his attempt to win her back. After all, he properly proposed and she didn't accept. She remembered that he said he didn't trust her in the first place simply because she was a Yank.

Sam couldn't describe this strange possession of her mind and soul. She talked to some third-party people. One friend said, "Well, it seems you have a choice of picking the good apple or the bad apple." *Was I consciously picking the bad apple?* Sam began to imagine that this seemed predestined somehow. This whole scenario of Wyatt coming into her life so unexpectedly was like a Pacman game. He hit her from the side and diverted her path to a completely opposite direction, one she could never imagine. Was this what they called destiny?

Patty and Holly spent most of their time with Brad over the next two weeks. They listened to all his stories about Canada from the mind of an Aussie whose country they had enjoyed and explored themselves these past months. Sam thought they both secretly fell in love with him.

Brad came by the house, as he had promised, to watch Toby escape. He fixed the exit point. Brad was such a good man. Sam clearly still loved him. She was even jealous of the time he was spending with everyone else, but she was controlled by forces greater than herself. She needed to pursue a steady course right now or she would go crazy. She believed she deserved all that was destined on the path ahead of her.

One night before Brad left, he called, "Is it possible to see you before I head back to Canada?"

"Of course."

"I'd like to take you to dinner. Will Wyatt let you join me?"

"Of course, I can answer that without asking him. I'd like that actually. I'm feeling terrible about how things ended the day you came back."

As a rule, Brad did not like to spend money on restaurants. They didn't go out much when they lived together. Brad picked her up in Cassie's jeep and drove to the new Centrepoint Tower. It was the most popular new trendy spot for tourists; it opened just last year. It revolved 360 degrees every hour giving tourists amazing views of Sydney.

Sam had never been there and was taken aback by Brad's gesture to create a moment for them to remember. They sat and enjoyed a beautiful dinner together draped by incredible views.

"Listen, Sam, I'm determined to understand that time will decide how this plays out. I'll return to live in Balmain for a while and reside in the Carrington Street house sometime in January. I hope we can catch up then. I'm heading back to Canada in two days. Wyatt is leaving for the States soon. Let's see where things go after the dust settles."

Sam nodded in agreement. "Listen, Brad, I hope you know I never meant to hurt you. I never want to hurt you in the future either. I *do* love you. I always will. But this other kind of love has taken possession of me."

"Okay . . . well for now I'll accept it. I have no choice. Just always know I loved you enough to fly across time and space to ask you to marry me. No one else will ever do that for you and I'll guarantee I'll never do it again for anyone else."

"I've also been thinking a lot about how you felt when you said you haven't been compensated enough for your work on the house. I know when you left that things happened rather quickly around the issue of compensation and the titles for both houses. Have you thought any more about what you feel would be a more appropriate settlement?"

"I actually have and I'm glad you mentioned it," replied Brad.

Sam knew in the past two weeks he had access to many opinions on the matter. He had Cassie's and his parents to name a few. More money was now put on the table as compensation to be paid over the next ten years or payment on the sale of the house or whatever came first.

She was not one for arguing over peace of mind. They had bought the house for $29,000 and only owned it three years. It could not erase all the blood, sweat, and tears he had put in, or the three jobs she worked to pay the bills for the building supplies or the compensation for buying a second house.

"I know we both probably wish things were going to turn out differently for us. God knows when you left, I was hoping you would come back and we'd drift easily into a happily ever after story. We would've had two houses and your property up north to give us a good start."

"Fair dinkum," he said. "Who wrote this ugly chapter?"

I don't know," Sam said turning her eyes downward. "I didn't write it. I couldn't have even imagined any of this."

They finished the evening on an even keel. Brad dropped Sam off at Gladstone Street and kissed her goodbye softly on the cheek. He slowly drove down the street as she had seen him leave for school for many years. He moved slowly away from her and around the corner in Cassie's Jeep. She instantly began missing him.

26

Another Knock on the Door

As September approached, Sam waited for the roller coaster to plunge to the bottom. She tried to spend every night going to the restaurant. She was just trying to cling a little longer to what was left of an extraordinary moment. Only a year ago, she felt that very same sense of loss as Brad got ready to leave and now it was happening again as Wyatt was moving out of her life.

Others were trying to hold onto the moment, too. Many of Wyatt's friends came nightly to eat and party with him. If she hadn't met them before, she was meeting them all now.

There were dozens of his old girlfriends that she recognized from parties from the past. Everyone was sad to see Wyatt's dream disintegrate. He was the Texas golden boy. Many of the contents of the restaurant began to disappear as Wyatt invited people to take the things they wanted.

One day Sam got to the restaurant early. She sat at the bar waiting for Wyatt. A waitress named Rita came over and sat by her. She ordered them both a drink; her shift was soon to begin. She was a perky little blonde with short hair. "Listen, I was hoping to get a moment alone with you before the restaurant closed," she said. "Do you have a minute?" she asked as she bounced up onto the barstool.

"Sure," Sam replied. "Thanks for the cocktail."

"I like you," she said. "You are a real class act, Sam, and believe me, I've seen all types walk through these doors in the past two years." Sam smiled back, with an appropriate response to the compliment.

"I don't know if you know this, but you have a scorpion by the tail," she said looking Sam directly in the eye.

Sam glanced over to her with a perplexed look. She was unaware of where she was going with this, but she was getting the gist. "Do you know what that means?" she asked.

"I think so," Sam answered.

"Simply, Wyatt is ONE MEAN son of a bitch."

Sam gulped, "Well, I've heard he can get angry, I've seen him get angry with staff, but I have never personally experienced it."

"Oh, no, it's a lot more than just frustration and anger," she said. "He's an outrageous bully and vindictively mean. There's *no* end to the torment he can bestow on people he feels have betrayed him or those he wants to get even with. My suggestion to you, Sam, is *run* while you still can."

Sam looked down sadly into the depths of her drink. She felt Rita had nothing to gain by giving her this warning. After all, she had no relationship with Wyatt other than as an employee.

"Listen, I can't tell you how much I appreciate you taking the time to talk to me. I know your words *will* echo in my head for the rest of my life. I can't explain for a moment the spell that's holding me so close to him. My head has absolutely no control over my heart at this point."

Rita slowly finished her drink and got down from the stool looking sadly back at Sam.

"Sam, I wish you the best." she said. "You're a fine lady. You deserve so much better than him."

In the end, Rita didn't do her shift that night. She finished their conversation, waved goodbye to the bartender and walked out the front door of the Brig.

The following Friday, Wyatt put a sign on the door saying the Brig was now permanently closed, thanking customers for their patronage.

It was terribly sad. Wyatt was trying not to appear depressed, but Sam could tell he was. The wind had left his sails.

One of his long-time buddies called her one evening and said he was going to throw a surprise farewell party for Wyatt in about a week's time. He asked if he could get Sam to deliver him to the Woollahra Eating House at about seven in the evening in Rose Bay. He told her to invite everyone she knew who would like to say goodbye. Patty, Holly, and Lyndsey came, but Lacy did not. Sam was surprised—she thought Lacy would at least bid him farewell.

The party was huge. Half of Sydney was there. Sam hung around her group of friends letting Wyatt whoop and holler with his. She recognized some, but most were unfamiliar to her. The Cousners were there and so were her neighbors, Rachael and Bob. All the bigwig owners of local Sydney pubs, restaurants, and bars from the Cross were there, too. The party was spectacular and everyone had fun.

Wyatt and Sam rode back together to the house.

"Well, I guess that's that," he said. "I just need to start packing up my things by the end of the week and tidy up some loose ends. I'll be in and out saying goodbyes, Sam. I'll try to let you know if I'm not going to make it back in the evening."

She could feel the wind shifting again. In his mind, he had already left and their life together here was no more. He was on to the next chapter of his life, whatever that would be.

Parent conferences were held over the next two evenings. Patty and Sam were going to be pretty busy as well. Wyatt was antsy. She and Patty didn't get home until 8:30 that evening and there was a note on the butcher block counter saying, "Visiting old friends, see you sometime tomorrow." It was signed ME.

Sam and Patty were pretty beat from the conferences. They made dinner and went to bed. About six the next morning, there was a knock at the door. Maybe Wyatt had lost his key. She opened the door wide. A man dressed in a brown suit stood at the front door.

"Are you Samantha Rothbauer?" he asked.

"Yes," Sam answered cautiously.

He pulled out a badge and introduced himself as Detective Flint.

"I'm with the C.I.B." he said. "I'm looking for a man whom you may know named Wyatt Stetson. Do you know him?"

Sam felt she was on the verge of an earthquake. Nothing could have prepared her for this moment. She was nauseous and her face showed it. She wasn't a very good actor or liar. The only solace she had was that by some freak quirk of fate, Wyatt wasn't at the house and she truly had *no* idea where he was. *We always said he had nine lives—how many was this now?*

"Yes, I know him. He's a friend of mine," she replied in earnest. He probably already had that information. "What is the C.I.B.?" asked Sam.

"I believe you call it the C.I.A. in your country." *What ... oh my God, this is far more serious than Wyatt described.*

"I think he's more than a friend of yours. We have information that he lives here with you."

Sam tried to look shocked, "Wyatt doesn't live here. He's a friend and I haven't seen him in a while."

"When was the last time he was here?" he asked continuing to write Sam's responses in a small black notebook.

"I haven't seen him in days," she lied. "I know he has been busy closing his restaurant."

"Well then, this can be over quickly if you will just cooperate and permit me to come in and take a look."

Sam began to think of all the incriminating evidence around the house and remembered Wyatt's suggestion. So she asked, "Do you have a search warrant?"

The officer became agitated. "*No*, I don't, but let me tell you some details, Miss. You, Samantha Rothbauer, have a Migrant Visa to teach in Australia. From what I can tell, you have taught school here for over seven years and have no criminal record. If I have to go downtown and get a warrant, I will be immediately revoking your Visa and you'll have forty-eight hours to leave this country. So, what do you say?" he asked.

Sam took a deep breath. She wanted to cry and throw up at the same time. "Listen, I wish to cooperate and I'll let you in, but I don't want you to think I'm a bad person. I know if you have information about Wyatt Stetson, you probably know he has more than one girlfriend. I know it may make me look bad as well, but I also have more than one boyfriend," she admitted uncomfortably to the officer.

Sam looked nervously around her. She just remembered that Wyatt left a joint on the dresser upstairs and she also remembered stories of officers taking you in and charging you with possession of an illegal substance.

"I understand, but there may just be things around I don't wish you to see," she said.

The officer seemed to back off slightly and seemed pleased she was going to let him in and cooperate.

"Listen, Miss. I'm looking for a *man*, nothing else."

"Okay . . . ," she said, and slowly stepped aside and let him in the front door. Poor Patty hadn't come out of her bedroom yet. She was probably listening to the whole awful dialog. Another chapter for her book, Sam thought. The officer turned to her. "Who's in *this* room," he asked.

"Well . . . that would be my flatmate, Patty." The officer proceeded to knock on the door.

"Is anyone in there?" he asked.

"Yes," Patty answered in a small voice.

"Are you alone?" he asked.

"Yes, *damn it*," answered Patty quickly. Sam had to chuckle. It took Patty's witty response to lighten the moment. Sam put her hand over her mouth to muffle a snicker.

"Okay, Miss, but I'm going to need you to come out. I need to search the room."

"Please give me a minute," Patty responded.

She slipped on a robe and came out over to the middle of the living room while the officer searched the room. There really wasn't much to search. It was all built-ins. He opened the closet went around the bed, looked under the bed and exited the room. Sam took her first sigh of relief. The officer never looked under the mattress where Brad had built a hidden chamber for his collection of rifles from three generations of war. Easily over a dozen rifles were stashed in there.

"Okay, Miss, you can go back."

"Thanks," she said. "I better get ready for school."

The detective stepped into the kitchen/family room and commented, "Nice." He walked to where the bathroom was and conducted a quick search. As he exited, he saw the gallery of photos that Sam pinned on the diagonal pine boards that lined the kitchen wall. It was a collection of friends and parties. Of course, Wyatt was in several. As he looked at the photos more closely, Sam spied Wyatt's note on the butcher block counter and threw her hand on top of it. The officer turned suddenly and asked, "Is that him?" he pointed to Wyatt's picture on the wall.

Sam stood motionless and answered, "Yes sir." When he turned back to the wall Sam slid the note under a box of tissues at the far end of the counter.

The officer proceeded to open the back door and searched the yard. She watched him through the beautiful lead light windows. *This is crazy.* He was checking out the height of walls which were over eight feet tall and surrounded the property—*and* not easily scalable even for a bobcat.

He walked the path to the old outhouse which was now a shed for Brad's tools and looked around and came back in the house. "Okay, what's upstairs?"

"My bedroom," she answered.

"Is that all?" he asked.

"Yes, and it is quite messy at the moment."

She followed behind the officer as he wound his way up the spiral staircase. He went straight to the queen size bed and looked under it. Toby was laying quietly on top of the already made bed taking in the whole scene.

"Cute dog."

"Yeah, he's a stray." She realized the officer was trained to watch behavior and check words. She tried not to say too much. He opened the closet to the left of the bed. He saw that it spanned the length of the house.

"Is there anything back there?" he asked.

"No, sir," she replied, "It's just used for storage."

"Okay if I take a look?" he asked searching her eyes.

"Go ahead," she sighed. If Wyatt was in the house, this would have been the place he would have thought to hide. He went inside and crawled all the way back inspecting everything, returning in a few minutes.

"Well, I'm beginning to believe that he isn't here and you aren't hiding him."

Sam didn't say anything. She just wanted this ugliness to be over. There was only one closet left on the opposite side of the room. He walked directly over to it and opened both louver doors together quickly revealing the contents inside. There, ready for the world to see, was the evidence of Sam's other boyfriend. Brad's Commando uniforms and all his shiny boots were lined below in perfect order. While the officer's back was to her, Sam grinned to herself.

Shocked, the officer turned and asked, "*What* is all this?"

"Well, sir, I tried to tell you I had more than one boyfriend."

"So what does he do?" asked the officer inquisitively.

"He's a school teacher and a weekend Commando."

"Where is he now?" he asked, as he moved Brad's things around.

"He is away right now and I'm minding his clothes for him," she offered truthfully.

"Wow," he shook his head. "I'm rarely surprised." He walked over to the pew that had Wyatt's jeans flung over the rail, a giant framed color picture of him and a banker, the brass bell, and a pair of cowboy boots beneath. "I'm going to guess these are Wyatt's things," he commented as he rustled through them.

"Yes," she answered. "He asked if he could store some things here from his restaurant."

They turned and walked down the stairs to the door. The officer took out a card. "Listen, you're not off the hook yet. Here's my card. If he comes back or tries to contact you, you are to contact me immediately, understand."

She nodded still shaking. "Yes sir."

She closed the door behind him and took a deep breath. She sank to the floor just sitting there and then proceeded to lie down on her back with her arms out like she was just crucified.

Patty came out of her room and peered down at her. "What are you going to do, Sam?" she asked.

"Die . . . no, breathe, I need to try to breathe. Just don't get involved with men, Patty, it isn't worth it." She slowly sat up taking slow breaths trying to think as she positioned her head in her hands. "Okay . . . I'm going to call Miss. Find again and tell her that I had another emergency and for her to get a sub. I need to somehow find Wyatt and warn him not to come back here. I think it best that you go on to school. Do you think you can drive my car yourself?"

"Maybe," Patty answered guardedly.

"There's a car across the street that's probably a stake-out. I think it's best if the car and you go to school. I want it to appear that it is business as usual. I know it's going to be hard but please do not say anything to anyone at school."

Patty nodded in agreement. "Nobody would believe me if I did," she said.

"How are you going to find Wyatt?" asked Patty.

"I don't know. I'm just going to call everyone I know."

Sam called Lacy's house first. She didn't know where else to start. She needed to rule out any possibility that Wyatt was there. Lyndsey answered.

"Hi, Lyndsey, this is Sam. I know this may be an odd question to ask but by any chance is Wyatt over there?" She asked the question thinking Lacy was on his list of old friends who hadn't shown up at the party the other evening. There was just a small chance he may have visited her.

"No, of *course* not," answered Lyndsey.

"Well, he didn't come home last night and the police were just here looking for him."

Lyndsey responded with the most appropriate response. "Oh my God, that man *does* have nine lives."

"Yeah, I agree. Listen, I know you're getting ready for work but I need to find him. Do you have the phone numbers of some of his friends who I can call, like his good buddy, Ken?" Sam knew Lyndsey had worked for Ken at one time. She waited for a long moment. Lyndsey told her, "I have a couple of numbers. Oh, and good luck, Sam."

"Yeah, I think I'll need it."

Sam said goodbye to Patty and told her she would call her later if she wasn't returning home. Her first call was to her neighbors, Rachael and Bob. She told Rachael the whole story.

"Could I please ask a *huge* favor. I have a lot of Wyatt's personal items that he'll need. The police have a car outside observing things in front of my house. Can I possibly put them in a garbage bag and lower it from the balcony over your fence to your backyard?"

"Sure," Rachael said. "Before I go to school, I'll put it out on the front stoop area on Jane Street like I was putting out the garbage. Maybe you can have one of Wyatt's friends come pick it up during the day."

"Thanks, Rachael, you're a doll," she answered gratefully.

Next she called the Cousners.

"Hi, Tom. The police were just here looking for Wyatt. Luckily, he wasn't at my house last night. He has a bunch of clothes and his passport here. I need to get them to him quickly, as soon as I can figure out where he is."

"Are you okay?" Tom asked.

"Yeah, a little shaky, but we just need to make sure Wyatt doesn't come back here. A stake-out car is in the front of the street watching everything."

"Were they Balmain police?" asked Tom.

"No, the officer was dressed in a suit and flashed a badge and said he worked for the C.I.B.," said Sam.

"Crikey . . . that's a different story. I wonder who or what he was involved with to get that kind of recognition? We need to find a way to get him out of the country fast," said Tom.

"Do you have any of his friends' numbers?" asked Sam.

"No," said Tom, "but I'll drive by Jane Street in an hour and pick up the bag. I'll keep the bag at my house until you let me know where you want me to drop it off."

Then she called Wyatt's good buddy Ken. "Ken, was Wyatt at your pub last night?" she asked trembling.

"Yeah, for a little bit, but he left about nine."

"Did he say where he was going?" she asked excitedly. There was a pause from Ken. "Listen, Ken, this is urgent; the police were here. I need to talk to him right away, please, any ideas?"

"Okay, I understand," he said. "Wyatt said something about visiting Eileen." Like the news of her brother's death, Sam was shocked but somehow not surprised.

"Do you happen to have Eileen's number," she asked pleading.

"No, I don't, but I'll do my best to get it. Stay by the phone."

Within thirty minutes, Ken got back to her with the number. She took a deep breath and called Eileen—the girl she hadn't talked to since Wyatt's partner's wedding, the girl whose diamond earrings she returned after Eileen lost them in *Sam's* bedroom!

"Hi, Eileen, this is Sam. Is Wyatt there?" she asked cautiously.

Eileen immediately was guarded. "Why do you want to know?" she answered curtly. Her response gave Sam hope.

"The police came here this morning looking for Wyatt. They searched the entire house and have a car out front. He can't come back to *my* house for any reason. Do you understand?" She seemed relieved that Sam wasn't trying to tear him away from her. "Do you mind if I talk to him?" Sam asked.

"Okay, I'll get him," she said, and called for Wyatt. It was now about ten in the morning.

"Hi Wyatt, it's Sam. The police were here. It was pretty intense. You can't come back to my house." She went on to tell him how she got the bag to the Cousners with all his belongings. "Let me know if there's anything else you need before things get transported to Eileen's."

"Okay," Wyatt said. "Thanks, Sam. Let me call you back after I think things through a bit."

The song "Gimme Shelter" by The Rolling Stones was playing on the radio as she began gathering up Wyatt's things. She thought it odd since the radio seemed to be only playing ABBA songs. Wyatt had put a wallet with three thousand in cash in her top drawer along with his passport and some photographs. She tried to gather up things he would pack in a suitcase. The ship's bell and large picture would need to be sent later.

She washed up, threw on some clothes, and tidied up the house. She looked around sadly realizing that Wyatt would never be stepping foot in her house again. Any other keepsakes he might want? She took some of the pictures off the wall for him to have and just a few more items that could fit in her purse and waited for the phone to ring. About noon Wyatt called.

"Okay. We're all going to meet tonight at Eileen's for dinner. You and the Cousners. We're going to need to make some arrangements to help me disappear." He gave Sam Eileen's address.

She called Tom Cousner and told him the plan. Tom was very excited to be involved. "Do you want us to come by and pick you up, Sam?" asked Tom.

"No thanks," she said. "I'm going to take a couple of cabs and pretend I am going shopping and see if I can throw the police off. If I think they're still following me, I won't go ahead with plans to meet at Eileen's." After all this, she couldn't risk Wyatt getting caught.

✈ 27

The Exit

Sam knew she was being overly cautious. She must have taken four cabs that evening. She first went to the food market on Darling Street, bought some items, and slipped through the rear door heading to a local chemist. She caught another cab and went to Double Bay and shopped there. Finally, she got a cab driver to drop her off at the top of the street leading to Eileen's house in Paddington. She slipped behind bushes to see if any cars would pull up and when she thought it was safe, knocked on Eileen's back door.

Everyone was in the parlor of Eileen's prestigious home drinking and discussing the next steps for Wyatt's escape route. It had become obvious that if the C.I.B. were involved, the airports would be under scrutiny. There was no way he was leaving Friday with an airline ticket under Wyatt Stetson from Sydney or even Melbourne's Airports. There needed to be an alternate ticket, airport, and date of departure.

Eileen, of course, volunteered quickly to keep Wyatt under wraps until he figured out when and where he was going to exit. Ken warned her that the police might be heading to her house next.

"No, he won't be here. I have a perfect hideaway ranch far out in the Outback; no one will find him there."

Although this wasn't an ideal situation by her standards, Sam was relieved he had somewhere else to go and be safe. Eileen knew the police wouldn't be kicking her out of her own country. There was a break in the conversation as everyone got up and headed to the dining room. Wyatt waved for Sam to follow him to the back den where Eileen stored her music.

"This is how she and I first met," he said. "She came to my restaurant hearing I was from Texas. She introduced herself as having the largest country western collection in the Southern Hemisphere. Of course, I had to follow her back to her house to check out the music. Look at this," he pointed to shelves. There were countless original LPs of Waylon Jennings, Hank Williams, Hank Williams, Jr., Merle Haggard, George Strait, George Jones, among multiple others.

Now she understood why he had invited Eileen to attend the Willie Nelson Concert. However, Sam was wondering how far back this relationship had stretched into his relationship with Lacy. Was this one of the reasons Lacy left town? It is hard to compete with a rich beautiful woman whose power reaches into the soul of country music.

Sam was resigned to let things unfold as they would. She was back to her personal belief to let butterflies fly free. The Cousners arrived with the black garbage bag she threw over the balcony into her neighbor's backyard. Wyatt pulled out the contents. A couple of pairs of jeans, his boots, his shirts, his cowboy hat, some toiletries. She handed him the billfold with his money, his airline ticket, and passport.

"Thanks, Sam, this is great. I can't thank everyone enough for coming to my rescue right now. I knew I pissed off a few people by not paying my bills, but their arms seem pretty long right now. I couldn't have survived this without your help."

All of a sudden Tom Cousner stepped over to Wyatt. "Here," handing him a brown paper bag.

"What's this?" asked Wyatt.

"Open it," said Tom.

Wyatt opened the bag and took out Tom's passport. "What!" he said.

"Just in case it is too hot to get out under your own passport, you can use mine," suggested Tom.

They all looked from Wyatt to Tom thinking they didn't even look alike. However, when you looked at the photos on each separate passport, they all agreed he might just get away with it.

Someone said, "Yeah, but if they decide it isn't him and trace it back to you . . . then what?"

"Then I'll just say someone must have stolen my passport at one of my parties." Tom was definitely the hero of this night. What a gift for a friend. It was one not to be forgotten.

They agreed that Sam should return the airline ticket and get a refund from the travel agent. Folks began planning a good exit strategy for Wyatt. The conversation went everywhere including the proposed suspicion about who turned Wyatt's location in to the police. Lacy's name came up more than once and Wyatt believed that it could only have been her. She hadn't come to his send-off party, and, after all, she was a woman scorned.

Sam found herself defending her. "Lacy wouldn't do that," she said.

"Don't be so sure, Sam. If you recall only a year ago, she wanted to use you to press charges against me and send me to jail. She'd love to see me behind bars and maybe even you too. Just saying," said Wyatt.

No one tried to contradict the accusation. Sam was beginning to feel uncomfortable. She would never believe she'd do such a thing. Eileen wouldn't disclose the location she was taking Wyatt to but felt he would be safe there for perhaps a month. Everyone in the room swore that they would only share that he was staying with friends but would not mention who.

Friends would report to Wyatt which location would be best to fly out of. Darwin was one possible location as well as Brisbane.

"Look, Wyatt, whatever you do, please don't wear your cowboy hat on the plane. Just pack it in your bag," Sam pleaded.

"No," he said stubbornly. "I'm definitely wearing the cowboy hat out. Fuck those bastards."

It was getting late and Sam needed to get back. She *had* to go to work tomorrow.

Tom and Karee asked if they could drive her back to Balmain.

"Ta, I'll take you up on that, but I'm going to ask you to drop me off on the top of Darling Street. I'll walk back to Gladstone Street. If there is a police car still observing the house, I want it to look like a cab had dropped me off at the corner."

Sam went up to Eileen first and said thanks. "Please take good care of him."

Then she turned to Wyatt. "I fear this may be the last time I'll ever see you."

"No, Sam, this is not the last time. We have a lifetime ahead of us," he said assuredly. Wyatt wasn't big on reassurances, but his words comforted her somehow.

"I know communication isn't a big thing in your life, but please promise me you'll stay in touch," she pleaded. "I'll die wondering whether you're safe and where you are."

He promised he would and she left the front door of Eileen's house wondering if this was the end.

During the weeks ahead, Lyndsey and others wanted to know about Wyatt. Sam just said she thought he was laying low with friends.

One Saturday, Lyndsey came over for a Happy Hour drink. "Lacy believes everyone thinks she turned in Wyatt." Sam wondered if the Cousners had shared the group's suspicions to Lacy.

"Well, what do you think?" Sam asked inquisitively. Lyndsey seemed to ponder.

"Maybe, I don't know," she said, "If she did, she isn't bragging about it. In fact, she's downright nervous that Wyatt *may* think she did."

"Well, I can't believe she would do it myself, if that's any consolation. I'm a hopeless romantic and feel there is honor among thieves."

"Really," she said, "After all this, you feel she wouldn't do it?"

"I personally *choose* to believe she wouldn't do it," Sam explained. "You know we all have a sense of Irish Catholic guilt in our lives. How do people live with themselves when they put a friend behind bars for twenty years? It is one thing to teach someone a lesson for home invasion with a night in jail, but condemning someone to a felony and ruining their entire life . . . ?"

"Maybe someday we'll know the whole truth," Lyndsey said. "But I have to tell you about a funny incident that happened a few nights ago at Campbell Street."

Sam was glad the topic had changed from Wyatt. She was getting more depressed by the moment. It was two weeks since she left Wyatt with Eileen and hadn't heard a thing. She had returned the ticket to the agent and gave the money to Eileen to take to Wyatt. But there was no word on his safety or exit plan. She convinced herself that her life lesson here was to learn patience. Lyndsey lit up a smoke and poured herself a shot. "Let's go outside to the deck."

A week later, Eileen called on Sam's home phone. "Wyatt is leaving next week. Don't say anything to anyone. He asked me to contact you. He will call you when he's safe."

Before the week was out Wyatt called. "Howdy." he snorted with laughter.

"Where are you?" Sam asked.

"Fiji. I've been catching up with some old friends."

"How was the flight," she asked. "Any problem at the airport?"

"Nope, not a thing. I walked up, had my cowboy hat on, and used my own passport. They just processed me through. Piece of cake."

"God, you are a lucky man," she said. "What are your plans now?"

"I'll head to Los Angeles in a week and then onto San Antonio to my mom's house for the holidays. From there, I'm going to try to figure out the rest. Listen, Sam, just remember I love you. I don't communicate much, but I'll write you when I get situated and know what I'm doing."

"Promise?"

28

The Dearly Departed

It was the end of October and close to Halloween. Patty and Holly begged Sam to attend a fancy-dress party with them. The theme was to look like flower children of the sixties. It was a bit like old times. The Canadians were also getting saddened by the fact that their year was quickly coming to an end.

Patty announced that her mum and Aunt Ellen were coming to Sydney and asked if they could stay at the house.

"Of course," Sam said. "I can't guarantee it'll be as exciting as when your uncle and sister stayed with us though. Life is pretty dull now that Wyatt has gone back to the States."

Patty's mum was adorable and all the conversations between them were about her boy, Brad. After a few stories, Aunt Ellen took Sam aside.

"I hope this isn't making you too uncomfortable, dear," she said. "My sister has had the best year of her life having Brad living with her on the farm."

"No, it's not a problem. We all love Brad."

One evening Cassie had the group for dinner at her house on Mort Street. They all made a plan to take turns touring the old girls around Sydney. They went to school with them and they took trains into the city to walk around. Patty broke the news to Sam that everyone was going to pile in Cassie's car and head up to Brad's family property in Maitland the last weekend. Sam knew she'd be staying behind. The news was out that she had broken Brad's heart.

Sam was somewhat heartbroken herself that she couldn't join them, but she knew the need for Patty's mum to meet Brad's mum. She was dying to see their faces when they met and hear the conversations of the two white-haired ladies. She was missing it all.

It was over a month and Sam hadn't heard a word from Wyatt. He had warned her he wasn't a writer or for that matter even a good communicator, but her insecurities were surfacing.

On Saturday, the pair were leaving, and they took a picture of all of them lined up behind Sam's Corolla as they loaded up the boot with Aunt Ellen and Patty's mum's bags. Toby sensed the heaviness in the air and went over to the last bag and sat on it in protest. *That dog must be half human.*

The week before Christmas, Cassie and Sam drove Patty and Holly to the airport. There was hugging and crying and promises that they would see each other again. Then Cassie dropped Sam off at her quiet, empty house.

Time passed. Sam continued her three jobs knowing she was going to need money for Brad and perhaps for getting ready to sustain a stay in the States. During the holidays, Wyatt called from San Antonio, Texas. He was at his mother's house. He had Sam talk with his mom for the first time. She had a sweet Texas drawl and said, "Wyatt has told me all about your plans. I just can't wait to meet you." They had the nicest conversation and it helped Sam feel connected.

Wyatt said he had been to Ruidoso and was working on putting a deal together to open a small restaurant there. Sam asked if he had seen his dad since his return. He just said, "Nope." She told him the earliest she could come would be the end of June. She needed to apply for a leave with the New South Wales Government and it usually took six months to process. If things went wrong in the States, she needed to know she still had a job. She would get the paperwork done and put the house up for rent and join him in El Paso when she was able to secure a date to fly. Again, she made him promise to write.

A fortnight before school was back in session, Sam asked for a meeting with Miss. Find requesting a transfer knowing things would be uncomfortable for everyone at the school when Brad returned. Miss. Find found Sam a third-grade position in Leichardt. She was counting the months, weeks, and days, until her flight to Los Angeles. She stayed low key and busy with work.

The next Saturday there was a knock on the front door. It was Brad. She knew better than to ask what he was doing there. "Come on in. Would you like me to warm up one of my spinach pies? I'll put on the kettle for tea. It is *so* good to see you. You look great," she said. She truly missed him. She heated the pie and asked him about his house on Carrington Street. "How are the renovations going? Have you met people in the neighborhood?"

"Good enough," he said. They made small talk about glitches in plans and approvals. The conversation was so familiar it was like a year and half had never passed. They were eating pie and talking about renovation problems like they did every Saturday before he left. Then Sam shifted the conversation to school.

"It isn't the same without you there," he said. "I miss you teaching in the same room with me and piling me high with your 'contract system' to grade every weekend. I miss it all," he said. His eyes looked up as he began to explore the beams he had put in, the boards on the walls, the jars and dishes lining the floating shelves above the Kookaburra stove.

He dropped the fork on the remainder of the pie, lowered his head and began to sob. Sam's heart seemed to break. She had only seen him cry once, when their dog Fritz had died. Instinctively she ran over from the opposite side of the counter and gently put her arms around him. *I was hoping he wouldn't push me away again.* "Brad, don't cry," she said as she rocked him in her arms.

"I still love you *so* much, Sam. I just don't know what to do," Brad uttered.

"Well, I still love and miss you too, more than you know. I've always loved you from the day I started working at that school," she sobbed. He had her crying, too. He turned her around and was kissing her furiously.

"What are we going to do about this bloody situation?" he questioned in desperation. "I'll leave here and go back home to an empty half renovated house. I just want to be sick."

"Well, you probably already know from Miss. Find that I've applied for a leave at the end of June. I need to head to the States and figure this all out. I love you both differently. I don't know what to do about anything. I'm frozen with indecision. I feel like I can't breathe."

"Well, can I ask you if you ever heard from him?"

"I received a call around Christmas, and he was going to contact me when he had an address where he hoped to start another business."

"That's it? He doesn't write you every other week like I did?" he said sarcastically.

"He told me he wasn't much of a writer," Sam replied. "I know this is not much to pin one's heart on. I'm just moving forward, it's what I do." She was sitting on the stool next to him realizing how pathetic she looked and sounded.

He turned to her slowly. "Okay, I'm going to make a suggestion here. You don't even know if he has moved in with another girl or not, right?" he questioned. She shook her head. "And we both know him. He must be with someone. We're both sitting here with two shattered lives in two lonely houses. Oh, and by the way, we *still* love each other. Isn't that worth exploring before you take that plane ride to visit your American Hero?"

"Please don't call him my American Hero," she begged. "We both know that is definitely not what he is."

"Well, would you mind if I spend the night? We could just snuggle and we'll see how that goes. If we both feel good about it in the morning, maybe I can move some things over. I know all my bloody weapons and uniforms are still here."

Sam nodded. "You know, I'd like that, actually," she said without any further discussion. They were together again and she was the happiest she had been in months.

29

Pandora's Box

Her road was paved and the tickets bought. She could always alter things if she changed her mind. Brad and Sam tried not to talk much about the new elephant in the room. She was secretly torn and not trying to think much about her decision to leave.

She continued to work three jobs. The Honest Irishman Pub was one of the nicest pubs for a barmaid, however, the management changed and she was forced to find another situation. It wasn't long before she found new employment in a tavern in Redfern. She was given the lounge in the back of the pub to manage. The new crowd wasn't the cozy neighborhood couples she had come to know in her previous employment. A group of Middle Eastern men seemed to call it their territory. Instead of coming up to the bar for a pint, they demanded that she come to the table and wait on them. Sam waited on those at the bar first which angered them. They called her names like you bloody sheila, filthy Yank, and other lewder descriptions.

Sam complained to Brad about the crass remarks when she came home one night.

"Bloody well quit."

"I need this job," she said annoyed.

"You don't *need* it that much."

"Well, I want to keep paying you for the house while you're renovating," she argued, knowing that it was a sore topic and not one open for discussion.

"S'truth, Rothbauer, there are plenty of other jobs in this city."

"Not *this* week," she argued back. It wasn't that easy finding a new job while working three jobs.

By the time she returned home the next evening, she had to agree with him. She was going to have to get other employment. The Middle Eastern men were getting more abusive. She had to go in Thursday and Friday but told the manager she needed to find something closer to home. Brad sighed with relief.

"I do have a favor to ask though. One of them put his hand on my arse (ass) tonight while I served his table," I told the manager.

"So, what's the favor?" he asked.

"I expect my last two nights are going to be bloody hell."

"The manager will have your back, right," he suggested knowing that she was probably requesting his presence in some capacity.

"He might check in periodically, but I guarantee he's not going to ask these hoods to leave," she sighed. The tone of the last two nights had her feeling ill.

"So what do you want *me* to do?" he questioned. "Just remember, I'm not your American Hero type. I'm not going to walk in there, guns blazing, and have it out with them. Isn't that what Texans do," he challenged.

Sam balked. "I'm not asking you to come in with guns drawn. I just think that if they knew I had some kind of man in my life, they'd back off."

"Well, I can't Thursday night. I have a planned meeting with some friends."

"Okay, then," she said. "Could I suggest that Friday you come in around 9:30? The Pub's lounge closes at ten p.m. I'll treat you to a beer. You can watch me close out and walk me to my car. Easy . . . okay?"

He thought for a long moment. "Okay." he said at last.

Sam wondered what he would do if they were married? This was not his comfort zone. He would fight the enemy in the battlefield but not the locals in the pubs of Sydney.

Thursday night things got worse at the pub. It was ten minutes to closing and Sam announced last call. When no one answered, she closed the till out. One of the drunken fools came up to the bar right after ten p.m. and demanded another beer. Sam argued with him that the till was closed out and suggested he try for one more in the Public Bar. She turned to put the money in the bag and he threw a full ashtray at her back. It hit her and it smashed to the floor with all its messy cigarette butts flying all over. Sam quickly picked up the money bag and moved to the back room to count the cash which was her job for closing each night. She was sick to her stomach. Gary, the manager, came in. He could see Sam was distraught. He went back to the lounge to confront the mob but the group of four had gone.

"Listen, Gary, my boyfriend, Brad, will be coming at the end of my shift tomorrow night but could you walk me to my car tonight as a special favor?"

"Where's your car?" he asked.

"Just across the street. Those jerks have it out for me. If you want to know, this is the real reason for my leaving," she muttered.

"Sure, Sam, I understand. I'll get someone to cover the front bar. I'll be right back," he said.

She let out a long sigh of relief. She debated whether to tell Brad anything when she got home. She decided he needed to know what he was walking into.

"Okay, I'm going to ask Val to join me," he suggested. "He lives close by. It'll be like two mates having a schooner together after work. We'll get there about 8:00 and sit at the bar with you. How does that sound? This way if the four of them want to take us on, we can handle it while you call the police."

"Are the two of you planning to wear your Commando uniforms?" Sam asked sarcastically.

"No, just rolling up our sleeves," he laughed.

"Okay," she said. "It would be fun to see Val again and I'm sure these idiots wouldn't mess with two men chatting with me during my shift."

Brad walked in first. Within twenty minutes, so did Val. They laughed together and the team of four left early. It ended well but it caused her to wonder how Wyatt would have handled it. It's really not fair to compare the response of the two of them, she thought. This was Wyatt's wheelhouse, wasn't it, dealing with drunken idiots, while Brad's was dealing with kids.

As she looked for another job, Sam spent more time working hours in Kings Cross at the Health Food Restaurant run by Jasmin and her boyfriend. Jasmin was a prostitute who disguised her finances with her wonderful culinary skills in her little health food shop. All the ladies of the night came through each night for their smoothies before they headed for the streets. One Friday evening, when Brad was heading for a Commando weekend, Jasmin said she was having some friends over for tea at her flat and asked Sam to join them.

Sam was more than curious about her life. She drove her car to a two-story Victorian house in a neighborhood nestled with enormous trees. She walked upstairs into a room that was centered with a long low table surrounded by well-dressed women sitting on pillows on the floor. The flat had Jasmin's taste. Handmade New Zealand lace accented by Indonesian batiks. She said hello to Jasmin and nodded to the girls. She walked over to sit on the floor next to a very attractive brunette who was professionally dressed. She was about thirty years old. Sam wondered how they all knew Jasmin.

"Hi, I'm Nancy," she said cheerfully. "You?"

"I'm Sam. I run Jasmin's Health Food Restaurant several nights a week."

"Well, I manage the events at the Sydney Opera House."

"Really," Sam said. "What's that like?"

"Well, it is not just a very interesting job, but it gives me access to many interesting clients."

"What do you mean, clients," Sam asked rather surprised.

"You know 'Johns,' regular clients," she laughed.

"So, I'm curious. If you have such a good job working at the Opera House, why would you need to seek paying customers for sex?" Sam asked perplexed.

She looked at her curiously, "Well, what else do *you* do for money, Sam?" she asked. "I'm sure you don't just run a health food restaurant."

"No, you're right, I teach school."

"And . . . is that all?" she asked.

"No, I also tend bar in various establishments."

"Well," she laughed, "I believe you are the only woman at this table who doesn't have a John."

"Really?" Sam said, looking around at the twenty or so beautiful women sitting around the table.

Once again, she commented out loud, "I wonder why she invited *me* here."

Nancy replied, "Well, you are a very attractive girl, Sam. You are easily sitting on a grand a week, my friend. Maybe she feels you might be tempted to stockpile some money away like the rest of us and buy up some expensive real estate in this town."

"I already own a house, thanks."

"Well, pay it off and enjoy yourself while you are doing it," she suggested.

"Do you really *enjoy* that kind of work?" Sam asked.

"Oh, yeah." she said. "This is the most profitable way to live out your fantasies."

"If you don't mind me asking, what kind of fantasies?" Sam probed.

"You know, adventures with men, adventures with women. The truth is this is a familiar Meet-Up group. We usually call on each other to work up fantasy groups."

Sam was not one for passing judgement on people. She didn't really care what people did as long as they were nice people. Jasmin was a nice red-headed flower child from New Zealand who enjoyed walking on the wild side. Nancy seemed friendly, honest, and classy. She often found herself in colorful situations due to her lack of discrimination.

"What are you thinking?" she asked politely.

Sam shook her head. "I'm thinking I'm at the wrong table," she said. "No offense, but this kind of work would cause me to self-destruct. Nothing against you gals, but I'm not wired that way. Wouldn't life be much simpler if I were? Could you let Jasmin know I needed to leave?" she said. "It was a pleasure meeting you, Nancy."

Sam continued at the health food restaurant and found another situation several afternoons and Saturday mornings working for a high-end butcher in North Sydney. She received her first and only letter from Wyatt when Jasmin walked into her shop one afternoon. Sam asked Jasmin if she could share it with her. *She was craving some feedback.*

It was a simple one-page letter. Wyatt started the letter with the announcement that he would begin each letter with Dear Honey from now on, instead of Dear Sam. It wasn't much, but it somehow echoed a sincerity and a continuation of commitment to their plan to meet at the end of June. He said he had settled in Ruidoso and was starting a restaurant named 'Diablos' with a partner named John.

Sam was happy to know he still waited for her, but he suggested he was going to be very busy and not to expect another letter. He gave her a number to call when she got to the States. Jasmin smiled. "I truly believe he loves you, Sam. I've always seen you two connected. I know love can be confusing," she stated. "But really it is quite simple, just follow your heart." *Sure, easy for her to say. My heart was split in two directions.*

Sam loved two men and her heart kept telling her to keep to the plan. The biggest regret she would have in life was to just play it safe. She hoped the passion she had with Wyatt might have disappeared by now, but it hadn't. It still controlled the compass in her brain. She needed to figure her life out on another continent. The odds were that Wyatt would never go through with getting married, but she would never know if she didn't go the distance. When she got home from work, Brad made an announcement.

"After you leave, I'm going to quit Commandos."

"What . . . why?"

"Because it's time," he said. "I played at it long enough. Time to get into other things."

"Like what?"

"I don't know yet," he said. "But I might just buy a boat and take up sailing." This was *bait* for Sam. She always wanted to be a better sailor and he knew it. It would be something they could explore together.

"Perhaps if you return, we could explore building that place we wanted on a lake or on the coast north of Maitland." Brad was smart. He was setting images in Sam's head to hook onto. She didn't know how to respond.

"Brad," she said. "You know I don't know what to say or how to feel right now. What we have now is beautiful and comfortable, but I couldn't go through life wondering whether I made the right decision and neither could you. I have to go and figure this out. I hope and pray you can understand. I know this is craziness and none of this has been fair to you."

"I understand the logic, but I'll never understand the decision," he said.

They began having dinners again with Rachael and Bob, the neighbors next door. It was beginning to feel like old times—*the story of US.* They decided to have all of them over for a large family-styled Easter dinner. They also invited Val and his girlfriend.

It was a beautiful day which led to a beautiful evening. Sam took Rachael aside while doing dishes and asked if she could take Toby when she left.

"Why not let Brad take him," she suggested.

"I've already mentioned it to him. It's a poor subject. I just want Toby to have a good home."

"Well, honestly, Sam, Bob and I really don't want any pets. But if you're hard up for a home, we'll take him and promise you we'll find someone who will truly enjoy him."

"Thanks, Rachael, you've always been such a good friend."

"Are you sure you really want to leave, Sam?" she asked. "You and Brad seemed to be back where you were before he left."

"I'm not sure of anything. All I know is I can't commit to anything until I get some questions off my plate. Wyatt wrote me and left a number for me to call him at his new restaurant in a town called Ruidoso, New Mexico."

"Ruidoso . . . really? I know that mountain town. Bob and I visited there one weekend during our honeymoon that went around the world. It's absolutely beautiful."

At least I wasn't headed for a dust bowl filled with rattlesnakes.

"No, without a doubt it's a memorable place. Beautiful snow-capped mountains, Aspen trees. I think the name means noisy river. It even has an Apache Indian reservation close by if I remember correctly."

"Thank you, Rachael. I need to take the leap. It'll probably lead nowhere but the journey will be worth the time and maybe I'll experience something beautiful along the way."

"I get it. We'll always love you no matter what," the two girls hugged. The clock ticked and the time got closer to June. Brad and Sam had been here before. Brad was slowly beginning to move his belongings back to Carrington Street. She reminded him, "Not long ago *you* were leaving. This time it's me."

"Right, I was leaving to go live with somebody's mother and you're leaving to go live with the man of your dreams." He paused.

"Sorry, bad analogy. I'm not betting on the outcome of any of this. We know how he is. I so appreciate your simple tenacity and persistence. It speaks volumes to me and I'll always love you, no matter what."

The month of May was filled with packing, selling off furnishings, and renting the house. The last Saturday, Sam hosted a garage sale. A young couple wandered in and purchased almost everything and offered $50 for Toby. "Toby is a dog who knows what he wants. He found you just like he found me. He is not for sale. He's yours if you want him."

They pulled up with their truck and carted away most of Sam's belongings including the dog, his dishes, food, and leash. It was a sign. Whatever was happening here had a destination of its own. It saddened her that she didn't get to have one final night of cuddling up with Toby.

Brad and Sam made it through the next few weeks. They brought up nothing and enjoyed their last moments together. She planned to take a taxi to the airport but Brad insisted that he'd drive her. He knew she was heading to visit her family first. "If it's not too much trouble could you let me know when you arrive in New Jersey."

"Of course," said Sam turning her eyes downward.

He handed her a sealed envelope, "Don't open this till you get to the States, just a few last minute thoughts."

"I don't know what more to say. You know I'm trying to move on from all this by moving forward somehow." *If I were to bet money on Wyatt right now, I would probably lose.*

"We both know Wyatt. He isn't predictable which should make any decision to stay or leave much easier." She stopped herself from saying more. She was afraid she was saying too much. She didn't want to cause more damage by making any suggested promises.

"Well, in that card are hand-drawn directions on how to find your way home," said Brad. They were standing by the window watching as a Qantas 747 pulled into a hangar.

"Wow, that's the 747 I took to England," he said pointing at one of the aircraft.

She turned and looked, "How did you know that was the exact one? No . . . wait, I know, you memorized the serial number of the aircraft, didn't you?"

He nodded.

"You are an amazing man, Brad Smith."

They hugged a long lingering hug. They kissed longingly and finally said goodbye.

As Sam boarded the aircraft, they were playing the new song by Men At Work, "Down Under." Sam laughed and thought she'd share it with Wyatt when she saw him. He'd enjoy it. She placed Brad's letter slowly in her pocket. She realized instantly that her destiny was either in her pocket or on another continent. Like the game of Two Up she was tossing destiny in the air and letting it fall where it may.

As she took her seat by the window, she began to question herself . . . *why am I doing this? Is it because I'm stubborn and can only allow myself to move forward and never look back? Was this all-consuming passion going to lead me anywhere? Would any of Wyatt's words really become our future? And . . . if they didn't, would I ever be able to face Brad again . . . would his actions speak to taking me back?* It was all so muddled and complicated with no assurances.

Yet, she knew that her destiny lay somewhere in the near future on the other side of the aircraft door.

✈ 30

The Reunion–September 2017

It was the third day of the reunion. Sam and the girls awoke to another warm day with autumn-like undertones. The leaves were beginning to change and the temperatures on the late September morning called for a sweatshirt. Sam took off for a brisk morning walk before the other girls got up. She walked up and down roads that said Line 1 and Line 2. Patty told her this was Brad's walk. She thought of him constantly knowing he was arriving sometime that evening.

After Patty brought her to her beautiful sunny bedroom with its white iron bed, she shared with Sam that Brad would be assigned to the room directly across from her. She wondered what had gone through her mind when she made that decision. Holly obviously picked the upstairs bedroom closest to the bathroom and Cassie, who was booked for an extended stay, chose the downstairs master bedroom.

After the walk, the girls decided to spend the day visiting a donkey rescue farm. The docent even mentioned Ruidoso, New Mexico, the mountain town where Wyatt and Sam first settled and where their two boys were born. It was a famous place for mule races, but more importantly hosted the World's Richest Quarter Horse Race.

They returned to the farmhouse in the late afternoon and Sam begged Patty to take them for a walk down to the lake. It was stunning with the light filtering through the leaves.

Again, no one spoke of Brad or even mentioned he was arriving someime that evening.

It was late by the time they returned to the farmhouse after an evening dining out at a local inn. Sam pulled Patty aside before she returned to Guelph. Earlier that day, Sam called Air Canada to confirm her return e-ticket for Sunday morning and they were unable to bring up her confirmation number. "Good thing I checked," said Sam.

"Would it be okay if you came by and collected me before you headed to the airport to pick up Brad? I'm worried that something is dreadfully wrong. If you don't want me to be staying for at least another week, I better get to the airport and fix this problem."

"It's no problem," Patty said. "I just received a text from Brad. He got in safely and will be waiting for me in the hotel lobby around 9:30 in the morning."

Old memories began to flood Sam's mind going over the old photos once again. Memories she wouldn't even allow herself to remember all these years. Everyone was aware of the magnitude of this reunion. She hadn't spent any time in Brad's presence in thirty-six years. He was aware that she had spent most of those years as a single mom and educator through Christmas notes from Patty. She knew he spent most of his as a happily married man with two daughters.

Sam was always the last to go to bed. She pulled the covers over her and laid still in the calm quiet of the friendly room she had claimed as hers for the past few evenings. Tomorrow, Brad might be sleeping in the room across from her. How would that feel? *Close but so far away.* No matter what, she had no intention of allowing anything bad to happen to his life again. She carried a lot of guilt around with her for way too many years. She had once read a sign in a small village in Europe. The author was unknown. It said, *"Don't cling to a mistake just because you spent a lot of time making it."*

She finally fell asleep anxiously anticipating the next day. It would be the real start to the long-awaited reunion. She moved herself into the middle of the bed and cuddled up to the second pillow pretending she was back in Brad's arms. She always loved how they cuddled and slept together.

Leaving promptly at seven, Sam and Patty traveled toward the airport. She was a stickler for being on time. It was their first chance to be alone since the reunion began. They talked casually about their last visit together.

They got to the hotel area that surrounded the airport. It was precisely 9:30. They were on time but the strip of road they were on was ravaged by construction. They pulled into several side roads.

"According to the GPS, we're close. Let's pull into this parking spot." Suddenly, Patty yelled, "Yea, this is the hotel." Sam got out walking anxiously around the back of the car. They got to the double doors leading into the hotel. Patty extended her arm blocking her way. "Listen," she said in a whisper, "Brad doesn't know you're here."

"What . . . !" Sam gasped in disbelief grabbing her chest. "You didn't tell him I was coming." Sam turned white. *What kind of reaction would she get?* "Should I go back and wait in the car?" She was beginning to shake.

"No, come with me, but let me say hello first. I just told him there *might* be a surprise."

She pushed open the double doors to the hotel lobby and followed a safe ten feet behind. Many people sat around with bags hoping to be picked up or discovered by someone. Patty walked up in front of a man who had his back to them. He had a baseball cap on and his nose was buried in a book. Patty slowly approached him from his right side and carefully placed herself squarely in front of him.

Sam stood ten feet behind the back of his chair feeling an eruption of butterflies in her gut. It took a moment for Brad to register that someone was directly across from him. Suddenly, he recognized Patty and jumped out of his seat dropping the book to the chair.

"Bloody hell, you could've given me a heart attack."

They hugged and Patty asked, "How was your flight?"

"Good, but long. I was able to read four books on the way over."

Patty slowly turned her gaze toward Sam not saying a word. This was it, the long awaited moment. Sam took a deep breath. Brad followed her gaze and noticed Sam. There was *NO* reaction.

"Do you know who this is?" Patty asked pointing at me.

He looked again deepening his gaze. *I'm only ten feet away.*

"My, I must have gotten old, he doesn't even recognize my face," Sam said.

"Yes, I do," he sounded annoyed. "What the bloody hell are *you* doing here?"

Shit, this isn't the reaction I hoped for. Karma, this was the same reaction I gave him thirty-six years ago when he came to the front door to propose. A knot developed in the middle of her stomach. He needed to create a mind shift, this wasn't the tour he signed up for.

Sam walked closer to him. "Well . . . I don't know how this whole event happened for you, but for me I got an e-mail from Patty about eight weeks ago when I was in Wales visiting friends. She said there was going to be a big reunion in Ontario at the farmhouse and was hoping I could make it. It was during my return trip back to the States when I decided that I would be back East around the same time for my sister's sixtieth birthday and the birth of my new grandson in Atlanta. I decided to take advantage of the opportunity to see everyone again. Life is just too short."

She took a deep breath and paused and looked up to see if he had any reaction to what she just said.

He looked at her and seemed to accept the explanation. "You know my wife predicted that you might be the surprise. I actually dismissed the entire thought myself." He gathered his things and moved to the left side of the car.

Sam smiled and said, "You ride shotgun."

Brad moved automatically to the wrong side of the car.

"It's the front seat and you need to walk to the other side of the car," Sam said pointing.

He chuckled, "I always forget that it's the other side of the car. By the way, when are you leaving?" he asked.

"Sunday morning, that is, if I can verify that I have a ticket. Air Canada can't find the one I reserved four weeks ago. We're heading over to the airport to see if I can straighten this out."

Patty dropped Sam in front of the airport door and said they would move a little farther up to wait for her. Fifteen minutes later Sam returned with bad news.

"Sorry, Patty, I need to get on my mobile and see if I can arrange a reservation on another airline. Is there any place that has internet?" Patty's farmhouse was not set up for the twenty-first century.

"We can drive into Guelph. I know a small coffee shop that might have internet. We'll go check it out, eh. This way I can give Brad a tour and revisit his old haunts."

Sam bought a large venti coffee and began the tedious work of downloading flights. She found a few that could work. Brad and Patty walked into the shop as she finished up.

"Were you able to make any progress?" Brad asked.

"Yeah, I think so. I just got off the phone with United Airlines. I believe I have one for Sunday around 11:00 in the morning. It will get me into San Diego around eight p.m. with a three-hour layover in Houston. At least it's in my price range."

"We're going to get a coffee," Patty said, "Do you want another one?"

"No, I still have a little in my cup. Any more than that and I'll be up all night."

Brad walked to the clerk and said in his distinctive Australian accent, "Do you have any white coffee, mate?"

That's an odd request. He always wanted her to drink coffee black when they lived together. Both Patty and Brad grabbed their cups and they walked outside to a sunny table.

"So how is Guelph," Sam asked. "Is it the same as you remember?"

"Pretty much," he commented. "I saw just a few things that were different."

The ride back to the farmhouse was filled with tiny conversations between Patty and Brad about the local people and teachers that he knew. Sam just listened to understand better what Brad had been looking forward to doing during his stay at the farmhouse.

Through the dialog, she learned that ten years ago, Brad brought his wife and their two daughters to Ontario. As they approached the farmhouse, there was a lull in the conversation.

"So, how mischievous do you feel like being this afternoon?" Sam asked. It was a great leading question.

There was a pause. "Well, it depends on what you're suggesting."

"Well, Holly says she needs to leave today right after lunch. Her brother is expecting her to return to care for their mother. I thought you might be able to disconnect her battery cable so that her car wouldn't start. This way, she'd have to call her brother and delay going home until the car gets fixed sometime tomorrow," she said smiling.

"I know how to disconnect it, if that's what you're suggesting, but maybe we need to be sure this is what Holly wants first."

"Yeah . . . I agree."

They pulled up in the driveway. The girls ran out of the farmhouse and gathered around Brad with hugs and kisses, asking how his flight was. They walked in with his gear and saw the table set for lunch. The large tea pot brewed its Earl Grey.

Brad playfully set his gear down and turned to Patty.

"Can I take my gear up to *MY* bedroom?" He obviously meant the room he had occupied the year of 1981. Patty turned to Sam who had absolutely *no* idea which of the four bedrooms had been his.

"Well, you could put them up in *your* room but there's no furniture in it."

"What," Brad shouted aghast. "No furniture, where did it bloody well go?"

"My niece needed a bedroom set, and that was the set she chose. We didn't have time to move other furniture around upstairs when we were getting ready for this reunion," replied Patty.

A look of disappointment came over his face, but he realized quickly that if that was the biggest disappointment he would have, it would still be an amazing trip.

"Okay, I'll just put it upstairs and you can point me to a room later."

Holly's suitcases were already packed by the front door. Sam took Holly aside and shared the magnificent plot she had come up with to keep her with them one more day.

"I *can't* Sam. I was lucky I got four days off from caring for my mother. If I ever need my brother to help again, he may refuse me because I pushed this one."

Sam realized she could not argue the case any further. She resigned herself to having just this one special moment of time to share with everyone together.

Cassie began asking how Brad's family was doing? He updated her on some recent events. They hadn't seen each other in a few months. However, Cassie owned a second home at the lake right down from Brad's family. They all spent a lot of time together but recently Cassie said she moved back to her house in Balmain. She mentioned that her friends were getting older and it was much easier to see them while residing closer to town.

They caught up with questions about family and then the conversation shifted to old times. A couple of light remembrances came from Patty and Holly. Then they began discussing the parties from the past.

Perhaps it was Brad's way to include her in the conversation but he turned to everyone.

"I can recall episodes of me holding Sam's head over the sink when she got sick."

"Episodes . . . ?" Sam questioned gazing over at him. "I only recall one." *Actually, I could recall two times, once Wyatt had to hold my hair back as well.* She looked at him and thought, *so these are the colorful stories you shared with people after I left.* Everyone at the table knew her better than that. In fact, sitting in front of her were some of her biggest fans. Then he lit into the next brooding question that may have haunted him for the past thirty-six years.

"What really happened between you and my brother Eric while I was away at Commandos that weekend? How the bloody hell did we happen to have an explosion in our new kitchen?"

Sam began to wonder whether she would even survive their first lunch together. The ugly questions were flying out of his mouth right from the start. *I probably deserve all of this. After all, I did break his heart.*

Truth be Told

Brad's question was disarming and was met with a gaping silence from all of them. His brother had an excuse for his behavior that weekend. Brad had later shared that his younger brother had some medical issues.

"I told you the story as soon as you got back that Sunday," Sam said, searching his eyes.

"Well, I want to hear it again. How does a can of spaghetti explode on a stove?"

"Let's see, it was a Friday night. You left for Commandos and I was alone with Fritz. No one knew your brother was coming. I had only met him once before and I felt awkward about letting him in that evening and told him he just missed you."

"Eric pleaded with me to let him in because he was so tired from travelling," Sam continued. "I figured it would be okay to let him stay. I trusted myself enough to handle things." *Big mistake.*

Sam went on, "I guess Eric was self-medicating. It was hard to know in those days. It was the seventies and everybody under thirty was doing some sort of recreational drug, except for Brad." *It was one of the many reasons Sam was drawn to Brad. She loved that he grounded her.*

"Your brother made himself right at home. He was curled up on the sofa and had built a large fire in the hearth in the living room. The next thing I knew he had lit up a joint that looked like a cigar. Later in the day, Eric decided he had the munchies and asked if he could make himself something to eat. I told him to help himself."

"I didn't budge off the couch to supervise what he was doing. For some unknown reason, Eric found a tin of Chef Boyardee spaghetti in a cupboard instead of grabbing something from the fridge. He cut a hole in the top, Bush style, and placed it in a sauce pan of boiling water. Then Eric came back to the living room and began another discussion about world events. Within minutes, there was an enormous explosion in the kitchen," Sam said.

"Rachael and Bob ran over after hearing the explosion and helped us clean up the glutinous mess that hung from every rafter. I apologize," said Sam. "I should have supervised your brother better." *Sam had been extremely relieved when Brad's brother left. He made her feel uncomfortable.*

Sitting around the lunch table on the first day of their reunion, Sam was beginning to pick up on the theme that the lunch conversation was going to be centered around her past with Brad. Over the years, Brad had multiple reunions with the other three girls, but Sam hadn't seen Brad in thirty-six years. Sam was sure during some of those occasions he justified *millions* of reasons why he and Sam could have never worked as a married couple.

As they finished lunch, Brad looked at the girls and shared another story of Sam, much to her dismay.

"Oh, then there was the time when Sam lost her temper while we were renovating. I had pulled the tub up at the edge of the family room, which by the way was still in pretty good nick. All of a sudden Sam got mad and began kicking the tub." Everyone giggled.

Sam turned to Brad and looked at him incredulously, "How *long* have you told *that* story *that* way?"

"Why?" he asked.

"Well, did you ever tell the others the details as to *why* I was so upset and kicked the tub?" *Sam knew she had him over the rails now.*

"I don't bloody hell remember the reason. I don't remember half the reasons you did what you did back then," Brad retorted.

"Well, it was the day I was going to grout the entire 700-square foot family room and kitchen floor with this brown muddy muck. You went about showing me how to mix the grout and clean the tools between each back-breaking application. You watched me start, then you spent the day in the attic laying wire. Is this coming back to you yet?"

"Yeah, a little," he began to squirm. "Vaguely." The girls sat forward.

"Well, about six hours later I called up to you in the rafters and asked if you might be ready to break for lunch. You said you'd be down in a few minutes. I made our traditional lunch—roll-up of Lebanese flat bread, cut turkey, and mayonnaise. I smiled as you descended the spiral staircase, hoping you'd admire my hard work and see that I had finished it all."

Sam turned to the girls, "Mind you, this was the first time I had ever grouted anything." She turned back to Brad, "You got to the bottom of the steps and bent down to examine the floor and looked up annoyed. And then you said, 'Bloody hell, Rothbauer, what have you done?' I groaned in reply that I had just finished grouting two rooms of floor tiles in six hours. Then you said, 'This is bloody awful. You didn't put nearly enough grout between these tiles. You'll have to do the entire floor again.'" Sam paused for impact.

"My back was aching, and I went to the card table we set up to eat lunch on the verge of tears. We began to eat the sandwiches in rigid silence."

"I told him he should have come down and tried to look at my work before he decided it was so bloody awful. He just stared at his food saying I was a big girl and if I needed his approval I should have asked for it."

"*Now* I was really pissed. I got up from the table and began kicking the tub of muddy water. It seemed like a better idea than throwing over the table with the food."

"Well, he didn't leave it there," Sam said turning to the group. "He came over to the other side of the tub, put his hands into the water and scooped what would be close to a gallon of brown muddy water and threw it all over me from head to toe. The tub never fell off the edge, but the water sure did, all over me."

Sam turned to Brad sitting rather still at the table, "And do you remember what happened next?"

"I haven't a clue," he said. "This is *your* story now, but I kind of remember it didn't end there. It's coming back," he smiled.

"There was a knock at the front door. I remember us looking at each other, wondering what to do. I looked like a melted Easter Bunny and you were caught in the questionable act of retaliation on a woman. I remember you saying, 'Don't answer it, they'll go away.' And I said, 'No way, I'm answering it.'"

"It was Lyndsey. She stood at the door, looking at the perfect mess of me and saw you in the background. Softly she said, 'I'll come back later. I can see this isn't a good time.'

"I remember grabbing her by the collar and saying, 'No, this is a *great* time. Please come in. I'll heat up one of my spinach pies and make us all some tea. We're done for the day.'

"Whether Lyndsey knew it or not, she saved the day. Who knows where that day could have gone? But we were able to calm down and get over our bad selves as we explained the events of the day to Lyndsey."

Everyone at the table laughed. Holly spoke up first. "I know we heard this and other stories over the years, but it is always good to know there were two sides to every story, eh." We all agreed and laughed.

Everyone got up from the table and helped Patty clean up. After Holly faded down the road, they went back inside. Cassie and Patty suggested they take a ride into the little tourist town of Elmira. Brad was up for doing most anything that would get him to see the sights he had missed for ten years.

Brad and Sam began walking along shopping together. Cassie and Patty went on ahead on a quest to find a special beer opener. Brad did a superb job crafting an easy-going conversation that led them through a smooth journey for the next couple of hours.

Sam turned to him. "Do you mind shopping?" They had never really shared the experience except to buy her ring.

"I know Cassie can spend hours shopping. We did a lot of traveling together and I now live in a house with three women who drag me along all the time," stated Brad.

When they got back to the farmhouse, Brad grabbed his camera and headed to the side door. He turned toward Sam. "I'm going to go around the property and take some pictures. Care to join me?"

"Sure . . . " she said with a smile. She went back for a jacket and caught up to him.

"So, where is your other half?" he asked.

Sam naively turned around thinking he might be alluding to a boyfriend. "What other half?"

"No, the other half of you. In Australia you were twice the size you are now."

Brad knew Sam for a period of almost eight years in Sydney. In the first two years of teaching, Sam had gained two stone (28 pounds) and through the following five years worked hard to take it off.

"Remember the Israeli Army diets? You were on that bloody diet every other week." He began to rattle off the sequence almost to the tee.

"Well, I did take half of it off when I was living with you, but I finally figured out what my body wanted to digest more efficiently over the last thirty years. In truth, it continues to be a work in progress as my metabolism is continuously slowing down these days."

He smiled, "You look good. In fact, you look bloody great. I'm so happy you're here."

"I wasn't too sure about that, especially after I heard your first reaction to seeing me. I just wanted to melt away."

"No, I don't feel that way. I love the fact you're here to share time with us. I was just shocked at first."

They walked around the entire perimeter of the farmhouse sharing smiles. He was amazing at photography, always was. He was out there because the light was perfect. He took dozens of photos of the house. He talked about the winter he was at the farm as they walked down to the lake. He described how he would take a dip in the pond in the summer months. Thoughts flooded back to Sam about the time they saved a cow while boar hunting in New Angledool.

"Do you remember the calf that got stuck in a watering hole," she asked.

"Remember how you masterfully lassoed a noose around his neck and you hauled out the wailing calf by tying the rope to the roo bar of the Holden?"

There seemed to be nothing practical that he couldn't do or solve. *I wondered why he couldn't save us.* Sam couldn't get enough of his Canadian stories. She felt like she was peeking inside the box of the man who had vanished from her life in 1981.

Soon after dinner, Patty and her husband left to go back to their house, Cassie went to bed leaving Brad and Sam alone at the dining room table in the old farmhouse. People seemed to be giving them space to catch up. Sam was grateful for the opportunity for some sort of closure.

"I see you drink red wine now. Do you have any extra? That's what I drink too," said Brad.

Sam was shocked, "Seriously, *you* drink?" Not only did he drink, but now they were able to share a bottle of wine together. They spent the evening talking about drinking habits and years of absence. They didn't speak of Wyatt or Brad's wife but more about his two girls and her two boys. They shared pictures of family and pictures of boats. They discussed questions that lingered with him all these years.

"Do you still smoke weed," he asked glancing up from his glass of wine.

"No," Sam said screwing up her face. "Not at all. I became a mother soon after I married and then later a school principal. I don't know if you knew this, but I never bought *any* weed in my entire life. My only use, even then, was what my friends would offer me at a party. It wasn't my thing really; they were fresh out of college and I was just catching up."

He recreated images and impressions of Sam from the seventies when they were all trying to grow up. The hours flew by. Being educators, their conversation naturally wandered to school. They were both good at it and had been amazing partners, a bonafide team. They created *experiences* for kids. He shared that he now was currently involved with Career Technical Education.

"No way," she said in amazement. "I just spent the last two years coordinating our CTE pathway programs in San Diego."

They were always on the same wavelength with kids and Sam silently mourned not having children with him and sharing a lifetime raising their own. *All the experiences we could have created with them.*

"You know, I still have every one of the letters you wrote me while I was in Canada," he said looking up at her. They stared surprisingly into each other's eyes.

"And I still have every one of yours."

"Hmm," he said. "That says a lot."

They looked at the clock.

"Midnight, maybe we should retire. Patty wants to make sure you have the whole tour while you're here. She said something about a visit to Mennonite Country tomorrow. I'm pretty excited about that. I've never seen their lifestyle before," Sam said.

"You'll like it, I'm sure." He followed her up the steep creaky stairs to the second floor. They were the only ones sharing the four second floor rooms.

"Do you happen to know where I'm supposed to sleep? *"Should I say over here with me as a joke . . . no, better not."*

"I dropped my bags in the only room up here that doesn't seem to have a bed," Brad said.

"Patty made up the room across from mine for you a day ago, but Holly occupied the one next to the bathroom down the hall and I *think* she may have changed the sheets."

Sam wanted Brad to know he had options. He didn't need to feel uncomfortable taking the room directly across from hers.

"Good, I'll take the one Patty made up for me." He placed his two little bags on the floor of his room. "What time are you getting up in the morning?" he asked.

"I'm still getting up when the sun rises. I've been trying to take walks each morning. Patty told me I should go on Brad's walk, but not knowing where you walked, I've been wandering around on different roads."

"That's easy. If you like, we'll do one of *my* walks first thing in the morning. Do you want to meet downstairs at seven?" he asked.

"Sure, that'll work. Patty said she'll pick us up at ten."

Sam snuggled up to her pillow dreaming of all the perfect moments they shared that day. *Oh, don't let this end.*

✈ 32

Through His Eyes

The next morning, like the day before, there was a cool nip in the morning air. Some of the towering canopy trees were turning color. Brad was already at the back door waiting for Sam wearing Nike running gear and white sneakers. She had on black tights, a long sleeve shirt and a pair of comfortable dock shoes.

They walked up the long driveway to the mailbox and made a left down Line 1. He pointed to the mailbox and described running for the letters in the snow each day, hoping to find letters from her early in 1981. They sauntered along kicking rocks and making light conversation. After a mile, they made another left turn and began the long stretch to the right of Patty's farmhouse property. Brad turned and instantly asked, "I have just *one burning* question. Why . . . oh, why, did you sell the house?"

Sam stared back at him. "Believe me, I *never ever* wanted to sell that house. It was out of sheer repetitive harassment that I felt I had to. Wyatt saw it as accessible money for him to tap into to support other businesses that he wanted to start. He wanted me to take loans out against it. I told him that it was my retirement money comparing it to his undivided trust left to him by his family, but he didn't see it that way. He kept saying if *my* house was going to be an issue, we could end the marriage immediately.

He was a bully. By then we already had our first baby. It got ugly, the bullying continued, and finally I said that I'd only sell the house to finance a home we could build for our family to live in New Mexico.

"Wyatt put together a bad deal with a suspect builder. Nobody was overseeing how this builder was doing business. At the same time what also happened was the oil crises of the mid-eighties in West Texas. To make a long story short, all the Savings and Loans in the area failed which my mortgage was tied to and my loan was considered a bad loan. (Mainly because the builder had used my money to complete another house and had liens on all the building material for ours.) No banks would pick it up. Within three short years, I lost everything, not to mention our marriage was failing from the start. I believed I was well and truly *cursed*.

"Thinking back, I wish you and I could have kept the title in both our names, then I wouldn't have been able to sell without your permission. Hindsight, spilled milk," she said.

There was a long silence.

"It took me twenty years of agonizing anger to get over you selling that house. My wife kept telling me that I needed to forget the past."

"Well, I would have advised you the same way if the tables were turned. Did you finally put it behind you?" Sam asked.

"Yeah. Like you said, spilled milk."

"If it's any consolation, I couldn't have picked a harder life. The marriage ended after 12 long years.

Bringing up two boys alone was hard. I had nothing, no support of any kind, but I was determined that my most important job in life was to bring up two fine men. I worked hard supporting two special people who would make amazing fathers and husbands. I got lucky. All my hard work paid off."

He kept walking silently processing Sam's life.

"Lacy shared some time with me when our children were very young, but then she moved from San Diego back to Sydney. Do you ever see her?"

"No, I moved north. I really didn't stay in the Sydney area too long after you left. I actually dated a blonde for a year or two but that was pretty disastrous. Then Cassie and I hooked up, traveled, and then moved to the lake area where I met my wife while teaching school up there.

"Did Wyatt ever give you anything to help with the boys?"

"No, not a dime."

"Why didn't you fight for it? You always fought for everything else."

"Well, the truth is I was afraid of him. The scorpion came out in him pretty quickly. If I insisted on fighting for money, there would have been no end to the hell those kids and I would have to endure. I wanted to raise the boys in peace. I always knew my purpose in life was to help mold children.

"A year ago, my younger son got married. Wyatt was there, and after he saw how in love our son was with his wife and watched how happy the two boys were with their families, he turned to me and gave me a big thumb's up. I guess that was the most I'll ever get from him."

"There has never been anyone else?"

"No, not really, I dated some people for a few years, but I never found the closeness that *we* had. I guess once you've felt that closeness, you don't want to settle for less."

"Why do you suppose it all happened this way?" he asked.

"Well, it's a plaguing question that's been left for both of us to ponder for thirty-six years, but I can only believe that it was partly our *destiny*. I believe you were supposed to have those two beautiful girls of yours and live a life in Australia and for some indescribable twist of fate, I was destined to end up back in the States raising my two gifts, my beautiful sons."

The walk was almost at an end and Sam felt Brad had gotten the biggest burning issue off his plate. She ran back into the farmhouse to change and told Patty and Cassie she was ready to meet the Mennonites.

Sam and Cassie got into the back of the car. They headed first for the town of St Jacobs.

"I want to go to this famous bakery my sister loves before we get to St Jacobs." Patty said.

After cleaning them out of custard tarts, they piled back into the car and kept an eye out for black horse-drawn carriages. As they got closer to the town, the carts began to appear trotting down the main roads.

Before they reached Main Street, Patty spied a small general store that had its clotheslines full of house dresses and men's shirts all plain, the same, and in various shades of blue, grays, lavenders, and burgundies. She parked the car.

"Come on, let's go in here and see what kind of goodies we can buy from their General Store." They walked into the quaint little store that reminded Sam of the old local Five and Dimes in the States fifty years ago. Cassie went to the aisles with trinkets looking for gifts for family and friends. Patty saw a small bakery section at the back of the store and looked for a fruit pie to take home for evening tea.

Brad looked through the assortment of pies as well, "I don't see my favorite." He walked up to the Mennonite mother and daughter baking pies in the back and cleared his throat.

"Excuse me, ladies, would you happen to have some shoofly pie?"

"No, sir, sorry, none today, but," they looked over at each other and said, "We could make you one." They looked around to check they had the ingredients.

"S'truth, really you could make one?" They both nodded.

"How long would it take? We're only planning to be in St Jacobs a couple of hours."

The mother answered,"If you give us two hours, we'll have it ready for you."

"Righty-oh, that'll be perfect. Do you need the money now?" asked Brad.

"No, sir," the mother answered again. "You pay when you pick it up." Brad left smiling from ear-to-ear.

"So, what exactly is in shoofly pie?" Sam asked inquisitively as they walked out the front door of the shop. "I've heard of it and there are songs about it but what the hell is in it?"

"Well, it is a careful blend of molasses, brown sugar, and butter."

"Oh my, it sounds incredibly sweet, a little like the pecan pies we have at our Thanksgiving but without the pecans." We walked around the store waiting for the girls when Brad spied a small barn with a horse.

He walked over to the window stall just as the horse stuck his head out. Brad began to stroke its snout. The horse hoped for a treat and nudged Brad's arm. Brad bent down to the horse's face and began to snort gently in his nostrils. The horse replied by nuzzling to Brad's face.

Sam remembered something like this when they were in New Angledool and she watched him communicate with the stallion. He blew her away with these tricks and he hadn't lost his touch. He may have done it to impress Sam, but it saddened her once again that she had the choice of watching him pass it on to their children.

Patty drove into St. Jacobs and found a suitable parking spot. Brad wanted to head to the famous Hamel Broom Store where he spent time during his last visit. The shop was closed till noon, so they busied themselves visiting gift stores, art galleries, and the historical center where a map for touring the adjacent areas surrounding Woolwich was available.

Supposedly, the Mennonites settled in Pennsylvania in 1680, but many went north prior to the Revolutionary War for fear they would be pressed into service.

After an hour, Sam got map reading duty, pointing out spots of interest. Along the ride, they went back to the General Store to pick up Brad's pie. It was massive.

"Well thank you very much," Brad said to the ladies.

Patty chimed in, "Thank you, You've spoiled him rotten."

"Yes, you certainly have," he said again. "You made my entire trip."

"Now he can go home," Patty said to the ladies.

Again Brad grinned as he carried his prize to the car configuring a way to keep it guarded and safe for the rest of the journey. After several hours of touring, Patty headed the car back to the village of Elmira. On the way, Brad turned to Patty. "Are we far from the covered bridge?"

"Not too far," said Patty. "Is that where you want to go next?"

"Sure, it's a great time of the day to get some shots of the bridge."

Sam thought, *oh my God, am I actually going to experience a scene from The Bridges Of Madison County?*

The bridge had a long span over a fast-running river into a thicket of tall trees. They went through the bridge to find a small parking area on the other side. They could hear the clank, clank, clank of the wooden boards.

Patty chimed in, "We used to call this the kissing bridge when I was a girl."

"Really, why?" asked Cassie.

"Well, as soon as the boys could drive, they'd take their dates to the other side of the crossing and steal their first kiss while going through the covered bridge."

Sam's thoughts immediately had gone back to Brad's first kiss. She wished in some way they could steal one now. *You're shameless, Sam.* They all piled out of the car and circled back to the bridge.

Brad took his camera gear and began shooting every angle of the bridge. Sam went up to a brass sign that described The West Montross Bridge.

It stated that it was a two-span hybrid bridge spanning 205 feet long and 17 feet wide and originally made from painted pine.

It was the biggest covered bridge she had ever seen. After taking a group picture at the beginning of the bridge, Brad walked beside Sam pointing to the struts and beams, showing her which were original and which were altered. There was a gift shop at the other side.

Sam walked into the shop and the shopkeeper told them the bridge had some mystery.

"You will notice at the end of the entrance of the bridge there is a floating red balloon. Someone replaces that balloon each day. This is the bridge where they filmed the horror movie "IT" written by Stephen King.

They got back to the farmhouse. "I can't possibly wait 'til dinner for a piece of this pie," Brad said. "Anyone want to join me for a bite?"

They all shouted, "Yes!" and Cassie put on the kettle for tea. They sat around the table anxious for their slice.

Brad took a small bite and smiled proudly saying, "Ah . . . tis the nectar of the gods."

Patty took a bite and shuddered, "Now that will perk up your fillings."

Brad laughed, responding, "Yes, it will."

They all did a small walk about the property again after dinner. Dark came early. Patty headed back to her house and Cassie stayed up to reminisce with Brad about their lives at the lake.

They caught Sam up on how she and Brad decided to travel together sometime after Sam left. They remained close and lived together for a while at the lake where they both taught school and joined a local theater group.

Sam imagined that if Brad and she had moved up there as planned, Cassie would have certainly come up and built her house close to theirs as well. She was always a dear friend to both of them.

Cassie retired to bed anxiously getting ready for the big flight on the Lancaster in the morning. Brad stayed up and shared pictures of his sweet little self-made steamboat.

They talked about his sailboat and Sam shared her sailing adventures. The great thing about an iPhone is she could easily share all the pictures of the Alden schooner, the Frey, and the fifty foot Columbia that she often sailed. She also shared pictures of her two 1400-mile journeys at sea.

"Thanks to you, Sam, I learned to appreciate sailing."

"I've been fortunate to get the opportunities I had to sail with friends."

"I've taught my whole family how to sail on the lake," he said. "My girls used to go when they were younger, but no one seems to want to go out anymore."

"Well, it *is* work," Sam said. "My boys were never interested in sailing with me. They found it too boring and it wasn't cool to learn something your mother did."

"It gets blustery out on the lake. You start out early thinking it will be an easy beautiful sail and then the winds hit and it can be a gale in minutes. I think it scares most people, but I love it."

"The sea is the same," she said.

"I did get the opportunity to travel with my daughters. Now that they're older I can see things are changing. They're off to college now."

"Well, I'm a little ahead of you. My boys recently married and gifted me five grandchildren under the age of four. So now I share time with their babies and their families."

Sam mused to herself that grandchildren certainly give one perspective about your role in this cycle of life. She still struggled with the question about how she *knew* she would live her life in Australia and in the course of six months, ended up raising two boys all alone in the States.

✈ 33

The Flight

If Cassie was anxious about her flight on one of the biggest bombers the Royal Airforce produced, she hid it well. Cassie was usually pretty even-keeled. Brad was poised with anticipation. You could tell he wanted the experience to be perfect.

They took photos in front of the sign that marked the entrance to the air museum and their troop marched into the front desk to check in and get the day's agenda. They were told Cassie and Brad needed to attend a briefing about an hour before the scheduled flight which was scheduled at ten.

They all headed to the expansive hangar that housed the Lancaster. It stood majestically near the massive doors awaiting its scheduled flight. It seemed even larger today than it did on Tuesday when the girls first visited the museum. *Maybe because today it was living and breathing.* Brad was sizing things up looking inside the crew seats trying to imagine what they might be experiencing during the flight.

"Where do you look out to take a good shot of the landscape below?" Sam asked.

"Those little portholes on the side. If you notice, there is only one little jump seat next to each porthole."

Sam looked in and thought six people, six seats. However, when they got to the briefing table, it looked like only four people were booked to go—one local older gentleman, Cassie, Brad, and a 50-something contractor from England.

Brad intended to only be the facilitator of the Lancaster trip. However, Cassie refused to do the flight alone and insisted that he needed to come with her. She paid his $2500 fare. It was a handsome gift for a lifetime friendship, a gift you didn't refuse.

Sam took a short video of the briefing, especially when Cassie shared the articles and pictures of her father and her uncle with their crew.

"You'll have an opportunity to come up and spend time in the cockpit." announced the pilot. "There will be a lot of noise in the aircraft as well. The air crew will issue headphones to each of you, so you'll be able to speak and hear what the flight deck crew is saying."

They walked around the hangar when Brad excitedly pointed out the Spitfire.

"God, that Spitty is the aircraft I'd *really* love to fly on." When Sam asked him why, he rattled off at least two dozen reasons.

Trying to make Brad's dream come true, Sam walked up to the desk and asked about the Spitfire. They said it was grounded. It was having work done on the engine. Since it could only fly one passenger at a time, a flight for thirty minutes would cost upwards of $6,000. *That might call for winning the lottery.*

"Well, I did notice that some folks are taking rides on some of your WWII bi-planes today. I have been jealous of everyone else flying. I just wondered if there was any possibility of purchasing a ride on one of those?"

"Let me check, what's your name? All right, Sam, I'll page you if I find out more."

Sam ran back to Brad and told him about the Spitfire and excitedly shared the news that she might be able to ride on a bi-plane.

"Believe it or not, I've had this on my bucket list for over thirty years," she said.

Within a few minutes, the clerk called Sam's name. She said a thirty-minute ride on a Tiger Moth that was used by the Royal Navy for training their WWII pilots would cost $300. It would leave at 11:30 and return at noon right at the same time Brad and Cassie returned from their hour flight on the Lancaster.

This was *so* perfect. Now Sam could be part of the excitement of the day. She ran back to Brad and jumped up and down. He was actually very excited for her, "I see you never lost your spontaneity!"

By 10:15, they were out on the tarmac taking photos of the crew. Cassie and Brad had a chance to speak to the captain for a while. This was a big day for him as well. It was announced earlier that it would be his last flight as Captain of the Lancaster after thirty years of service.

Patty and Sam ran to the observation deck to take a video of the 'Lanc' revving up. It took fifteen minutes for the plane to warm up engines and begin rolling down to the air strip. Then it took another fifteen minutes for it to take off. As Patty and Sam stood on the highest point of the deck, the Lancaster circled and flew directly over their heads. The roar of the bomber's engines shook the tower. It sent shivers up their spines.

After the plane disappeared into the horizon, Patty and Sam went below and had a cup of warm tea and one of the pastries she bought at the Mennonite bakery. Within thirty minutes they announced Sam's briefing. She took Patty with her so that she could meet her handsome captain and experience the excitement.

Before they knew it, Sam was climbing on the wing to get into the open cockpit. Patty took photos of her with Sam's I-phone.

"Hey Patty, don't leave yet, I need my phone to take video inside the plane from the air."

"Oh, yeah, huh." she said smiling as she ran back, "That might come in handy, eh."

The Tiger Moth was like an old model T. The ground assistant took hold of the propeller by hand and yanked it to try to get it to spin on its own. After the sixth try, it was rather iffy about getting the aircraft started to go anywhere.

"Okay. Give it a minute, let's try it again," the pilot said. At one point he asked, "Did we refuel the plane after the last flight?"

Sam thought *seriously, don't they check these things before passengers get on?*

Just when she thought she'd have to get out, the propeller caught. "You ready?" asked the pilot.

"You bet, I was born ready."

"No second thoughts, right?" he asked.

"No, sir, as long as I don't have to get out on the struts and jump off this plane I will be just fine." Her mindset for the day was drink in every minute of this flight.

They reached 2000 feet quickly. Sam took photos of the cockpit. There was a plaque that said 21 April, 1941, and another describing the craft as Gypsy Major 1 C, cruising speed maximum 2100 feet.

The pilot spoke through Sam's head phones.

"If you want to catch a glimpse of the Lancaster, it's approaching the left side of our aircraft about 400 yards ahead." Sam stretched her neck to see if she could get a picture, but she could only see a glimpse.

They cruised over farm properties and open fields and then set over a very large river system.

"What river is this below us?"

"That's the St. Lawrence Seaway, Miss, the largest river system in Canada. It takes you downstream from Niagara Falls to the Gulf of St. Lawrence past New Brunswick."

"I'm familiar with it. I actually sailed 1400 miles north on the St. Lawrence last year."

"How far did you go?" asked the captain.

"All the way . . . up to the Gulf of St. Lawrence. It's amazing to see how small it is from this height though," she said stretching her neck out farther.

"What size boat?" asked the captain.

"It was a beautiful 45-foot sloop."

Finally, they set down and taxied into the space just beside the Lancaster that was sitting stately and quietly back on the tarmac. Sam got out and saw Patty by the fence and next to her was Brad firing off pictures on his Nikon. She ran to them excitedly giving them both a big hug.

"How was the ride on the Lancaster?"

"Amazing, everything you would hope for and more." He described that each of them was given quite a lot of time in the cockpit with the pilot.

They walked through the hangar together when the pilot ran over to Sam with her certificate that proved she completed the flight. Brad insisted on getting a photo of her with the certificate next to the Tiger Moth. It reminded Sam when he took the other picture of her with the certificate shortly after they jumped from a Bonanza Beechcraft in Australia. The photos may have been taken over thirty-six years apart but the high pitch excitement they shared was the same.

They walked around the museum together laughing and smiling. He gave Sam the grand tour of over two dozen aircraft in the hangar. He wanted to go back to visit the Spitfire.

His love for history and the amount of information he stored in his brain on everything military had always been fascinating.

"I hope I'm not boring you. I sometimes bore myself."

"No, on the contrary," Sam said, "It's like getting a personal tour with the Discovery Channel. I'm just remembering back to one of the arguments we had at Gladstone Street."

"Which one?" he said.

"OUCH . . . come on, Brad, we really didn't have that many. It was the day I spent decorating the living room after you finished the bookcases. I carefully placed pictures, knick-knacks, and books into a carefully laid out décor."

"Yup, I remember that. I had gone away for a Commando weekend and came back to my books all amuck. The aircraft books were mixed with the Civil War arms and ammunition books. It was bloody awful."

"Exactly," she said. "It was the first time I ever thought that books needed to be appropriately placed for finding information outside placing a set of encyclopedia books on shelves. I remember you spent the rest of the evening repositioning all the books."

They laughed together and delighted in the memory that they really didn't have that many heavy scars from their years together.

They left the museum about 1:30 p.m. Patty informed them that they had an invitation to join her sister and their family for lunch. It would only be an hour ride north.

"I'm so excited to see your sister again," said Sam. "Are we going to that same lake house we visited when I came to see you and your mum in the late eighties? Brad turned around. "You visited Ontario in the late eighties?"

"Yes, I was on my way to visit my sister in Jersey. Patty had visited me in New Mexico and I got to visit her mum at the farm house and have lunch at her sister's lake house. It has been that long since I've seen them."

As they rode off, the museum began to fade in the rearview window. Everyone in the car recognized they had left a very special moment in their lives behind.

They rolled up into the driveway. Patty brought them up to speed that her brother-in-law had suffered an inoperable brain tumor that winter. As soon as they arrived, Brad went into the family room where her brother-in-law sat and spoke with him at length about the trip on the Lancaster.

Later Brad joined the rest of them with a full plate of food out on the patio. He took the seat next to Sam. It was a strange but familiar feeling. For a moment Sam was feeling very much like the couple they were in 1980.

Patty's family begged Sam to talk about Africa since she had traveled to West Kenya only two months before. Sam explained that she was working on some projects with a school built by a large non-profit called Kids for Peace. One of her nieces asked, "Do you have any regrets about making such an arduous trip?"

"Well, I think the only regret I really have is that I can't give blood for another year. The blood bank insists that when you visit countries that have high incidences of malaria, they want to make sure you are free from transmission." Immediately Brad spun around to face Sam.

"Do you really give blood?" he asked excitedly.

"Why yes, I've given blood every eight weeks for over 25 years. I feel guilty that I can't this year. I always figured it was one of those things I could do to give to others who needed it. I never had enough time to volunteer much during my years as a full-time mother and principal."

"What blood type are you?" he asked.

"O positive."

"Me too." he said. "I've been giving blood every eight weeks for over thirty years."

They sat and stared at each other, speechless. It was beginning to get dark and they needed to get back to the farmhouse.

Brad and Sam didn't speak much on the way back. This was her last night and she was already mourning the end of the reunion.

They already had dinner, so they poured some wine for the last evening together and reminisced about the day. She left everyone early to start packing. It took an hour for her to pack things up and she headed to the bathroom at the end of the hall to get ready for bed.

On the way back to her room, she passed Brad's room. His door was ajar. Though she felt guilty, she took a peek. He was lying fully clothed on top of the covers reading a book. Sam stopped for a long moment embarrassed as he stared back at her without saying a word. She was plagued by inappropriate thoughts but refused to give in to them for fear she could leave more devastation.

Finally, Sam broke the silence. "Do you think we'll have enough time for another walk tomorrow?" she asked.

"I think so. Patty isn't coming 'til ten, right?"

"That's right.

"Okay, then, see you in the morning. Sweet dreams."

She got into bed snuggling around the other pillow lying beside her. She half hoped there might be a soft knock on the door just for the chance to talk some more, but of course there wasn't. It was the way it had to be. Clearly, she was still in love with Brad—always had been and always will be.

34

The Final Moments

Brad was downstairs when Sam got there. "Are you ready? These dogs are already barking," he said looking at his feet.

"Too tight?" she asked.

"Too loose. I keep stepping right out of these bloody runners."

They stepped off the porch and headed in the same direction they journeyed over the past two days. She needed to be at the airport at eleven and was pretty sure everyone would be coming to bid farewell. She was also certain any last words or memories shared between Brad and herself would take place in these final few moments of the five-mile walk. She sensed nothing dramatic was coming. Brad had already asked the hard questions.

They didn't make it to the gate when Brad bent down and took off one of his sneakers. A pebble had already lodged itself in his shoe. He adjusted his Nike and they sprinted off taking a left turn again on the road named Line 1. They kept a steady pace until Sam noticed he disappeared. He had gone back to the side of the road to examine a carcass of an animal that had obviously been hit by a car. It was flattened like a pancake and unrecognizable. More like a smudge on the road. "What d'ya think it is?" he quizzed.

Sam shook her head, "I haven't a clue, mate."

"Look again, look at the tail," he pointed.

She followed his finger but couldn't see a tail in that smudge.

"Here," he pointed. "The tail has black and gray horizontal stripes," he said. "It is obviously a raccoon." He was always teaching.

Sam didn't even want to think about how many things she missed by not catching life through his eyes. They walked at a steady pace commenting about the beauty in nature surrounding them, until they came to the little bridge that spanned over the stream that emptied into the pond behind Patty's house.

Brad slowed his pace and came to a complete halt walking over to the side of the bridge. He stood quietly taking in the scenery below. Sam pulled up to the right side of him and peered at the water gushing under the bridge.

"Isn't it funny what a big role water has played in both our lives," Brad said.

She sensed he was taking a moment to be introspective. His observation was true enough, both their lives evolved around boats and water. They began their lives envisioning a future life around it and both ended up pursuing it separately. Sam just kept staring down at the glistening rush of cascading water. "Hmm," she said, nodding in agreement.

He cleared his throat still staring at the water. "You know, there hasn't been a *single day* in my life I don't think of you."

His words jolted her while, at the same time, flowed over her like a cool wave of velvety water.

She remained motionless for a moment and replied slowly, "Well, there isn't a day that goes by that I don't think of you either. It isn't so much about simply thinking *of* you, it's more like thinking about what 'WE' would be doing, or better yet how we would have developed together as a couple, you know, where we would be now and what we would be working on next."

"You just said it better than I did. I think that describes exactly what I do as well," he added. "You know, Sam, I think our circumstances were just a product of bad timing. I had just gotten out of a marriage of ten years when we became intimate and fell in love. I wasn't ready for the idea of another marriage.

She nodded, having surmised this on her own at the time. It is the main reason she said nothing and she let him go with no guilt attachments and no ties going to Canada. When he left, she wanted so much for him to come back and be hers. That, no matter what happened, their love could withstand the test of time. It was like tossing a feather into the wind and expecting that it would return.

In a split second, Brad created a simple observation around thirty-six years of reflection and emotion. It was, in fact, that simple and that complex. Their love *was* a product of bad timing. *Timing had never been Sam's friend.*

She shared with Brad that Wyatt recognized he wanted children but really had no desire to engage in the process of being a husband or a father in their lives. He was absent pretty quickly.

"You know, my sister Dina still greets Wyatt with a warm hug when she sees him. She tells him that she's forever grateful for him being the catalyst that brought her sister back to live in the States. She feels we would have never gotten to know each other as sisters had I stayed in Oz.

"Something I have often wondered is when we first began to talk about marriage in those early days, even in the lightest sense, you would joke about it. Do you remember what you'd tell me?"

"No."

"You'd joke and say, 'Why would I marry you, you're a Yank and will just leave me someday and go back to the States.' I often wondered then, did you *really* think that at the time or were you just avoiding commitment in your humorous way?"

"I guess it was my way of joking away the prospect because I wasn't ready to talk about it. It wasn't because I didn't love you."

"Well, I really didn't think I was ready yet either, but I was reaching for a hopeful sign to hold onto, just reaching to see if there was a future vision for US. When you were joking it away, I began second guessing where things were going. I have to agree with you it certainly was a timing issue. I did live with years of guilt over breaking your heart though.

I felt I deserved the life that I had without a partner. The pure and simple truth is I didn't make the right choice and we just have to live with our choices."

There was a long silence. She turned to Brad and looked into his eyes. "I just want you to *always know*, I loved you *then* . . . I love you *now* . . . and I will *always* love you."

He turned to her and smiled. "This calls for a hug, don't you think," he said.

She walked up to him. She was certainly in need of a hug. They embraced in a sweet lingering-but-not-too-long hug. They kept to the boundaries of their current world.

They walked along happily thinking they were able to resolve many questions they carried for years. She stepped alongside of him holding onto the feeling of *US. I may have robbed it for a minute, but this moment was truly OURS.*

That same day Sam wandered back to San Diego on a United Airline flight to return to her lovely world of yacht clubs, warm sunny climate, and her single world. It was enough to keep her busy. She walked the long stretches of beautiful beach in front of the Hotel Del Coronado and continually wondered about all that happened in that reunion and the endless questions that still haunt her.

It was Saturday morning of the next week. It was the day of Brad's departure. She had given him a hug at the airport and just whispered, "Stay in touch, *please*."

She was lying in her bed on her boat when her cell phone rang. "Hello."

"I'm leaving North America today heading back to Oz and I thought I'd see how you're doing?"

"I'm good," she answered with hesitation, "How about you?" She wanted to say a myriad of things, but what was there to say? He was masterful at it. He knew his place but felt the moment. "I just want to say again because of you, this trip was magic for me, Sam."

She paused, "For me too. It'll be forever lodged in my heart."

"I promise to keep in touch. I'll miss *this* moment."

"Me too," she said.

"I love you," he said.

"I love *you*," she answered slowly, hating to hang up.

She fell silent and saddened, thinking of how stupid she felt about her lack of words. All the things she wanted to say to him but knowing she shouldn't. He made an effort to grab one more moment of "*US*" while on this continent. She so wished she could have embraced it more, even help give it a bigger moment.

Sam soon realized it was so much more than special, it was a gift. She also realized at that moment their love had always been *real* for both of them.

Several weeks later, she had dinner in a local Italian eatery in San Diego with Lyndsey's daughter, Bella. Sam always noted how beautiful Bella was when she walked into any space. She always exuded such confidence while lighting up a room. Each month while Bella lived in San Diego studying law, they got together to catch up with each other's lives. Sam began giving her details of the reunion.

Bella lived with Sam for six months while she was in her freshman year of high school. She knew Sam dated people in the past but spent most of her life alone.

People would often ask Sam what was up with that? 'Why would a woman like you end up alone?' Sam's answer was always the same. "Well, I'm just unlucky in love and real estate." *Bad timing.*

Bella often shared she didn't know where her life was going either, but wondered for her sake what fate would bring to her. It was very clear to everyone she wasn't going to settle for less than she deserved. Wise beyond her years, sometimes she would say, "Sam, men are just stupid."

After hearing her story, she asked, "So, Sam let me ask you a question?"

"Oh, isn't that what you lawyers love to do, ask questions?"

"No, *really*, if all of a sudden Brad called you wanting you back, what would you do?"

"Well, that isn't going to happen," she said. "It isn't a real question. He's a happily married man with two beautiful daughters."

"No, Sam, *anything* can happen. All that could end and he could want to spend the rest of his life with you. Come on, what would you say?" she pulled herself upright reaching for an answer in Sam's eyes.

"I would say **yes,** in a heartbeat."

"Okay, *why*," she probed, I really *need* to know . . . why," she said leaning forward in her chair.

Sam could tell she hoped to gather some insight for her own life based on the perceptions of those who had already gone through theirs. "Well, simply, you search for a meaningful love in your life. I know I'm a romantic, but to have a moment of seeing life through the eyes of someone you love is truly magic. I missed all that. I missed *so* much. If there was a moment left to indulge in such an opportunity again, I'd take it in a heartbeat. He should have been my life partner. I guess I will always struggle with why."

⸺•⸺

Three years later, during the spring of the COVID 19 virus, Sam was nestled in the aft cabin of her boat feeling safe and secure despite the midnight storm predictions. She was on her iPhone checking the internet for messages and a quote suddenly appeared like many of them often did. She was dumbstruck. It was like the answer to all her questions fell from the Universe at one time and she clearly understood why things happened as they did. She read the words over and over again. It was a Eureka! moment.

The anonymous quote said, *"A friend once told me that the biggest danger to an adventurous-spirit is stability and security. A free-spirit needs to look to a new horizon every morning."*

Sam knew early in life that she was an adventurous, free-spirited woman, but when faced with the biggest decision in her life, she now understood she couldn't choose her anchor because it meant stability and security. She *feared* it would be the death of her free spirit.

They say it is our fears that guide our lives, and so Sam *instantly* understood why she jumped on a plane to pursue the one person who would never provide her *any* stability and security. She suddenly realized it wasn't just fate or destiny that drove her north. It did come down to her choice and getting on that plane was *her* fault. She was playing with Pandora's Box. Her curiosity had pulled her to seek the meaning behind Wyatt's words, and as soon as she had gotten off the aircraft, Wyatt took her to Mexico and asked her to marry him. Believing it was fate, she made a spontaneous choice based on her fears. It happened that quick, with no further thought, and she let destiny take a hand.

Now, forty years later, she understood where her fear had always lived. Wyatt's lack of stability wasn't a threat, she knew she could make it on her own, Brad's anchor and stability was.

She also realized that her decision to live on a boat for the last fifteen years resonated through these choices as well. The new horizon reached her door each morning and her life attached to a deteriorating boat on a floating dock wasn't at all secure. Every day was an adventure. Evidence of her choices were all around her lapping at the walls of her partially submerged home.

As a wise sage once shared with Sam, "Love can't always set us straight, at its worst it can leave us blindsided. It is always best to love yourself - it can set you free."

Navigating one's happiness would always be a tricky business for Sam.

Australian Slang Glossary

A cold one – beer

Aussie Salute – a wave to scare the flies

Barbie – barbecue

Beauty! – Great!

Billabong – a pond in a dry river bank

Billy – teapot used on the fire in the Outback

Bloody – used to accentuate a thought

Bloody Oath – it is true. You're right mate.

Brekky – breakfast

Brolly – umbrella

Bush -meaning out in the bush, the wild

Chockers – full

Chook – chicken

Crikey – means surprised

Crook – tired, ill, or angry

Dead set – true

Dunny – toilet

Dinky-dy – the real thing

Fair Dinkum – honestly

Flat out – really busy

Footy – football

Fortnight- two weeks

G'day – Hello

Galah – stupid person (actually a type of Australian cockatoo)

Good on Ya – Good work

Heaps – lots

Knickers – lady's underwear

Lollies – sweets

Mossies' – mosquitos

No worries – no problem

Outback – the interior, remote area of the bush

Piss off – get lost

Ripper – fantastic

Rooted – tired

Runners – sneakers

Sheila – a woman

Snag – a sausage

S'truth – exclamation of surprise

Stuffed – tired

Swag – a single bed roll

Swagman –a drifter

Tea – dinner

Torch- flashlight

Tucker – food, or Outback food

Two-Up – a gambling game typically played on Anzac Day

Acknowledgments

I will always be eternally grateful for my sister, who's the voice in my head, my sons and their wives who became my heart and soul, my grandchildren who fill my heart with joy, and *all* my special friends (you know who you are) who have always supported me in my gypsy-style life. Your love and support have allowed me to experience the world and its children.

In addition, very special thanks to everyone who helped me in developing and editing this story: Jo Ann Glaccum, Jo Anne Scuderi, Denise Conti, Breda Curran, Heather Cardinal, Betty Sproule, Susie Schaefer, Ruth Chapman, Beth Conard, Janet Paulovich, James Hallman, Eddie Ashmore, Joan McConville, and Pendleton Wallace.

One fall evening in 2017, I was sharing the events surrounding a reunion in Canada with my friend Cheryl, having a glass of wine on the back porch of her beautiful boat *Lolita*. Cheryl had been diagnosed with cancer and immediately encouraged me to write this story as a novel. "I always thought I had at least one book in me. I have so many stories," I said.

"Well, life's too short, you need to start that book tomorrow. I'll never forgive you if you don't finish it," she said. *I was never one to disappoint Cheryl.*

Now three years later, Cheryl has since passed, but I will never forget our visits as she checked weekly on my progress. I loved that woman. I only wish she was here to read it on a warm summer's eve.

My life in education was truly my passion and purpose. There wasn't a day I didn't love my job. I am so grateful for all the hundreds of teachers I have had the privilege to work with over my extensive career. *I could always see in each of their faces that it was a calling to be a teacher.* The school was my second home, my wheelhouse. It has been the connective tissue of most of my relationships. I was lost when I retired, and writing filled up the void, thanks to Cheryl. Whether fiction or nonfiction, there are stories in all of us that need to be shared.

As for all the children, literally thousands that I have come to know: Bless you and thank you for the memories we shared. Each of you were a *gift* to my life. You gave me far more than I gave you. You taught me everything I needed to learn.

About the Author

A New Jersey native, Georgia Faye flew off to travel the world and find herself. In 1975, she answered an ad advertising a teaching job in Sydney, Australia, which was experiencing a severe teacher shortage. She lived in Sydney for eight years.

Today, Georgia has made her home in the San Diego area for thirty years and lives on a forty-year-old motor yacht. Her forty-five-year career in education led her to be recognized for community and global development, including major awards for Zero Waste programs, school development, innovative farm to table programs, and two Distinguished School Awards, which ultimately earned her the title of Southern California's "Principal of the Year."

She is the proud mother of two handsome sons and six beautiful grandchildren. Georgia continues to pursue an adventurous life traveling the world and volunteering for international volunteer programs in Europe, Croatia, Greece, and West Kenya. Her love of chess is often referred to in her writing.

Although Georgia has been writing for years, she finished her novel *Down Under* after being published in *The Pivot Project* anthology during the pandemic, which featured her chapter "Navigating Happiness" as the first chapter of the book. Georgia is a member of the San Diego Writers and Editors Guild, The Writer Digest Guild, The Wild Atlantic Writers Association, The Author's Guild, and The Romance Writers Guild of America.

Printed in Great Britain
by Amazon